Inside the Blowholes

A young adult novel by Thomas Davis

Four Windows Press, PO Box 13, Continental Divide, NM 87312

January 2013

Photograph of Four Windows Cave on the cover
by Kevin Davis

Copyright ©2013 by Thomas Davis

All rights reserved. No part of this book may be used or reproduced by any means, including photocopying, recording, taping, or by an information storage retrieval system without the written permission of the publisher except in the case of brief quotations embodied in critical articles or reviews.

Four Windows Press books may be ordered by contacting

Four Windows Press
PO Box 13
Continental Divide, NM 87312

davisethel@gmail.com

www.fourwindowspressbooks.com
www.fourwindowspress.com

Printed in the United States of America

Dedication

To Ethel, whom I have always loved, and Sonja, Mary, and Kevin, as always, and the grandchildren, Phoebe, Sophia, William, and Joey, and all those who love dragons….

And to the Zuni Mountain poets who, during their Sunday meetings at the Inscription Rock Trading Post and Coffee Company, listened to me reading *Inside the Blowholes* as it was written for months on end

Table of Contents

Contents

Dedication 3
Table of Contents 4
Chapter I 6
Chapter II 13
Chapter III 19
Chapter IV 26
Chapter V 35
Chapter VI 40
Chapter VII 47
Chapter VIII 53
Chapter IX 60
Chapter X 66
Chapter XI 73
Chapter XII 80
Chapter XIII 87
Chapter XIV 94
Chapter XV 102
Chapter XVI 109
Chapter XVII 119
Chapter XVIII 127
Chapter XIX 134
Chapter XX 141
Chapter XXI 147
Chapter XXII 155
Chapter XXIII 161
Chapter XXIV 167
Chapter XXV 176
Chapter XXVI 183
Chapter XXVII 191
Chapter XXVIII 198

Chapter XXIX 205
Chapter XXX 209
Chapter XXXI 216
Chapter XXXII 223
Chapter XXXIII 229
Chapter XXXIV 236
Chapter XXXV 243
Chapter XXXVI 250
Chapter XXXVII 256
Chapter XXXVIII 262
Chapter XXX*IX* 269

Chapter I

Only one other person lived inside El Malpais. She was the most beautiful woman Juniper Window had ever seen. She lived in a treehouse built in branches of El Malpais' largest Douglas fir. Neither Juniper nor his father saw her very often. She had long silver hair and eyes so bright and wild they shivered through you when she glanced your way. Mostly Juniper saw her on full moon nights when pahoehoe lava shined black with a faint silver sheen. His father, kind, dark brown eyes piercing his son's spirit, always told Juniper to avoid the woman, that her craziness was even deeper than his craziness, and that she could be unpredictable.

Sometimes, when Juniper was feeling lonelier than usual, he would use trails shielding him from raven's eyes noticing everything that moved and go to where Sheena lived. He would sit in the crook of a pinyon tree's branches snaked into clear New Mexico light and look at the wonderful treehouse, its round windows and always freshly painted silver, blue, and yellow walls.

He would wonder why he was afraid to leave his hidden perch and go and have a conversation with the only neighbor he and his father had. But during these musings a vision of Sheena's eyes would come to him, he would shiver, and then slip from the pinyon and walk trails other than the one he had come by to go home.

His father always knew when he had gone to his pinyon perch, and he always told him, "Avoid Sheena. She can explode and scald you so deeply your heart will never be the same."

Juniper always listened to his father. He loved how his father looked, bushy eyebrows and a smile that lit up his craggy face and made the day brighter. Father loved him notwithstanding how they lived, and Juniper believed he would move to Ramah, the nearest town, if Juniper insisted.

But there came a day….

At school Juniper had tried talking to Lily Smallhand, a dark Navajo girl as silent as he was, as wonderful as the underground river's dark waters. He had been in classes with her for two years. She had moved home from Albuquerque after being raised in the city and had struggled, the way Juniper struggled, to fit in with local kids. Whenever she answered questions in class her musical voice conveyed thoughts and ideas seldom heard inside the high school. When Juniper had tried saying hello to Lily, asking her how her day was going, she had stared at him with a dark anger.

"What do you care?" she had said in a flat, cold voice.

Juniper had fled down tiled school halls. What had he done to Lily Smallhand to make her hate him? he asked himself. Even though most students thought he was weirder than a green faced Martian, why couldn't he make at least one friend? He had been going to school in Ramah most of his life.

After the long bus ride and the longer hike down the dirt road and over the Cairn Trail to home, he felt even more isolated and alone. He had tried talking to Sam Maryboy, but Sam had stared out the bus window without acknowledging him. The walk in the spring evening, as dark clouds scuttled through blazing red and orange skies, winds howling like coyotes serenading the full moon, made him feel lost.

Once inside the small cave where he and his father lived, with its rough-planed ponderosa floor and walls constructed from knotty cedar hauled from a canyon near Bandera caldera, his desolation deepened. His father was not home. The black-enameled wood cooking stove was waiting to be stoked for supper. Juniper stared at it and thought about the crawl to the small ice cave so that he could get elk hamburger for their evening meal.

Then, as aimless as a falling aspen leaf on Mount Taylor in late fall, he left the cave, climbed out of the collapse's wall of black boulders, and wandered away from the road, school, Sam Maryboy, and Lily Smallhand. A huge golden moon sailed dark skies.

Shadows elongated every stone, bush, and tree. Clouds danced with light as the moon dodged tangles of cloud.

Suddenly, Sheena, dressed in brilliant white, unearthly in her beauty, was on the trail in front of him standing on a Douglas fir's broad branches. He stopped and thought about what his father always told him, "Stay away from Sheena, especially on the night of a full moon," but he felt rebellious.

"What can she do?" he asked himself. "You're worthless anyway."

Sheena shifted in the great tree. He could feel her stare from two hundred feet away. Her white dress and pale face shimmered in moonlight. Pouting, he walked toward her, staring back at her staring. She lifted her left arm.

"Stop!" she commanded. "Stop now!"

He kept moving toward a woman so beautiful she diminished the moon's orange brightness. She laughed, her laughter a song across lava fields.

"Ahhh, a man," she said, her voice menacing. "Come to my house, little man," she said. "I'll show you how black widow spiders swallow their prey."

Her laughter was loud and wild, tinged with madness. Juniper's arms shivered, unnaturally cold.

When Sheena leaped from tree to lava, he turned and ran, his body whipped by winds suddenly sweeping black fields. He breathed hard and felt paralyzed even though he was running as if escaping a terrible danger. Why was he so frightened? he asked himself.

At first he thought he could easily outrun Sheena. She was a woman and could not know El Malpais' trails as well as he did, but he glanced over his shoulder and saw her running as fast as he could, feet confident in moonlight. Even when, a minute later, a black cloud collided with the moon and lava fields plunged into absolute darkness, Sheena kept after him.

"Wait!" she called. "Wait for the black widow and her web!"

"Go away!" Juniper yelled back. "Leave me alone!"

"Join me in my parlor!" the woman screeched. "In my house that navigates stars!"

Juniper tried to feel where his father was. He kept hoping his father would appear and stop the wild chase. He ran into the blowhole field not far from where they lived. Oozed-up mounds of centuries-old lava with small and large openings surrounded him. Without thinking he skewed toward one of the largest blowholes and scrambled into darkness more intense than the night. He crawled like a crazy man into tubes running hundreds of miles beneath lava fields.

A hundred feet into the lava tube he stopped and listened. His heart sank into his stomach when he heard Sheena behind him, scrambling like he was scrambling. In front of him the tube branched four ways. Which way? he asked himself. He crawled toward an opening that led to a series of squeezers that would let a boy through, but would block an adult woman's body.

He slipped through one squeezer, then another, then another. He stopped to listen. The tube's air was close and choking with a faint whiff of sulfur. His eyes grew large when he heard Sheena slip through a squeezer behind him.

"Come boy," she said, voice muted by stone. "You walked to me on the trail. Come."

Juniper put his hand on aa lava and pulled back. Small, sharp stones cut him. He hesitated, caught between the sharp lava floor and the sounds of the mad woman.

"Why am I afraid of her?" he asked himself.

Father answered in his head.

"She's crazy," he'd said. "Stay away from her. She's dangerous."

Juniper scurried madly across aa lava, ignoring pain in his hands and knees. He squeezed through an opening so small he barely scraped through, going deeper into the tubes than he had ever gone before. He came to another fork in the tunnel and took the right fork. He crawled downward. He stopped again and listened.

Silence. Sheena was no longer behind him.

The tube he was in was larger than those he'd scrambled down. Water dripped onto glass-smooth lava. Hearing no sound behind him, he realized he was lost in a dark maze without light or a way to get back to the surface. He touched stinging hands to his face. "What have I done to myself now?" he said out-loud.

He crawled over smooth stone until he found himself on an overhang's lip above an immense cavern. Distant, ruddy-red lava light flickered at irregular intervals.

Then he saw the great lizards moving in darkness. Tongues flickered in and out of huge mouths with rows of razor sharp teeth. White skins flickered whenever lava lit the darkness. The lizards had small, scaly patches of pale skin where eyes should have been. They were lying beside a dark underground river and its powerful current.

"Christ," he whispered to himself. "What are those?"

The largest lizard turned toward the sound Juniper had made. Juniper's heart pounded in his ears.

"You're lost," Juniper thought to himself, but the voice he heard in his head was not his voice. "You are not where you belong."

He backed away from the cavern's ledge. "You must follow me," the voice not his voice said in his head.

The big lizard moved. It was fourteen feet long and had a long neck and legs, bowed out from bunched-up shoulders as thick as a pinyon's trunk.

Juniper slowly backed into the lava tube's darkness. He was not afraid the way he had been running from Sheena, but the situation seemed unreal, bizarre.

"You must not be afraid," the voice said. "You must follow me or die in the volcanic earth's depths without food or water. No one will hurt you. You must climb a lava tube that leads to the surface."

Juniper glanced behind him. He whimpered to himself.

"Follow me," the voice insisted.

Tentatively Juniper moved toward the ledge's rim again. The great lizard moved down the river bank, leaving the other lizards behind. Sightless eyes looked at Juniper and the ledge, but the lizards were as still as stone, waiting for him to decide.

Slowly, fiercely, watching the big lizard, ready to flee, Juniper crawled off the ledge to the cavern floor. Ruddy light flickered on his arm's bare skin. He got to the floor and sidled against cavern walls as he followed the lizard. It did not turn its head toward him, but moved down the river bank.

The cavern wound around a corner; he could no longer see the other lizards. Juniper relaxed, abruptly aware of tight knots in his shoulders. The big lizard kept moving as Juniper tried to keep up. It stopped twice and lapped river water. The lava fire's glow strengthened and lit the cavern's glassy floor. Descending from the ceiling great yellow and white stalactites created a stone forest, pointed ends near the cavern floor as sharp as spear points.

At last, after what seemed to be forever, the lizard stopped. It looked back at Juniper with sightless eyes.

"There," it said in Juniper's head. "Above you."

Juniper tried to watch the lizard while looking at the ledge above his head. He turned and started climbing the smooth wall, feeling for bumps adequate for footholds as he moved upward. Safely on the ledge he stopped and looked at the dark opening in front of him.

"That will lead to the surface, though it's a long climb," the voice in his head said.

Juniper gathered what courage he had left and put one knee into the tube.

"How can I understand a lizard?" he asked softly, speaking more to the darkness than to the reptile below him.

"A dragon," the dragon corrected firmly.

"A dragon then," Juniper agreed.

"Go to where you belong," the dragon said. "Forget we are here."

Juniper hesitated. "Thank you," he said at last.

Without looking back, he climbed upward. Inside the darkness he lost time. He moved hands and knees and pulled himself upward. Sometimes the climb was steep. His breath labored in darkness. At other times the tube leveled out, and he moved easily. Knees and hands stung with every move. Finally, not a hundred feet ahead, silver moonlight danced on smooth black lava.

He pushed forward until he was out of the tube. Wind howled across the badlands. Fresh air gulped into his lungs as he gasped and gasped. He'd survived!

He looked around and saw he was close to his cave and home. He saw his father above the collapse.

"Father!" he called. "Father!"

His father turned toward his voice and then ran the trail toward where Juniper stood in moonlight.

Chapter II

When Juniper woke the next morning his body was on fire. Father had bandaged his arms, knees, and shins once he'd got Juniper down the collapse's stairs into the cave. Blood had seeped through bandages and dried during the night. Juniper groaned as he shifted on the bed and forced himself to sit up. The dark mood that had led him to confront Sheena had been left behind in the lava tubes.

On the shelves above his head toys his father had carved for him from pine, cedar, Ponderosa, and Douglas fir, for Christmases and birthdays, lined eye-level shelves. Jackrabbits sat beneath carefully carved branches of Douglas firs placed beside a team of six elk with branching horns hauling a blue and silver sleigh filled with piles of tiny split wood. Juniper concentrated on the toys, forcing away pain.

Outside the Oglala Sioux star quilt hung across the corner where Juniper slept, Father was planing wood, the planer's rhythm steady. When Juniper groaned the planing stopped.

"Juniper?" father asked. His voice sounded troubled and sad.

"I'm up," Juniper answered. "Sort of."

Father pulled the quilt back and stuck his head into the small room. He looked somber; eyes ringed dark. He had not slept all night.

"I'll fix breakfast," Father said.

Juniper shook his head. "No," he said. "I'm not up to eating. Not yet."

"Come out then," Father said. "We need to talk."

Juniper looked curiously at his father. He seldom sat down just to talk. They talked while his father was working on his carvings or in El Malpais hunting elk or gathering roots or berries. Juniper wasn't sure he wanted to move from bed, but curiosity got him to his feet. He felt wobbly, uncertain, and could barely keep himself upright. A faint air of the fear he had felt fleeing from

Sheena and seeing the dragons in the underground cavern was still inside him. Father brought a chair close to the quilt and helped Juniper sit. The look on his face was as strange as Sheena's look had been when she had told Juniper to stop before leaping from the Douglas fir to lava.

After Juniper had sat on the rough, handmade chair, Father went back to his work bench. He looked in silence at Juniper, moments stretching into moments. At last he looked away and picked up the cedar he'd been shaping.

"We need to talk about last night," Father said.

He stopped, not wanting Juniper to respond. He tried to find elusive words, his forehead furrowed in intensity.

"I'm okay," Juniper said, breaking the uncomfortable silence. "I shouldn't have gone so deep into the tubes, but I'm okay."

Father looked at him and smiled. Powerful emotions flitted on and off his face as he struggled with whatever he wanted to say.

"I know," he said. He took a deep breath and sighed. "I should have talked to you years ago, but I suppose. . .living in El Malpais has come to seem to be okay."

"I've lived here all my life," Juniper replied. "I wouldn't know anyplace else."

His father looked at him. "But you've never known why we live here," he said. "And you deserve to know."

"What are you talking about, Father?" Juniper asked.

Father sighed again. "How am I going to tell you?" he asked, looking toward the cave's door. "I should have been brave." He shook his head. "There's no good way," he mumbled softly. He squared his shoulders and sat ram-rod straight.

Juniper suddenly felt like he had in the lava tube when he had realized Sheena was no longer following him. The house was too small; he needed to go into the collapse's scattered trees and breathe in the wilderness, away from the maze of emotions he was feeling.

"This is not easy," his father said. "But after last night…" His voice faltered. "She's never gone after you before. Not out here. I've believed…." His voice faltered again.

Juniper waited for whatever was to come. He shifted and grimaced from pain, but kept quiet.

"There's no good way to tell you," his father said, repeating himself. "But you need to know the story. You're old enough. God knows you've been a good son." He sighed again.

"The first thing, I guess, is what you already know. We used to live in Grants where…" He pointed at the chunk of cedar he had been working. "I made a living for you, your mother, and me by making fine wood furniture and selling it in Albuquerque. What you don't know…" His voice faltered again.

"What you don't know," he repeated. "You must have wondered," he said to himself. He looked at Juniper. "What you don't know is who your mother is, or why you've never sat with her and talked about who you are and what her life is like." He stopped again, eyes and frown puckering his face.

"There's no good way," he said again. He looked into Juniper's eyes. "You're mother's Sheena," he said quietly. "We live here because I've never been able to leave her, not even when she ran away from us and started living like an animal in a place where no sane person would choose to live."

Father looked away from Juniper. Juniper sat on his chair and felt distant, as if he had put away the pain he was feeling and left the house and was looking back at him and his father from somewhere else. He said nothing, felt nothing.

"Juniper?" Father asked after a long silence.

Juniper tried to shake the deadness he felt. "Why didn't you tell me?" he asked in a small voice. Sheena? His Mother? The woman-strange-spirit who had tried to kill him?

Juniper's words and the look on his face tore like a bullet into his father's stomach. He bent over and looked at the rough pine floor.

"Sheena lost her Mom and Dad in a terrible car accident," he said. "The accident caused her to go into labor too early, and she lost a baby girl who would have been your sister. It was too much."

"I had a sister?" Juniper asked, trying to absorb what he was being told. How could he understand all of this at once? What did it mean?

"I was wrong too," Father said. "I couldn't understand. Sheena's parents had always been mean, making her feel ugly even though she was beautiful and laughed like an angel come to earth. I understood her despair about the baby, but it ripped us apart. It tore up the life we'd made together. I couldn't understand about her parents--why she grieved for them the way she grieved."

Juniper looked at his father curiously. He was no longer talking to Juniper, but to a younger self that no longer existed. I should just get up and leave, Juniper thought. I should walk to Sheena's treehouse and get rid of my fear and confront her. I should go with her when she invites me into her spider web.

"Sheena's never hinted she's my mother," he said out-loud. "You've told me to be careful of her, to avoid her."

His father flinched. "I shouldn't have brought you here to live," Father said. "When she ran from the hospital and the medicines they'd given her, I was frightened..." His voice trailed away. "I couldn't find her, but at Inscription Rock Trading Post and Coffee Company John and Pam told me people were talking about seeing this woman near Big Skylight and Four Windows caves. She seemed to be living where nobody could live.

"I left you with Donald Sharp and started searching the lava fields. I found her finally, wild, dress torn, filthy, too skittish to approach. I tried to coach her near me for a month. I brought food I left out in the open. Every time I glimpsed her she was standing in a Douglas fir, so I built a treehouse so she'd have shelter and painted it rainbow colors because she'd always loved rainbows before our baby girl died. The first time I saw she'd found the treehouse and moved in was one of the greatest moments I've ever had."

"This is insane," Juniper said to himself, but then realized he was talking out-loud. "Insane. How can your mother be an El Malpais spirit who wants to hurt you?"

Father closed his eyes.

"I still love her," Father said. "I've loved her every day since we were young, and I saw her dancing alone in moonlight outside a party her parents wouldn't let her attend. We had a good life together until you were four years old."

Anger bubbled in Juniper as if he were a blowhole ready to spew molten lava into the air. He stared at his father. All the years he had spent at school in Ramah, trying to understand why other kids hated him, boiled into his eyes.

"She hates me, doesn't she?" he said, his voice hard and angry. "My Mother? Sheena?"

Father looked desperate. He moved the cedar block from one hand to another.

"I don't think she knows who you are," he said at last. "I don't think she recognizes who I am."

"What is she then?" Juniper asked, his anger building. "A woman who doesn't recognize her own son? If she was normal once, what has she become? A witch? A demon? A faery spirit? What?"

Father dropped the cedar and put his arms in the air in supplication. "I don't know," he wailed, startling Juniper. "God help me, I don't know!"

In the silence that followed Juniper stared at his father. Tears streamed down Father's face, his lips trembling.

Rage building in Juniper disappeared. His father sobbed, haltingly at first, but then uncontrollably. He bent over, head touching his knees.

Juniper got up from his chair and knelt by his father. He gasped from the pain in his knees as he knelt. He took Father's bowed head in his hands and said, over and over again, "I love you Father. I love you."

Then he paused. He thought about Sheena's eyes shivering through him in the moonlight.

"I'm sorry," his father gasped. "I'm so, so sorry."

"I love Sheena, mother, too," Juniper said out of a great sadness. He was on a roller coaster of emotions: Okay, dead, angry, sad… "I don't understand, but I love her too." He paused. "If you want me to."

Father had always been where he could help take the hurt away from school and the small cuts and bruises of living. He had always been unflappable even during the worst storms sweeping cold, snow, and winds over desolate lava flats.

Juniper was so upset he could hardly breathe. He could not hurt his father, but how could he accept that Sheena was his mother? He remembered how he'd felt in the lava tube realizing Sheena was still following him. He thought about the unreal moment when he had found the dragons. Nothing from the moment he had seen Sheena in the Douglas fir to this moment made sense.

Inside his arms, Juniper could feel his father getting control over himself. Father lifted his head slightly and put his arms around Juniper, burying his face in Juniper's shoulder.

"You deserve better," Father said. "A better home, a better father, a better mother, a better life."

Juniper thought about what his father was saying without moving, feeling his father's arms around him.

"I'm not like other people," he said at last. "I'm my father's and mother's child, son of El Malpais and volcanoes burning beneath the earth." His voice sounded forlorn and desperate.

Chapter III

On Monday Father tried to get Juniper to rest another day. Father had gotten up early, built a fire for a deer sausage breakfast, and started working on the chair he'd labored over Sunday. He was sanding the twisting curves of the chair's cedar wood arms. Juniper had mostly stayed in bed the day before and willed hands and legs to heal. He had brooded all day about Sheena and his father, trying to understand Saturday's revelations.

He had always believed his mother lived in Grants and stayed away because she disliked Father's life. Who would want to live in El Malpais? He'd believed his mother had rejected him and his father, and he'd gotten used to that idea.

But he had known his mother all his life. He had just not known that he knew her. She was not the normal, mousy mother he'd imagined, who baked chocolate chip cookies and attended church on Sundays, but a strange, frightening force who lived mostly in Douglas firs, a strange spirit who denied her son was her son.

Sunday afternoon Father had started talking about creating a one-of-a-kind kitchen table and chair set and selling it so they could move to Ramah or Grants away from Sheena, the treehouse, and the only home Juniper had ever known. Juniper had let his father talk. He had no desire to leave home and move to a place that would treat him and Father the way he'd always been treated at school.

When he had been younger he had dreamed of moving from El Malpais and becoming normal like the kids at school, but he had long since grown out of that dream. His life was not perfect, but he was who he was.

By Monday morning he was restless and desperate to leave the cave. He got up, dressed, forced himself to ignore pain as he buttoned his blue Levi shirt, came out of his corner, and told Father he was going to school.

"You're not well enough," Father said.

Juniper looked steadily into his father's eyes. "I know," he answered. He held up bandaged hands and looked at them. "But if I don't go I'll be as crazy as Sheena."

Father winced and looked at the cave. He seemed more unsure of himself than he had been before telling Juniper about Sheena.

"No one should have to live here," he said.

He looked away from Juniper and picked up the cedar he'd been sanding.

Juniper shook his head. "I didn't mean it that way," he answered, but then walked out of the rough pine door with its square windowpane and hiked through boulders to the stairs climbing out of the collapse. The piles of black lava stones marking the Cairn Trail's winding through the lava fields comforted him with their familiarity as he struggled to ignore the pain he was feeling.

After reaching County Road 42, wincing as pants rubbed bruised and torn skin, an immense shadow ran along the ground in front of him. He looked up. An albino golden eagle, wings trembling, hovered above his head. It was the largest eagle Juniper had ever seen. A moment after Juniper looked up, the eagle wheeled and flapped great wings upward and upward into the early morning sun's glare.

As Juniper watched, momentarily blinded by light, the eagle disappeared, wings flashing as it flew into the sun's fire. When the eagle was gone Juniper looked away, sunspots swimming in his eyes.

As his sight came back Juniper wondered about what he had seen. He felt dizzy from the experience. Eagles, hawks, and owls were not unusual in El Malpais, but an albino eagle? On this day? After Sheena? The blowhole? Dragons? His father's revelations? What was the meaning of a white eagle that disappeared in a flash of light as it flew into the sun?

Later at school, after an endless bus ride, the day's wonder continued. On the bus Sam Maryboy said "hi" to him, but then retreated into his silence. Even the Lowder twins, who more often than not loved to torment Juniper and Sam, were not as surly as usual. Then, at school, before the day's first class, English Composition, he was standing in front of his locker. He stared at bandaged hands, trying to force himself to use aching, stiff fingers to open the combination lock, and then Lily Smallhand stepped out of the hallway rush.

"You need help?" she asked.

Juniper's breath caught at the shock of Lily beside him, looking friendly. He looked into her black eyes, wrinkling his forehead, and nodded.

"Sure," he said.

Lily kept looking at him and then smiled. "Look, about Friday," she said. "I had a bad day at home. My grandfather got really mean, and I took it out on the first friendly person. Not very smart." She paused. "I'm sorry," she said. "You're the nicest boy in school."

Juniper suddenly felt like he could smile for the rest of his life. He dropped hands to his sides and glanced at his gray locker.

"The combination?" Lily asked.

"Oh, yeah, sure," Juniper said, suddenly tongue tied.

"6 right, 10 left, 1 right, then pull." He tried to think of something intelligent to say, but his thoughts were like molasses pouring through a thin-necked bottle.

Lily opened his locker, and he reached up and pulled out his books. Seeing his pain, Lily put her hand over his hand. In his confusion at feeling her hand on his bandages, Juniper blushed.

"I saw a white eagle this morning," he blurted out.

Lily looked at him, not moving her hand, her gaze steady. "A white eagle?" she asked. "A sign?"

"A sign?" Juniper said. "A white eagle's a sign?" holding his breath. He had never touched a girl's hand before. He could not remember touching his mother's hands in Grants before his grandparents and sister had died.

"Animals are part of the life force," Lily said softly. "The eagle was one of the animals that gave the world light. You need to talk to my grandmother. She knows these things."

"I have to take the bus home," Juniper said. "We don't have a car."

"I know," Lily said. The bell calling students to class rang. "I'll talk to you in math," she said. She was off into the last streams of students rushing to class.

Juniper stood still, feeling her hand on his bandage as halls emptied. Did her touching him mean she liked him? He tried to shake off surging ebullience. It probably meant nothing. He closed the locker and hurried to class.

Then, at lunch in the cafeteria, Lily came to his table and sat across from him.

"Hi," she said, looking at her canary-yellow tray and blue plate covered by an oversized Navajo taco with its beans, hamburger, green peppers, and tomato sauce.

Juniper smiled. "Hi," he answered.

Lily looked up from her food into his eyes.

"I've been thinking about the white eagle all morning," she said. "Eagles represent strength, endurance, and vision. If a person is given an eagle's feather they've been honored. White is a symbol of power. You've had a powerful vision. I'm sure it means something special."

"Like you suddenly sitting at lunch with me?" Juniper asked before he thought about what he was going to say.

Lily laughed. "No," she said. "Something much more special than that." She paused, turning serious. "I'm just…me. I belong amidst canyons and rocks even if I'm not always comfortable there."

Juniper could have looked at her the rest of his life. She was not beautiful the way Sheena, his mother, was beautiful. She was dark and still, and she thought long, deep thoughts that were part of earth's rhythm, the balance of living. She was not mystery and eerie laughter ringing over moonlit lava. She was normal the way he had once imagined his mother to be.

"I'm not much of a person," Juniper said softly. "I saw the eagle, but powerful visions come to important people, and I'm anything but important. I'm not sure anything important will ever happen to me."

"White's a color for healing," Lily said quietly, firmly. "An eagle disappearing into the sun would not seem to be about healing, but maybe the eagle's about you and healing."

Juniper blushed. The conversation was not going how he wanted it to go.

"I'm okay," he said louder than he intended. "You gotta be tough to live in the lava fields."

Lily smiled. She seemed wise, Juniper thought to himself. He'd never known anybody who was wise.

"Have there been other signs?" Lily asked. "Little ones. Like finding an eagle feather or seeing a bear or something else unusual?"

The vision of blind white dragons in deep caverns beside an underground river stunned Juniper inside the noisy cafeteria. He was in the blowhole climbing down lava tube darkness, trying to escape his mother, crawling away from wild laughter, El Malpais, himself. He looked into Lily's eyes. She was leaning toward him.

"There was something," she said, her voice intense. "You've seen something else."

Juniper shook his head.

"White dragons," he said so softly he could barely hear himself. "In a cavern flickering red from lava deep beneath the lava fields." He paused, looking frightened. "I'm supposed to forget they are there."

"Dragons? White dragons?" Lily asked, her voice puzzled.

"I was trying to escape my mother," Juniper explained. "I climbed into a blowhole and crawled through lemon-squeezers until I saw them. They were bigger than any lizards I've ever seen, and they called themselves dragons."

"You had a vision," Lily said uncertainly. "A vision. White dragons and a white eagle…" her voice trailed off. "I don't think my grandmother could help with all of that. We need a medicine man, someone who knows ancient ways. I don't know…"

The school bell rang. Neither had eaten their meal. Lily picked up her fork and cut off a piece of the fry bread taco and gulped a bite. "After school," she said. "Before the bus comes."

Juniper stopped chewing and looked at Lily. "You don't think I'm crazy do you?" he asked. "My mother's crazy."

Lily smiled at him. "I think you're having visions," she said. "You need to understand your visions or you'll go crazy, but you're not crazy now."

The bell rang again. They both stood.

"Later," Lily said, turning toward the hallway leading to American Studies.

"Later," Juniper said softly as she walked away.

After school Lily was waiting for him on Ramah High School's front steps. When she saw him she smiled and fell into step with him. He tried to take her waiting for him in stride and tried to act cool, but he grinned like a love sick fool.

"I've been thinking," she said. "The way to understand visions is to have guidance, or to seek more of them out until they make sense. I don't have anything to do with medicine men, but if you'll let me, I'll go with you while you try to find out what the eagle and dragons mean."

Juniper stopped. His school bus was in a line of buses waiting for the kids who lived away from Ramah in the country.

"Go with me?" he asked.

"My brother will drive me to the County 42 turnaround," she said. "You can meet me Saturday morning. He can pick me up before dark after we've spent the day together. We can look for the meaning of your visions."

"Saturday?" Juniper said blankly.

Lily smiled, bent toward him, and brushed her lips on his right cheek. He stood as rooted to the sidewalk as if he'd turned into a Douglas fir. Lily turned and walked swiftly away from him.

"Saturday," he said to himself. "Saturday."

She'd kissed him, he thought to himself. Lily Smallhand, a girl, had kissed him.

Chapter IV

The rest of that week changed Juniper's life. Lily thought he was important, partially because the eagle and dragons were powerful signs, but maybe a little bit for him too. In a week Lily became the most powerful meaning in his life. Before school, at lunch, and after school they snatched moments.

Juniper told Lily about Sheena and how she had acted the night he'd scrambled into the lava tube and found the dragons. Lily told him about her wonderful grandmother and her wisdom and her unpredictable grandfather, how he would turn on her and whip with harsh words that made her cry after drinking and losing control of himself. She told him how her father and mother had died in a car crash like the car crash that had killed Juniper's mother's parents and how her grandparents had taken her in and given her a home away from the city life she knew. Conversation gave them narratives that helped make sense out of what they were feeling.

When Juniper tried to tell Lily she was the miracle foretold by the eagle and dragons, she smiled and shook her head.

"I'm no miracle," she said. "I'm Lily."

"You've made me less lonely and helped me through a hard time."

"Eagle and dragon visions mean more than us," Lily insisted. "I've talked to Grandmother, and that's what she says. She said something important is about to happen, and you've been blessed by what the signs will reveal."

Finally, Saturday came. Nervous for reasons he could not explain, fearing Lily's reactions to the lava fields, his cave house, the coincidence of the white eagle and dragons in his life, the foolishness of exaggerating his importance, Juniper got up even earlier than he did on school days.

He had not told his father about Lily's visit, but Father seemed distracted by his work on his chairs and did not seem to notice that Juniper was not sleeping in the way he usually did on Saturday mornings.

Before dawn's first light he had already walked the Cairn Trail and watched as light lit the tops of tall ponderosas. Restless, unable to stay still, he walked back to the cave and helped fix breakfast, then was off again, looking in the blowhole field for the lava tube that led to the underground river's cavern.

By the time he was back at the Cairn Trail parking lot, watching as an ancient Buick crawled over the road, he was so nervous he felt sick. When Lily, smiling, got out of the Buick, he felt better, but still nervous. Her brother, long black hair tied into a ponytail, opened his car door and stood with one foot on the ground, the other in the car.

"You Juniper?" he asked Juniper, looking at him. Juniper nodded. "You be careful of my sister," he said. He got back into the car, turned around, and drove off.

"I don't believe you're here," he told Lily as she walked up to him. Her smile was excited and bright, making New Mexico's sunlight even brighter.

"I am here, aren't I?" she responded. "We're going to search for signs and meanings!"

She playfully punched Juniper on his shoulder.

"Where did you see the white eagle?" she asked.

Juniper nodded down the dusty road. "There," he said.

"Let's go," Lily said. "Let's see what we can see."

Juniper concentrated as they walked; trying to remember the exact spot he had seen the eagle. He kept looking at the ground as if he could reverse time and make the past the present. Then he stopped. He could almost see the eagle's shadow.

"Here," he said.

He looked into the clear sky.

They were standing in front of the immense black lava wall surging up from the small canyon they were standing in onto the lava field's plateau. It gleamed dully in the sun's light. He looked at Lily. She was slowly turning in a circle, arms outstretched. She was beautiful, Juniper thought.

"Why here? This spot by the lava wall?" she asked, talking to herself more than to Juniper. She completed the circle and looked at Juniper. "What did you feel when you saw the eagle?" she asked.

Juniper frowned, trying to remember. "I was pretty sore," he said. "I was forcing pain away when I saw the eagle's shadow and looked up and felt…" he paused. "I'm not sure…amazed, filled with wonder…I'd never seen an albino golden eagle before. I felt blessed, I guess."

Lily nodded, searching skies as if she was hoping to see the eagle.

"There's the lava wall," she said. "Trees and brush. Sky…"

She gasped and pointed.

Sheena was standing on the lava wall's rim, looking down at them. She looked small on the black wall's immensity and was so still she seemed a part of the landscape.

Anger surged inside Juniper, contradicted instantly by a more complex feeling: Confusion, a feeling of power followed by hopelessness.

"That's your mother, isn't it? Sheena," Lily said beneath her breath. "Here where you saw the white eagle."

Juniper nodded. "My mother?" he asked. "A mother's more than a woman standing in a Douglas fir, isn't she? A mother doesn't scare the beejesus out of her son."

"This means something," Lily said, ignoring the bitter tone in his voice. "The white eagle, you and I searching for more signs, and then your mother where you saw the eagle. The signs have something to do with your mother."

Sheena's unearthly beauty could not be made out from so far away. She stood on the wall's rim and looked at them, her look so malevolent Juniper could feel its power. To the right of Sheena a huge bull elk, eight points on each side of its horns, appeared on the rim.

"This couldn't be happening," Juniper thought to himself. "Not at this place. Not this moment."

Lily was holding her breath. The elk and Sheena, unaware of each other, stood still. Sheena leaned backward and screeched, the sound eerie and haunting.

The bull, startled, leapt backward from the wall's rim. Juniper shivered and looked at Lily. Why did his mother have to be insane? What was Lily going to think of him now? Lily did not flinch, but looked thoughtfully at Sheena.

The high pitched wailing stopped. Sheena was gone from the wall. Silence.

"You've met my mother," Juniper said at last.

Lily looked seriously at him.

"Let's go to the blowhole field," she said.

"You haven't seen enough?" Juniper asked, a touch of fear in his voice.

"Your signs have to do with your mother," Lily replied. "The bull elk was another sign. You're doing what you're supposed to do. That's what the bull elk told you."

"The lava fields are rough," Juniper said. "You aren't used to them."

Lily smiled mischievously. "Don't think a girl can keep up with you?" she asked.

Juniper blushed, his face hot.

"I didn't think Sheena could keep up with me," he answered. "I thought no one could know the trails through the lava as well as I did, but I was wrong."

Lily turned back the way they had come.

Nearly two hours later Juniper had led the way to the lava tube he had climbed out of after taking directions from the big dragon in the cavern. He was amazed Lily could follow him as easily as if she was moving through the school's halls.

"This is where I came out of the earth," he said. "The big dragon showed me this tube, and I crawled until I saw silver moonlight shining on black lava, and Father found me."

Lily looked around as if expecting to see the bull elk, Sheena, or the eagle, but the blowhole field with its dozens of twisted black mounds was empty.

"What's your father like?" Lily asked absently, as if she thought she had to say something.

Juniper looked up into late fall, early winter sky. Two ravens spiraled around each other, flying higher and higher in a wild dance. Lily looked up at the ravens and then at Juniper.

"Another sign," she said, her voice sounding satisfied.

"My father's like those ravens," Juniper said. "He's wild and free and filled with the poetry of movement that expresses itself as love for me…" He paused. "And love for Sheena, my mother, I guess, although he has mostly warned me to avoid her."

Lily carefully sat on the rounded top of one of the smaller blowholes. "I think I understand," she said. She looked at Juniper with round, excited eyes. "This is about your family, about your mother's, father's, and your pain." She paused. "Maybe about my family too," she added softly. "I'm seeing signs too."

The ravens reached the top of their sky dance, veered from each other and hurtled toward lava fields, swerving into another dance above black rock as they raced over pressure mounds, hills, and depressions.

"Arrack!" one sang. "Arrack," the other answered.

They flipped wings simultaneously, flashing behind a cinder hill, disappearing.

"Wow," Lily said. "I've never seen ravens dance like that."

Juniper laughed. "They're smart," he said. "I've spent hours watching pairs like that. They do their acrobatics, then fly off and find carrion, a jackrabbit or mouse, along a road to eat. Pairs spend their lives together. They never separate."

"You're going to have to see the white dragons again," Lily said suddenly. She looked at the dark lava tube near her hand. "I don't know how you can stand going into dark like that. I can follow where there's light and land, but I don't think I can follow you into a lightless hole."

"See the dragons again?" Juniper asked, startled. "I could, I guess, but do they want me to see them again?" He looked at his still healing hands.

"It doesn't matter," Lily said. "You have to follow your vision."

"You think the signs are about my family?" he asked.

"I want to see the treehouse," Lily said.

"If Sheena sees us you might have no other choice than to visit the dragons," Juniper said ominously.

Did he want to see the treehouse? He'd avoided it since Sheena had driven him into the lava tubes. Did he want Lily to see it? He tried to remember how he had described it to her, but gave up when he failed to remember if he had told her about it at all.

"If the signs are about your family, we need to see the treehouse," Lily said firmly.

"Sheena saw us. She could be waiting for us," he objected.

"She's never waited for you before," Lily said.

Juniper closed his eyes. "I'm afraid," he whispered, ashamed at voicing what he was thinking.

Lily lightly put her hands on his shoulders.

"I'm afraid of my grandfather sometimes," she said. "He's wonderful when he's not drinking, but then he'll start, and he gets dark and mean, and I want to run away from him forever, especially when he hits me. But Grandmother's there, and I can't leave her, so I go home every night with my brother and hope Grandfather's not drinking and that his good self will greet me when I come in the front door."

Juniper looked at her. "This has been the strangest day of my life," he said. "I've got a friend who doesn't think I'm a Martian, but we see signs and do things that make it seem as if I'm from Mars after all."

"The treehouse is part of your vision," Lily said. "I don't know why I know that, but I do."

"Probably because it's the color of rainbows," Juniper said. "When I was a kid I thought it was the world's most beautiful place. I never knew Father built it. He never told me."

The admission, for a moment, made him feel as empty as he had the night he had walked from his house in the cave toward where Sheena was waiting for him in the Douglas fir. He turned from the blowhole field and walked toward the treehouse.

Passing by the collapse, he stopped. "Do we have time for lunch?" he asked. "It's late, but I fixed lunch."

Lily shrugged. "Sure," she answered.

A few minutes later they were in the cave. Father had gone out, and the house was empty.

"I'm sorry your father's not home," Lily said as they ate cold elk steak sandwiches. "I was hoping to meet him."

"We have to be careful," Juniper answered. "Sheena's dangerous, and she knows the lava fields. We can't escape if she sees us."

Lily smiled. "We'll be careful," she said.

By the time they ate and climbed out of the collapse, the afternoon sun was climbing down the sky toward sunset. An early, waning moon was foretelling coming night. Juniper, as nervous as he ever remembered being, wound through the lava fields, leading to the pinyon above the treehouse. Forty-five minutes later they were on the hill, the rainbow colored treehouse below them.

"So that's the treehouse," Lily whispered.

Juniper was so tense his heart was beating in his ears. Sheena, looking too beautiful to be true, opened the treehouse door and looked at where they were hiding.

"You're out there," she said loudly. "Spying on me. You've been spying on me for years."

Slowly, Lily stood up. Juniper, frightened, grabbed her arm and tried to keep her in hiding, but she stood up anyway. Sheena smiled to see Lily, eyes wild in their madness.

"Ahhhh," she said. "Not the man, but a woman." She laughed. "Come to my web, little one," she said. "I'll make you a dress of spider silk and moonlight."

"Lily!" Juniper said desperately. "We've got to run."

Lily continued to look at Sheena.

"The man too!" Sheena exclaimed. "The man for my web!"

"Are you a spider?" Lily asked suddenly. "Is that what you think?"

"Wait for me!" Sheena exclaimed. "I'm coming!"

"Lily!" Juniper said, panicking. "We've got to go."

"She's beautiful, just the way you said," Lily answered.

"Lily!"

Sheena walked over to the steps and descended to the lava fields as if she was a royal princess. Head held high, she swept along as if she could sweep the universe before her.

"We're leaving!" Lily announced, her voice calm. "I'm glad to meet you."

Sheena stopped near the steps' bottom.

"Nobody's glad to meet me," she said. "Nobody's been glad to meet me for years."

Juniper, surprising himself, slowly stood up beside Lily. He looked at his mother and tried to see her as his mother.

"We've seen signs, Mother," he said. "Lily says the signs are about our family."

Sheena's face contorted.

"I'm not your Mother," she shrieked. "Don't call me that! Don't call me that!"

"We'll see you later," Lily said loudly, making herself heard over the shriek.

"Later?" Sheena said, her voice suddenly soft. "Later?"

"Let's go," Lily said.

Juniper, not waiting, turned and walked into the lava fields. Lily took hold of his arm and followed. Juniper felt inexpressively sad. He suddenly realized his mother felt an agony that… He had, for the first time, heard the agony in her voice. The only comfort he had was Lily's hand grasping his arm.

When they were halfway to County 42, Juniper stopped and listened as hard as he could to the wilderness.

"No one's behind us," he said.

Lily smiled. "I didn't think she would be," she said.

"Why did you let her see you?" Juniper asked.

Lily sighed. "I was thinking about you hiding behind the pinyon and looking down on her all these years," she said. "I decided you needed to stop hiding and confront her the way you've been confronting the signs you've seen."

Juniper frowned. "Isn't that my decision?" he asked. "Not yours?"

Lily's face fell. "Oh," she said.

A more powerful panic than he had felt at the treehouse welled into Juniper. After two years of trying he'd finally made Lily his friend. She'd kissed his cheek and held his hand. If he lost her…

"I'm sorry," he said quickly. He looked into her eyes. "You're the most important person in my life." He paused. "I need you to help me with all this."

Lily smiled. "I've always been headstrong," she admitted. "But this has been a powerful day. I don't think I'll ever forget it."

Juniper smiled back at her. "We'd better get back to the parking area," he said. "I don't want your brother thinking bad things about me."

She laughed, kissed his cheek, and took off down the Cairn Trail.

Chapter V

Father was working on the set's third chair when Juniper came home. The two weeks since Lily's visit had been a dream. He and Lily had spent every minute they could together, studying in the library, meeting at Lily's locker before school, talking until Juniper had to run for the bus before he was left behind, but the minute Juniper walked into the cave, he knew something was wrong.

For all Juniper's life, except when Sheena was revealed as his mother, Father had been unflappable, making sure wilderness lives were livable. Even when blizzards drove snow horizontal with forty mile winds, Father had made sure they had enough to eat and heat in the black cast iron stove. He was somber; a man who had made choices most men would not have made, following his wife into El Malpais with his young son and fighting to keep his family together. Walking into the cave, Juniper stopped in the doorway after closing the door against winter's first cold.

"Father?" he asked.

His father kept sanding cedar he'd fashioned into a chair, but looked up. He'd been crying. He looked haggard.

"There's no hope," he said, his voice bleak.

"No hope?" Juniper asked.

Father stopped sanding.

"I went to see your mother," he said. "I've hoped all these years she would find a way back to us, but she flew into a rage so awful I couldn't get near the treehouse. She knew I was coming. I don't know how she knew."

"I don't think about Sheena much," Juniper said carefully. He tried to avoid admitting to himself he had just been thinking about her. "Lily and I went to see her when Lily was here, but she wasn't sane. She didn't go completely crazy, but she made no sense."

Father looked at the chairs he'd finished. "She needs treatment," he said. "But she reacted so badly last time…" His voice trailed off. "I need to be near her, but you're a teenager and need a normal life."

"Can't the rescue squad come and get her?" Juniper asked.

He felt like a traitor asking the question. His father had, in some ways, given up life for his mother, but Juniper wanted a mother, not a dangerous, beautiful woman speaking in riddles, haunting El Malpais like an insubstantial spirit.

Father laughed. "Could you catch her if she didn't want to be caught? You and I know the lava fields better than anyone, but she was raised on Chain of Craters Road and has spent years exploring every collapse, cave, and lava tube."

"I don't want to move," Juniper volunteered. "My life's pretty good. I have you and Lily. That's enough."

Father looked at him without speaking.

"I've tried to mend a beautiful dream that life once was," he said at last. "Maybe I should I admit I've failed. Maybe I should realize I have responsibilities, not dreams."

Juniper walked over to the stove, putting split Ponderosa into its firebox. He lit a match and started the evening fire. The cave was never as cold as outside, but he could feel the coming night's frigid air.

Father put down his head and started sanding again, bringing out the cedar's grain and small, dark knots. The chair's curving legs and back were natural and elegant.

That night after Juniper had gone to bed, he dreamed of the big dragon and the cavern's underground river. He walked peacefully toward the dragon, feeling heat from lava flows deep beneath them warming his feet. The dragon was silent, concentrating on the river's dark flow.

The dragon stopped walking and looked at Juniper with sightless eyes.

"Do you know my name?" he asked.

"I didn't know dragons had names," Juniper answered.

The dragon sighed. In the sigh were memories longer than any ten humans' lives.

"Dragons have not always lived in this cavern under the earth above volcanoes building toward a thousand year explosion. We once terrorized humankind, building wealth inside hoard caves, fearing those who came to steal what we had stolen. As humans multiplied like rabbits in paradise, we grew fewer and more vulnerable to your weapons. The dragon race dwindled. We tried to make peace, developing skills that aided rather than destroyed humans, but that failed. Humans kept multiplying, and always a few hunted us, afraid of our gifts, reducing our numbers and making life a nightmare of ceaseless dwindling.

"Finally, under the leadership of the last dragon king, Grilgax, a conclave was held in Scotland's wilds. Explorers were sent with orders to find a place where humans would never come over tens of thousands of years. After a hundred years searching, we came to this place and hid, giving up flight, giving up the beauty of open-aired skies, accepting blindness in return for an existence we have come to love."

"You don't miss the surface away from caverns and lava tubes?"

"No," the dragon said. "Neither I, Simalucroix, Creleigh, nor my relatives want anything to do with the surface, although…"

"Yes?" Juniper prodded.

"We dream of starry nights and silver moons and of wings, long unused, stretched as we soar into endless skies."

"Simalucroix? That's your name?" Juniper asked.

Simalucroix did not answer, but looked with sightless eyes at Juniper.

"Why did you come?" he asked.

"I don't know," Juniper said. "Lily, my friend, said you are part of my vision and that I have to seek visions until their meanings become clear."

"Then you must come, not in your dreams, but in yourself," Simaucroix said. "You have troubles. The question is, do dragons in deep caverns care to resolve the troubles of any human, even one who would be our friend? We wish you no harm, but should we bear you good will with old gifts?"

Juniper woke. The cave was dark and cold. He got out of bed. Father was sleeping behind the storm pattern rug an old Navajo man had given him, snoring as he turned in his restlessness.

Juniper put clothes and boots on and went outside. The night felt like snow. Clouds covered the moon and stars. Once outside he thought he should go back inside and sleep. He had an Algebra exam tomorrow and would not do well without sleep, but instead of going back to the house he walked through the collapse's boulders to the steps. Before he put his first foot on the first step, he heard movement above him. Sheena was standing at the top of the stairs.

"Mother?" he said before he thought about the strangeness of Sheena being there.

The woman haunting him looked down, but kept still.

"I'm sorry," she said, her voice clear, rational. "I didn't want to upset your father. The only way I can live is to rage and wail at living."

Juniper had no idea how to respond. She stayed silent, waiting for him to answer. He stood as still as if he was in the line of sight of an antelope he and Father had spent days hunting.

"I wish I could rid myself of this sadness," Sheena said at last, her voice desperate. "I wish I could find the peace I had with your father."

"You know I'm your son?" Juniper asked at last.

A coyote yipped close by, causing both Sheena and Juniper to startle. Sheena's sadness fell from her as if it was a cloak shrugged to ground.

"You're a little man," she said, her voice mysterious, gentle, silver. "I live in a house that sails through stars."

She turned and started to walk away.

"Wait!" Juniper called.

She paused, looked like she was thinking about turning to Juniper's voice, but did not look back and disappeared over the collapse's rim.

Juniper tried to sort out his thoughts. He should go in and wake his father and tell him about Sheena, he told himself. Father deserved to know he'd awakened something in her. She had even recognized that Juniper was her son.

But then he saw Lily's eyes as she smiled at him. She could have been standing beside him on the bottom stair in the dark.

"You have to follow your vision," she said. "You have to see the dragons."

"But should we bear you good will with old gifts?" Simalucroix asked in his head. "Do dragons in deep caverns care to resolve the troubles of any human?"

Father's face when he had first walked into the cave had looked so troubled Juniper had wanted to heal his father's deep pain, but there was no solace for such pain. No end.

A gust of wind shuddered through his coat. He turned from the stairway and made his way back to the cave. How could he sleep? he asked himself. He had never once expected to have an understandable conversation with Sheena. Inside he looked at Father's corner and wondered if he should wake him. He'd tell him in the morning, he decided: When things would make more sense. He went to bed and quickly, unexpectedly, fell into dreamless sleep.

Chapter VI

A flash of anger flickered over Father's face when Juniper told him about his encounter with Sheena the night before. Juniper had woken feeling rested and energetic. The cave was warm from the morning fire. When Juniper came out from behind his quilt, he was surprised Father looked haggard, so instead of waiting to tell about Sheena at breakfast, he blurted it out, suddenly wanting to get it said.

"Why didn't you…" Father started to say, his voice harsh, but he paused. He sat on one of the roughly-made chairs near the stove. He breathed deeply, looked away from Juniper, looked back. "She spoke in a normal way?" he asked.

Juniper frowned, remembering his beautiful mother in the dark standing above him, sounding inexpressively sad.

"Mostly," he answered. "Though in the end she called me a 'little man' and said something about her house sailing through stars. She walked into the lava fields. I thought about waking you, but there's no finding her when she decides to disappear."

Father's face grew contemplative. "Is there hope after all this time?" he asked himself. He looked at Juniper, eyes shining. "She said she didn't mean to upset me?" he asked.

"That, and she wished she had the peace she once had," Juniper answered.

"I don't suppose I should go to the treehouse again," Father said, talking more to himself than to Juniper. "Still…" he paused. "I found her the other day. Maybe it did some good." He looked at Juniper. Elk sausage smoked in the frying pan. Juniper jumped up and took the pan off the fire. "Maybe we should go together," Father said. "Maybe that would mean more. When you and Lily went to the treehouse… Maybe what she's responding to is both of us."

Juniper shivered. He had been frightened when Lily had stood and let Sheena see her. He had been more frightened running from Sheena and crawling in absolute darkness to the dragons' cavern. He did not accept Sheena as his mother even though he had called her mother at the treehouse and when she had stood at the top of the stairs. His emotions rumbled like black thunderheads. What did he feel? he asked himself. Who was he?

Father stayed still on his chair, watching.

"This is hard on you," he said at last. "I can understand that."

Juniper shook his head, trying to feel his way through his emotions.

"You should have told me earlier," he said.

Pain flooded Father's eyes.

"Maybe so," he whispered. "But I didn't…think…I'd ever tell you. I told myself that telling you wouldn't bring your mother back. I didn't want her to hurt you. I don't know where her rage comes from, but until now I've never known it to lessen."

"You said you still love her?" Juniper said.

Father frowned, looking into himself, eyes distracted.

"You need to know why?" he asked.

Juniper nodded. Father looked at the floor, trying to find words he wanted.

"Not everybody's love is unconditional," he said at last. "Your grandfather, who you never met, always had a deal. He traded guns, whiskey, cars, anything he could lay his hands on. He was always coming and going, not paying attention to me and your uncle, ignoring your grandmother except when he wanted something.

"When I married Sheena I swore I wouldn't be like that. I wouldn't forget Christmas or make promises to her or our children I couldn't keep. I wouldn't brag about how shrewd I was when I couldn't support myself, my wife, and kids. I wasn't going to be like my father."

He looked around at the cave's one room.

"So here we are, trying to find a way through a maze that never ends, living a life not fair to you, me, or Sheena even though she's caused it all."

Juniper breathed deeply, his emotional tangle in his sigh.

"When I was little I thought Sheena was a witch," he said. "I thought you might be a wizard. I couldn't understand why anybody would live in a cave when they could live in a house and drive a car."

"Maybe my choices have been as irresponsible as my father's," Father said. "Maybe the other side of the same coin, but just as hurtful."

Juniper shook his head.

"Lily likes me," he said. "She knows about Sheena; she's been here."

"But if your mother…" Father stopped in mid-sentence. "I love you," he said. "I love Sheena. I'm strange and difficult. I don't think I've escaped the way my father made me, but I've kept my love for my family true."

"Are you going to try to find Sheena?"

Father shook his head. "I've dreamed of our family whole for a long, long time. But now…" His words hung in the air again. "Can you stand burnt cold sausage?" he asked, pointing at the frying pan.

Juniper smiled. "Sure," he said. He laughed. "It won't be the first time."

Later that day, at school, Juniper talked about Sheena with Lily. Lily wrinkled her forehead. "What do you think happened?" she asked.

"Father's hoping she's healing," he said. "That we might become a family again."

Lily's dark eyes looked into Juniper.

"Do you see last night's meeting as another sign?" she asked.

Juniper shook his head. "I don't know."

"Your father still loves your mother," Lily said wonderingly. "Even though she's not lived with him for years."

"He says his love is unconditional," Juniper agreed. "He talked about my grandfather and how he never loved anybody. He said he told himself when he was young he'd never be like that."

Lily ran her hand through raven black hair. They were standing by Lily's locker, waiting for classes to start.

"That's really romantic," she said. She paused. "Maybe that's what Sheena, the dragons, white eagle, elk, and ravens mean."

"What?" Juniper asked, puzzled.

"Look at my grandfather," Lily answered softly. "I think he loves my grandmother, brother, and me, but when he drinks love disappears into whiskey. He acts like he has no love for anybody, especially not for me, and not for himself."

"But what has my father's love accomplished?" Juniper asked carefully, not wanting to upset Lily, somehow knowing the discussion could upset her. "Sheena haunts lava fields on nights with a full moon like a beautiful ghost that doesn't have a life she wants to live."

Lily looked at him.

"When I talk to my grandmother about you, your mother and father, she doesn't say much," she said. "She looks at me, smiles, and says you have to find your own understanding. She says they're your signs, and you need to understand them. She says I'm part of the meaning since I've seen signs too, but your signs are yours and not anybody else's."

"I love Father," Juniper said. "He has a lot of pain. I'm not sure he sees his love for my mother as romantic. He can't let it go; it tortures him. He doesn't believe the dream that keeps us living in El Malpais."

He touched Lily's shoulder without realizing he'd touched her. "Since you've become my friend," he continued. "I don't mind living in the cave. I don't feel as alone."

Lily ignored the bell calling them to class.

"I wasn't sure I liked you or anybody," she said. She leaned over, lightly kissed his cheek, and backed away. "But my grandmother told me I had to reach out to somebody. You'd tried to be friendly, so I reached out to you."

Then she was gone down the hall toward her English class.

After school, on the way home, Juniper stopped by the lava wall where he had seen the white eagle. Without thinking, he walked over to the uplift and climbed. When he was on the wall's rim, he sat, dangling feet over the edge, and tried to think about his and his father's lives. His thoughts were as restless as wind skittering from Sheena to Father to the eagle to white dragons.

He wondered if Father had spent the day trying to find Sheena. He knew what had happened if his father had tried. Sheena's reason had disappeared the moment she had walked away from the stairs. She'd walked into rage and her treehouse's sailing through stars. She would not respond the way Father wanted. Rage, built out of a childhood Juniper could not imagine, would not release her.

What could he do? Juniper asked himself. He was happy in his friendship with Lily. He loved her, if he could love anybody the way Father loved his mother, willing to give up everything normal in the hope love someday would someday come back to him.

He suddenly felt dizzy and backed away from the lava wall's rim. The sun was setting in a blaze of oranges, reds, and yellows. Simalucroix was pacing through the cavern by the river, agitated and confused.

"Do dragons in deep caverns care to resolve the troubles of any human?" he said, a daytime vision. "Grilgax demanded humans not find us for tens of thousands of years, but we've been found," the great dragon said. "By a boy who should never have found us who needs skills long buried in memories."

Juniper fell to hard aa lava, his body trembling. "Simalucroix?" he called out-loud. "Simalucroix?"

The great dragon stopped pacing and looked at the cavern's dark ceiling. Blind eyes swept back and forth as if looking for bats in the dark.

"You're that close, Juniper?" he asked. "After one meeting? You can call me?"

Juniper looked wildly about him. He could feel the albino eagle's beating wings as it flew over lava fields looking for a rabbit. What's happening to me? he thought. What's happening?

Simalucroix radiated calm into Juniper the way he had before showing the way from the cavern to the surface. Juniper felt Simalucroix's effort and fought the calmness.

"What's going on?" he demanded in an angry, raging voice. "Why am I seeing you when you're not here?"

The great dragon wagged its huge head.

"This should not be happening," he said. "We are not ready to be known by humankind." He paused. "You've already told others of our existence."

The accusation stung Juniper.

"I don't believe you're real," he said, still speaking out-loud.

Simalucroix's sightless eyes blinked.

"That's true and not true," he said firmly. "You know we're real, but you do not want us to be real."

"I dreamed about you," Juniper said fiercely. "In the caverns when I needed a way out and then at home in bed."

"Your mother's mind flitters like starlight on shining lava," the dragon said. "Your father struggles to maintain who he is."

"Father's fine," Juniper whimpered, cowered by the dragon's deep voice. "He wants my mother to be the way she was when he married her, that's all."

"But you haven't answered the question," Simalucroix said. "Do dragons in deep caverns care to resolve the troubles of any human?"

"How do I know?" Juniper wailed, sounding like his mother standing in a Douglas fir in moonlight. "I'm not a dragon."

"You've found dragons," Simalucroix demanded. "After a thousand years you've found us where we couldn't be found. I rejoiced touching your mind in the cavern, but I've been troubled, remembering Grilgax, remembering so much we have been privileged to forget. Dragons are restless in ways not seen since we first walked into Big Skylight Cave and found our way in darkness to the river."

"Lily knows I was there," Juniper said, desperate to explain himself. "She's part of who I am. I had to tell her. Lily told her Grandmother who is part of who she is."

Simalucroix stared at the cavern's dark without focusing. Shadow thoughts danced through Juniper. Fire and smoke mixed with powerful feelings of freedom as great wings lifted up into thinner and thinner air. People in wooden villages screamed as bowmen shot useless arrows into the sky. Huge dragons slept on beds of gold and jewels that knights in gray armor searched for until they found where dragons slept and came at them with swords and shields, spilling dragon blood and making nights alive with the screams of dragons dying.

Shadows plummeted Juniper, battered him with terror deeper than humanity, the self he was.

"Peace, little one," Simalucroix said."You are a dragon sign," he said. "Like we and the eagle you saw are signs. When signs cross the world is about to change. Dragons know that. Let us hope change brings good, not bad."

The vision of Simalucroix faded. The moon, waning, was high in the eastern sky. Winter cold bit at Juniper with a ferociousness that weakened him. What in the world? he asked himself. How could he have seen and talked to Simalucroix in broad daylight?

He looked at his healed hands. I can't stay here all night, he thought. I need to see what Father did about Sheena. He got to his feet and walked along the wall's rim toward the Cairn Trail.

Chapter VII

That night Father was silent. He had started carving the fourth chair's legs and was deep in thought. Juniper asked if he had tried to find Sheena, but when Father shook his head, a smile quirking at his mouth's corners, Juniper understood that discussion needed to wait. He spent the evening inside Father's silence, thinking about the hours he had waited for conclusions to percolate thoughts his father could share. He finished math homework, then his English assignment, writing a four page essay about the differences between aa and pahoehoe lavae in neat, careful handwriting, said goodnight, and went to bed.

The next morning Sam Maryboy surprised him when he came and sat by Juniper on the bus. His round, dark face, eyes still sad, looked more alive than they had for weeks. He looked into Juniper's eyes with a stillness mirroring the ancient beauty of pink, green, and red rock walls rising into pinyon, ponderosa, and juniper hills near Ramah.

"I'm sorry," Sam said in his soft voice.

"Sorry?" Juniper asked.

Sam looked out the bus's window at the cinder hill they were passing.

"You've tried to talk to me," Sam answered. "I've been too depressed to respond. It's been a hard time."

Juniper tried to look into Sam's eyes looking out the bus window. Depression was a mental illness. Juniper thought about Sheena and her behavior. She was not like Sam. She did not sit immovable, staring into empty space. Still, a relationship had to exist between one mental illness and another—if only in that the illness was centered in a person's thoughts and emotions.

"What's it like to be depressed?" Juniper asked and then regretted the question. He did not want to upset Sam.

Sam, still looking out the bus window, shrugged.

"I'm not a very strong person," he said softly. "I want to be more. I want to accomplish good in the world, but I look at myself and see how I am. Hardly anybody likes me, and I brood about how that feels, and pretty soon I'm trying to find a way to get away from the pain of who I am. Failures dog me, like a dream, pressing down on me. I can't get away from them since I don't know how to wake up."

"You're one of the few people I talk to," Juniper objected softly. "We've known each other since we were little."

"I've always been depressed," Sam said. "I just haven't always known what to name my feelings. Sometimes, like today, I feel better and see what my mother, father, and you, and sometimes teachers, do to help me, but other times I only feel dead inside."

"There's help, medicines," Juniper suggested, his voice barely audible.

"I've been in programs," Sam said. "They help for a while. The medicines make me feel heavy. I feel calmer, but they don't feel right."

"There's got to be an answer," Juniper said. "Something." He paused, trying to make a thought hovering just outside his thinking clear. "My mother's ill," he said at last. "She's the woman that roams the lava fields."

Surprised, Sam looked at him, turning away from the window.

"Your mother?" he asked, surprise in his voice. "The witch?"

Juniper shifted restlessly in his seat. The witch? His mother? Sheena? When had he started thinking of Sheena as his mother? As if she was his mother and not a spirit burned into El Malpais' landscape? Why had he never thought about her as a human being?

Sam looked at him with an intensity usually reserved for the bus window.

"She's sicker than I am if she's your mother," he said, his voice shocked. "Does she even talk? I mean, I've seen her, but I've always moved away as she moved away from me."

Emotions stormed in Juniper's eyes and face. "Look," Sam said. "I don't mean anything bad if she's your Mom." He paused. "I should understand if anybody can." Revelations were making him nervous, excited, afraid… "At least I have my Mom," he said. "She loves me…" His voice trailed into uncomfortable silence.

Did Sheena, his mother, realize he existed? Juniper asked himself. He reached out and put his hand on Sam's shoulder. Sam flinched away from his touch.

"You're a good person, Sam," Juniper said. "You're my friend no matter what."

Sam, hesitantly, smiled.

Lily was waiting when Juniper got off the bus. Her smile took away his gloom. Juniper took Sam's arm when Sam started to fade into the school crowd. Lily, face alert, cocked her head slightly as Juniper brought Sam to her.

"Lily, say hello to Sam," Juniper said, smiling at her. "Sam's been my friend since grade school."

"I've seen Sam around," Lily said.

Sam hesitated, but then smiled too. "Lily," he said, his voice unemotional.

Lily laughed at him. "I understand," she said. "Hanging around with Juniper's sobering business."

She grabbed Juniper's hand, lighting up the day.

"Is it?" Sam asked.

"Depends on what sign he's seen today," Lily answered, looking at Juniper.

Juniper thought about Father's face at breakfast, eyes serious, face determined.

"Sam's the sign of the day," he said quietly.

"Signs?" Sam asked.

"He hasn't told you?" Lily asked.

Simalucroix's dragon voice was in Juniper's ear.

"But you've found dragons," Simalucroix had said. "After a thousand years you've found us where we couldn't be found."

Dread chilled Juniper. Thanksgiving was next week; winter chilled the air. In December the first snowfalls would come. How could he let more people know about the dragons?

But Lily was excited to tell his story to Sam. He shook his head at her, but she was looking at Sam, not him.

"Grandmother says Juniper's a focal point," she said. "He sees dragons, a white eagle, dancing ravens, and an elk at a significant place, each one building meaning, and in the meaning powerful changes."

Sam looked confused. Lily squeezed Juniper's hand. Would Sam feel hurt if he changed the conversation? Juniper thought.

"You're grandmother's wise?" Sam asked Lily.

Juniper stayed silent. The question seemed strange. How did Lily's Grandmother's wisdom relate to what Lily was telling Sam?

Lily nodded. "She has deep wisdom. She knows the drum reflects the beating of human hearts."

"We have to be careful," Juniper said, trying to get Sam's attention more than Lily's. "I don't really understand what's going on in my life."

"Dragons?" Sam asked in his quiet voice. "Like fire breathing lizards in the white man's storybooks? King Arthur and the round table?"

Juniper's heart sank. His heartbeat moved toward his stomach. Lily saw the look on his face, his concern.

"Your friends need to know," she said to him. "You're going to need your friends."

"Simalucroix is unhappy to be found," he said softly, aware of the moving crowd of students surrounding them. "He doesn't want me to remember. Now you, Lily, Lily's grandmother, and I know. Simalucroix seems frightened."

"You've seen him again?" Lily asked eagerly.

Sam was looking strangely at Juniper and Lily. He looked as if he was wondering if he was more normal than they were. A light Juniper had never seen in his eyes was burning.

"Only in a vision," Juniper answered.

"Dragons?" Sam asked softly again.

"Where?" Lily asked.

"On the uplift wall," Juniper said. "Where I saw the eagle, and we saw Sheena and the elk."

"Oh," Lily breathed.

"This is really interesting," Sam said. He looked like a different person, alive, fascinated.

"The secret's out," Juniper shrugged. "How do you put a secret back once it's been told?"

"How can this be real?" Sam asked. "Dragons don't belong in the land of the Diné[1]. They're European. Our people would know if they're here. There would be stories…"

"It's Juniper," Lily said. "He found them when they wanted to be hidden."

"Can we see them?" Sam asked. "You said Simul…"

"Simalucroix," Juniper said. "He's their leader."

"Simalucroix," Sam repeated. "You said you saw him in a vision."

"He's seen him in his flesh too," Lily said.

"In reality?" Sam asked, his voice skeptical.

"I climbed down a blowhole to a cavern where the underground river flows," Juniper said. "I saw dragons, white and blind and ancient."

"Visions are important," Sam said, more to himself than to Juniper and Lily.

Lily nodded. "They have meanings," she said emphatically.

The school bell rang.

---

[1] The name the Navajo people call themselves.

"I'll think about this," Sam said as he moved off toward class. "It's better than thinking about myself all the time."

He looked sad again, but his face looked more alive than before.

Lily hung back, looking at Juniper.

"I can't come out this weekend," she said. "But I can Thanksgiving weekend. My brother can drive me again. He's gone to Albuquerque this weekend."

"I wish we had a car, and I could drive," Juniper said wistfully.

Lily smiled. "How's your father?" she asked.

The vision of his mother standing at the top of the collapse's stairs flashed behind Juniper's eyes. He frowned.

"My mother was at the cave," he said. "Or at the top of the stairs," he said. "She talked to me."

Lily smiled excitedly. "That's good isn't it?" she asked.

"Father thinks she can be normal again," he said. "He's upset. I don't think he knows what to do, but he wants to do something."

"You'll confront the dragons while I'm there?" Lily asked.

A whistling started up in Juniper's head.

"What does all this mean?" he asked for the hundredth time. "I know we're seeing signs, but what does it mean?"

His voice's forcefulness startled him.

"You have to court signs and visions," Lily said calmly. She looked at the high school building. "We'd better get to class," she said. "We're already in trouble. School never allows room for what's important in life. Not really."

"School's taught me a lot," Juniper said. "It's just that it's not a good place. Not for me."

Lily tugged him toward the double doors.

"Not for me either," she said.

They walked into the empty halls together, watching for monitors and the inevitable visit to the principal's office, but no one was around as Lily, then Juniper, slipped into class.

Chapter VIII

When Juniper came home from school Father was not in the cave. When he woke the next morning, Father was still gone. Juniper thought about going to look for him even if he missed school, but his father had spent many nights quartering an elk or deer, preparing to haul the quarters to their ice cave. Juniper worried when Father was gone overnight, but he knew that looking in El Malpais was wasted effort. The wilderness was too big with too many depressions to find anyone. After tamping down old fears that Father was lying in a collapse injured and unable to move, he got ready for school.

The disappointment he felt when Lily was not waiting for his bus stopped him as Sam quietly waited for him to control his sense of loss. Lily had not missed school since they had struck up their friendship.

"I'm sorry she's not here," Sam told him as Juniper mustered resolve to face the school day.

That evening on the bus Sam tried to get him to talk about the dragons. Juniper, lonely in spite of Sam's friendship, wanted to sit and stare out the window the way Sam so often did. He especially did not want to talk about dragons, but Sam pestered him, and finally he talked about Simalucroix talking to him in his head while he looked at the cavern from the small ledge.

"He didn't move his lips?" Sam asked.

Juniper shook his head. "How can a dragon move its lips? The head's shaped wrong," he said. "When Simalucroix first talked to me I thought I was talking to myself. It took a while to realize words I was hearing were not mine."

"This is neat," Sam said. "Really neat." He smiled. "I don't think I'm ever going to be depressed again."

Sam's upbeat mood lifted Juniper's spirits. Lily would be at school tomorrow, he told himself. Things will be all right.

Smoke was rising from the cave when he came to the collapse's stairway. Juniper sighed relief, surprised at how worried he'd been. Once inside the cave, however, he was shocked. Father did not look like he had slept since Juniper had last seen him. He looked haggard, eyes bloodshot. He looked up when Juniper opened the cave's door.

"Father?" Juniper said when he took in the black rings around his father's eyes. "What?" He stopped.

"Sheena's not better," Father said in a worn-out voice. "Maybe worse. She ran me all night with the axe I got her for firewood. I almost waylaid her, but pulled back. I was afraid I'd have to hurt her to control her. She kept yelling over and over again to leave her alone."

"Are you all right?" Juniper asked.

Father shook his head. "Not really," he said. "After you told me she came to the stairs I thought maybe there was hope for her and our family, but I've never run so far. No wonder you scrambled into a blowhole. If I would have been near the blowhole field I might have tried that too."

"She's not getting well," Juniper said as gently as he knew how.

Father shook his head. "I'm not sure she can get well," he said. He buried his head in his hands. "I don't think there's anything I can do. I'd help her if I knew how, but I don't know how."

Juniper sat by his father and put his hand on his shoulder.

"There's still the two of us," he said.

Father looked at him. He looked sad.

"I still love her," he said. "I remember who she was—she is." Tears were in his eyes. "There's got to be a way…" he mumbled.

Juniper fixed supper and sat in darkness after Father had stumbled to bed. Worry gnawed him. What had happened to Lily? Had her grandfather been drinking again? Sheena's moods were fluctuating wildly, from a moment of lucidity to rage.

That night Juniper's dreams tossed and turned kaleidoscopes of images. Prussian blue skies alight with a full moon and galleons of clouds rushed, a palely lit river, toward black horizons. Sheena danced from the top branches of one Douglas fir to another, face alight with moon shadows. His father and mother met on a bleak plain without lava or forest and confronted each other, Father striving for sanity, his mother laughing uncontrollably.

Then, toward morning, Simalucroix came, calm, massive, eyes glittering with burning lava.

"Sleep, little one," the dragon said. "Sleep. Dragons will have a conclave and discuss this. Sleep. You have entered consciousness; I understand your meanings."

After Simalucroix faded, Juniper, at last, slept without dreams.

The next day was the day before Thanksgiving. Father was working on the fourth chair when Juniper stumbled from bed. Father looked like he'd spent another night mostly awake. Juniper felt the edge of panic; worries about Father and Lily dominated his thoughts. Father mumbled incomprehensible words when Juniper left the cave.

On the bus Sam sat beside him and smiled, looking relieved.

"I was afraid you wouldn't come," he said.

"Wouldn't come?" Juniper asked, puzzled.

"Lily was absent yesterday. You looked discouraged. I was afraid you'd get depressed and couldn't make yourself move."

The thought startled Juniper. Depressed? He'd been down, especially when Lily had not shown up for school. He sometimes felt as if a perpetual storm had buffeted him from the moment when Sheena had frightened him into the blowhole, but he didn't think he'd ever been depressed. Sam was thinking about how he reacted to stress and was projecting how he thought he would react onto Juniper. Juniper looked at his friend and smiled.

"I'll be okay," he said. "Things are complicated. I'm afraid Father's taking Sheena's behavior pretty hard, but I'll be okay. I have you and Lily. I'm not alone."

Sam smiled. "Good," he said, squeezing Juniper's arm. "I'm glad."

Lily was waiting at school, but when Juniper saw her, his exhilaration at seeing her died. She had a black eye and a purple-reddish bruise on her chin. Rage slammed through Juniper. He could hardly see he was so angry.

"Your grandfather did this," he said.

Several people looked at them as they filed from the buses. Juniper's voice had been louder than what was wise at school.

Sam took Juniper's arm. "Easy," he said. "Shouting never solves anything."

Lily looked at Juniper and smiled wanly.

"He did," she said softly. "But it doesn't matter. Grandmother moved us away from him yesterday. That's why I wasn't in school. She said she should have left the old man and his bitterness years ago, but she kept hoping for better."

"Moved?" A sharp feeling shot through Juniper. What would he do if Lily moved away? Now, when he and his father were in crisis?

Lily shook her head. "No, not away from here," she said, answering his unasked question. "Out on Grandmother's old ranch Hogan toward Zuni. It's primitive, but like Grandmother says, it'll do for now."

"Your grandfather has no right to hit you," Juniper said.

Lily stepped forward and took his other arm, smiling at Sam as she did so.

"Just because they hit you doesn't mean they don't love you," Sam said. "My parents have been good that way. They fight and have a hard time, but they've never hit each other or me. My grandfather used to hit my mother when she was young, but now he tells her he's sorry for the way he'd been. He hit her out of love, he says, even if that doesn't make sense. You can see he loves her, though. A lot."

"I wasn't coming to school," Lily said, pressing against Juniper's arm. "But then I thought about what you two would think. I decided I'd rather put up with stares all day than worry you."

"I'd like to smash his head," Juniper said angrily. "He shouldn't touch you. No one should touch you if they're angry."

Lily stopped and faced him. "It's okay, Juniper. It is. Grandmother and I moved to the ranch; we figured out how to get me to school, and the black eye and bruises won't last. He gets drunk, that's all, and he changes. Mostly he's the most wonderful grandfather you could have. He'll take me on a hike and tell me about every bird we see and talks about its life in woods or sagebrush meadows. When he's drunk you have to avoid him and what Grandmother calls his bitterness. It's over now, and I'm here."

"I can't stand to see you hurt," Juniper said.

The bell rang. "We'll talk about it at lunch," Lily said.

She let go of his arm, smiling at him again, and walked away.

At lunch Lily looked tired. She was hurting from her grandfather's beating. She smiled wanly when she slipped into an orange cafeteria chair, casserole lunch on her tray.

"I'll be glad when today's over," she said. "Mrs. Chancellor called me in at second period, and I thought she was never going to let me out of her office."

"The school counselor?" Juniper asked.

"I thought for a while they'd move me to a foster home," Lily said. "They're going to talk to Grandmother, but I think I convinced them we're safe in the Hogan away from Grandfather."

"They can do that?" Juniper asked. "Foster you away from your family even if you don't want that?"

"Social Services can do anything," Lily said bitterly. "That's part of why Grandmother moved us so quickly. She knew I was going to go to school today, and she wanted to put off Social Services."

Juniper wondered how Father had managed to keep Social Services away from them for all the years they'd lived in El Malpais. They lived anything but a normal life. He was pretty sure the cave's living arrangements would fail any code ever put into place, but he'd never known of any threat to his living with Father.

"I don't want you to move," Juniper said urgently.

"I'll run away if they come after me," Lily said. "I can come to El Malpais, or Grandmother knows a canyon place near the Hogan. She doesn't think they could find us there."

"But that would mean you couldn't come to school," Juniper said quickly. "El Malpais would be all right. We'd be together, but we'd never see each other if you hid in a canyon."

Lily shook her head.

"I think I convinced Mrs. Chancellor," she said. "She's not so bad for a counselor. She listens to what you say. She'll make Grandmother come to school, but she promised not to sic Social Services on me. Sammy's home tomorrow. Mrs. Chancellor said she'd meet Grandmother even though it's Thanksgiving. Saturday Sammy will drive me out to the lava fields. I wish I could come tomorrow, but Grandmother's fixing Thanksgiving dinner for Sammy, me, and Grandfather."

"Your Grandfather?" Juniper yelped, drawing attention to their table.

Lily shook her head.

"Don't worry. He'll be sober," she said. "He's promised to leave after the meal."

Juniper breathed relief, wondering about Lily's confidence about her grandfather. He had not known how tense he'd become thinking Lily was going to miss visiting on Saturday. She'd said her brother had promised, but Juniper knew how circumstances changed plans. He thought about Father and how he'd looked that morning after trying to convince Sheena to…what? He was unsure about what Father had been trying to achieve. The only time Juniper knew Sheena had ever spoken rationally was from the top of the stairs in moonlight when she'd talked to him.

"I've been hoping you'd be able to come," he said. "When you didn't show up at school I was scared something bad had happened, and I'd never see you again."

"Something bad happened," Lily winced. "But I'm here, and I'm glad I'm here in spite of the complications." She paused. Cafeteria noise rose and fell around him. "You have to see the dragons," she said at last, her voice intense. "I've had a dream, and they're the key. The bull elk told me that in a dream."

Juniper felt tingly all over. Lily was dreaming now? She still expected him to brave the blowhole and find Simalucroix? He shook his head. She was not a simple person. She was willing to forgive her grandfather's weaknesses, but expected him to act strong when he was not strong.

"The key to what?" he asked.

"To our problems," Lily said, looking up at him with her black eyes. "Yours and mine."

Juniper was silent. The bell rang. It always rang, or he had to get on the bus, just as he and Lily had reached a crucial moment.

"Maybe even Sam's," Lily said softly. "The dragons are the key."

Invisible pressures pressed down on Juniper, making it hard to breathe. "I don't want to go back down the blowhole," he said as quietly as Lily had whispered Sam's name.

Lily smiled. "You're my hero," she said. "I can feel it."

She tapped her chest above her heart. Juniper looked at her small breasts and looked away, excited and embarrassed.

"Whatever reason is behind you seeing the dragons and white eagle is for your family and friends, including me and Sam," she said.

"After school?" Juniper asked as they stood and picked up their trays.

Lily smiled, looking even more weary, and nodded.

Chapter IX

On Thanksgiving day Father and Juniper plucked two wild turkeys, shot while Juniper had been at school, and baked them in the wood-fired oven. After they'd eaten turkey, wild onions, and greens, Father took the second turkey and walked to Sheena's. Juniper wondered about Father's actions, but it turned out that Father had fixed Thanksgiving dinner for Sheena for years. He had fixed the extra bird and delivered it while Juniper was at school, determined to protect him from Sheena's craziness. He was not about to change his dedication to his wife just because she had chased him with an axe all night.

The time between school ending on Wednesday and Friday noon was endless. Juniper wandered lava fields aimlessly, at one point finding himself above the Ice Cave watching a family of tourists walk from the visitor's shop toward steep stairs that would let them see ancient blue and green ice frozen on the cave's floor and walls. He kept returning, however, to the blowhole field and the blowhole where he could climb from the surface to the cavern where dragons lived their long, sightless lives.

When Lily showed up Saturday afternoon Juniper was waiting for her, sitting on the parking lot's wooden curbs. Lily's brother Sammy paid no attention to him, but let Lily out of the car and drove away. Lily was somber, but came and touched his shoulder, smiling shyly.

"Ready?" she asked.

Juniper nodded.

"You don't need to be here," he said. "I don't want you in the blowhole. I can climb down it on my own."

Lily searched his eyes as she looked at him.

"I need to be here," she said. "Your white eagle came to me last night. He didn't say anything, but looked at me until I knew what he was saying. I'm supposed to be here."

Juniper took Lily's hand. "Come on then," he said.

They walked up the Cairn Trail and veered to the blowhole field over the natural bridge between two huge collapses. When they got to the black mound-rock with the right lava tube, Lily held Juniper back.

"Wait," she whispered, brushing her lips to his cheek.

Her gesture made him feel brave, like an adventurer.

"It'll take hours," Juniper said.

"I'll wait," Lily answered.

She looked hesitant. "Did you tell your father?" she asked.

Juniper shook his head.

"No," he said softly. "He doesn't know about the dragons."

He turned from Lily quickly before he lost his nerve and, headfirst, feeling awkward, climbed into darkness.

Inside the tube time disappeared. He climbed downward, dizzy when the descent was steepest, the slope at other times more gradual. Most of the tube's surfaces were smooth. Once they felt so glassy he thought he was going to start sliding and wondered if he'd stop before hurtling into the cavern.

He did not think about Lily waiting for him until he had been in the tube's timelessness for some time. The minute he thought about Lily, Simalucroix's deep dragon voice spoke.

"We have gathered for you," he said.

Juniper stopped crawling and strained to hear what had not been said.

"Simalucroix?" he asked out-loud, then grinned, feeling foolish. The dragon heard him, but did not hear his voice.

"Yes young human?" Simalucroix asked.

Juniper tried to find what he wanted to say. This time he thought his answer and did not speak.

"Should I be coming?" he asked.

Simalucroix was silent. Juniper climbed downward again.

"Your needs and dreams are great," the dragon said at last. "You should not have found us, but you did. Our long isolation made us careless. We, whose race has always prided itself on forever-memories. But now you come, and the conclave will meet you."

"The conclave?" Juniper asked as he crawled.

"Few humans have experienced a conclave," Simalucroix answered. "In these volcanic caverns we have grown into social creatures where once we were solitary, roaming the universe as individuals. In a dragon meeting of bodies and minds decisions are made that change what is and what will one day be."

In Simalucroix's voice high mountain peaks gleamed. Howling winds ran across fields of blue and green ice beneath a full silver moon. Juniper shuddered and thought about turning and climbing back to the surface, but even as he considered that possibility, an image of Lily's face with its black eyes and bruised chin came to him. Her grandfather lashed her with his fist in a drunken rage.

After a time of silence Simalucroix spoke again.

"Your mother haunts the caverns like a disembodied spirit," the dragon said. "She is beautiful for a human, but wails as she tries to meld emotions and thoughts together. We see her in trees, hair streaming in moonlight. She haunts us, but we have left her alone."

Juniper stayed silent, though he wondered why Simalucroix was talking about Sheena. He wondered how Father was doing as he finished the fourth chair. In the darkness thinking about his father's courage and loneliness seemed overwhelming. He could see anguish twisting Father's face as he sought help for his young wife when she could not shake sadness from bones leaden in her body. Father flinched as his wife screeched rage when nurses gave her anti-depressant pills and tried to watch her take them as she slipped them into her clothes.

Juniper tried to drive visions of Father and Sheena away. Sheena got out of bed, slipped into the hallway even though nurses were keeping close watch on her room, found hospital uniforms in a closet, dressed like a nurse, and slipped out of the hospital room's window into the night, triumphant after days of being unable to think or move. Free! she thought to herself. I am free!

A difference appeared in the darkness ahead. Flickering volcanic fires lit the tube's darkness. Juniper came to the ledge above the cavern's floor. On the dark river's banks a thousand dragons had gathered from the great underground lava tubes, caves, and caverns. They stretched for miles, long heads moving, great bodies twitching, whiteness stirring as tongues flickered, and the sound of a thousand dragons moving rumbled as loudly as clacking freight train wheels on old tracks.

Fear seized Juniper. He could see high mountain dragons on cliff rims leaping into dark skies and soaring like nightmare ravers. They looked like the dragons below him, but were different, larger and more ferocious, wings white, blue, red, brown, or green, leathery scales covering long, sinuous spines.

"The time to be afraid is past," Simalucroix said, voice stern. "You have found us; we have gathered into conclave. Come."

Juniper closed his eyes. The dragon smell was overpowering. Not unpleasant, but alien, power that clogged the cavern with life that belonged in open-aired wilderness.

"Come," Simalucroix commanded again. "You showed courage once and saved your life. You must find it again."

"I didn't expect so many," Juniper whispered. "How do I find you in the midst of so many?"

"Come," Simalucroix commanded again, but more gently. "I expected our clan, but the word went out, and dragonkind came. No one alive remembers when the last conclave, where all dragons were welcome, was held. It stirs ancient memories, dreams, ancient hopes."

"Will they hurt me?" Juniper asked, moving closer to the ledge. He tried to imagine how he could climb to the cavern floor without stepping on dragon backs. "I feel small."

"Come," Simalucroix commanded yet again. "We realize you are fragile and young. You'll be safe."

Juniper took a deep breath and climbed off the ledge. When his right foot touched the cavern floor the closest dragons moved, giving him a path to the river. He looked at sightless eyes as they looked at him through their eyelid's white membrane. He tried not to think, but moved forward. The dragon smell became even stronger as he walked. Dragons towered over him even though they were on four legs and looked, from the ledge, squatted on the ground. Each one was nine, ten, eleven, twelve feet long.

As he walked he tried to remember Father's, Lily's, Sam's voices.

"You're my hero," Lily had said, tapping her breasts.

"There's got to be a way," his father had mumbled.

"I don't think I'm ever going to be depressed again," Sam had said.

As the dragons parted, Simalucroix, luminescent, unlike the others, stood at the path's end between canyon walls of dragons by the river. The minute he saw him Juniper knew who he was.

"Welcome little one!" Simalucroix's voice boomed, loudness echoing over the river and through the cavern's chamber, silencing the conclave's rumbling movement.

Juniper's heart raced to hear the huge voice outside his head.

"You talk out-loud!" he said, surprise in his tiny voice.

"Few humans have been to a dragon conclave in all history," Simalucroix said. "No human has been to a conclave this large. Time is turning as wheels grind wheels, and treasures long lost come to life in a sighted eye's blink. Change has come, and we need to know what that change means."

A soft humming was on every side of Juniper as the dragons started singing. Juniper could hardly believe where he was, or that he was walking without buckling to the cavern floor.

"Why am I here?" he asked Simalucroix without speaking.

Simalucroix struggled, his body twitching powerfully as the dragons' humming increased in volume, becoming a powerful song.

"You know why you're here," the great dragon roared, almost knocking Juniper to the ground. "AAAaaacccchhh!" Simalucroix screeched, his screech making Juniper whimper.

Humming pitched into a tornado of sound. Juniper put hands over his ears and pressed as hard as he could, but sound vibrated his bones. He started sweating even though the cavern was cold. Simalucroix twisted and stood on his hind legs, stretching his long neck, breathing flame into the darkness.

Small puffs of flame emitted from dragon nostrils all over the cavern, glittering the ceiling alight with orange, yellow, white, and green colors from minerals never touched by light.

Simalucroix twisted again. Skin from his back parted. Wings unfolded and gushed wind toward Juniper.

"We are dragons again!" Simalucroix roared triumphantly. "Great dragons!"

The humming became a sound of joy not heard for millennia. A thousand dragon voices rumbled, chortled, and buffeted Juniper. He felt sick deep inside his heart and fell to the ground. He felt small, insignificant, a firefly's flicker in the universe's immensity.

"Enough!" Simalucroix roared.

Silence was immediate.

Simalucroix, looking like a dragon from the times when St. George had hunted them in silver armor and a black and red head metal visor, walked slowly to the fallen man-child. He bent his long neck toward the ground and wrinkled his great nostrils.

"We forget ourselves. We have a guest. He has had to find courage to be here to see ancient ways become new again. Juniper?" he asked.

Juniper looked up into the glittering eye of a great, winged dragon.

Chapter X

Lily could hardly stand still. Juniper disappeared into the blowhole's black stone headfirst, and worries swarmed like a dark mosquito cloud. Could he really climb to the cavern and underground river through a hole barely bigger than his body? What did they really know about the dragons? They were wild even though Juniper said one talked to him. Would they leave Juniper mangled in their deep cavern darkness? Were they even real? What if they were an evil sign rather than the good one she had assumed since being told about the white eagle?

Grandfather's image materialized, a ghost in her head, face dark and angry as he shouted wildly about her and her grandmother's evil woman ways. He balled his fist and started drunkenly stumbling toward them. The wonderful man who got up every morning, faced the sun, and said ancient prayers was gone; an old, angry man fumed about wrongs experienced during a long life.

To calm herself she leaned against the blowhole that had swallowed Juniper and conjured memories of Grandmother smiling as she picked wildflowers in fields around McGaffey. She imagined her voice as she sang lullabies to help Lily sleep, her steel when she got angry at her husband for striking Lily, her movements as she gathered clothes and food to move them to the canyon's Hogan.

Time crawled, Lily half dreaming, half thinking, waiting. . . Is that a woman's lot in life? she thought to herself. Not climbing into the blowhole, but retreating inside herself to wait? The blowhole behind her back sang with a thousand deep, inhuman voices. Lily started from where she had been leaning, turned, and stared fiercely at the blowhole's darkness.

A great roar rumbled out of the blowhole. Lily's heart hammered. Juniper! she murmured softly. Juniper! What could she do? What had she forced to happen? She crawled up to the blowhole and tried to force herself inside. The walls were polished black, shiny glass, once fire. She tried to force herself to crawl downward, but failed to move.

Behind her, outside the blowhole, a terrible screeching caused her to back out and look at the sky. Heart hammering, she felt blind, mindless panic.

A white eagle flapped heavily upward, an enormous white snake writhing in its talons. Lily stood transfixed as the eagle flew from her. An albino eagle and an albino snake? What did that mean? What did it mean that she, rather than Juniper, was seeing the sign? As the eagle got smaller with distance, Lily remembered the blowhole. The singing and loud sounds had ended.

How could she know Juniper was all right? What should she do? Wait? Crawl into the blowhole? She felt paralyzed. She could not climb into the lava tube. The eagle and snake had called her back. She was supposed to wait. Waiting was hard. Really hard. She wished she had crawled into the blowhole behind Juniper.

In the cavern Juniper, looking up into Simalucroix's eyes, could hardly believe he was looking at the same dragon. Wings as thin and delicate as silk flared off Simalucroix's shoulders. They were longer than his body's length. They looked enormously strong. His head even seemed proportioned differently, more of a triangle than a square, strong hind legs bunched below a long, scaly white chest as he stared at Juniper.

Juniper did not answer Simalucroix's query, but gawked, oblivious as sparks from the breath of dragons made it seem as if it was pre-dawn on a winter morning. The dragons around him were still in their old forms, bodies squat to the ground. Juniper's heart was beating thunderously.

Simalucroix rested on haunches in front of Juniper. "Christmas is coming," the great dragon said solemnly.

The words startled Juniper. Why would a dragon know about Christmas? Even more importantly, why would he care? The dragon race had been buried in caverns for over a thousand years. Christmas was a human holiday created after Grilgax had called a dragon conclave and found the safety of El Malpais' caverns, a celebration of a holy man, Jesus Christ.

"What do you know of Christmas?" he asked Simalucroix.

The great dragon sinuously moved his elongated neck, glittering eyes focused on Juniper. In the cavern's smallness Simalucroix's size was overwhelming.

"Specific times are magic over the ages. Miracles are born in special times, bringing spirit and goodness out of places where they are buried."

"And?" Juniper asked.

"And," Simalucroix said, his voice filled with the power of the cavern's thousand dragons. "You need and want something from the conclave. You have woken the dragon spirit and helped me find wings. Dragons sing of new millennia undreamed during our grandparent's grandparent's lives. On Christmas night humans wish for miracles."

Juniper stared at Simalucroix's eyes. They whirled with subtle colors in the darkness. Juniper was seeing things that could not be seen, trying to make sense out of a world that was not real.

"What kind of miracle?" he muttered more to himself than Simalucroix.

"That's for you to put into human words," the dragon answered without hesitation. "It is not for a dragon or the conclave to define your miracles."

"This is crazy," Juniper said.

He put his hand on his arm and squeezed. Was what he was experiencing real?

"Why did you come?" Simalucroix asked him. "Why have you kept talking with me even from the world's surface? Why not go on with your life and do as I asked and forget dragons live beneath the earth?"

"Early Christians believed you were demons," Juniper said.

"We are, in a human sense," Simalucroix said. "Humans never see a mother dragon with a clutch of eggs or feel the exhilaration of all dragons when a new dragon hatches. But there are times when miracles become possible."

Juniper looked from Simalucroix's eyes to the surrounding dragon wall. It moved endlessly as dragons breathed in and out and shifted as they awaited the conclave's ending.

"Are you telling me I can ask for a miracle?" he asked Simalucroix at last.

"You have already made a miracle," the great dragon answered, fanning his wings with furious movements that lifted him from the ground. He stretched his long neck and spoke, holding himself in the air, stirring the cavern's dust.

"No dragon has flown since Grilgax's time. No dragon has breathed air flowing with winds or seen earth beneath him as he is silhouetted dark against a full moon's shining silver."

The mention of a silver moon made Juniper flinch. Sheena stood in a Douglas fir's low branches; her eyes glittering the way Simalucroix's eyes were. Eerie madness in her laughter made Juniper's scalp tingle. Then he saw his father in the cabin after running all night from Sheena, eyes sunken and ringed dark purple. He looked so discouraged and weary death was an invisible black cloak over his shoulders.

"You said dragons once developed gifts for humans, but were too late in realizing the power humans had and that hunters kept hunting you," he said to Simalucroix. "What were the gifts?"

About him the gathered dragons hummed again. Their song entered Simalucroix and made him larger and more resplendent. His head waved gracefully at the top of his long neck.

"Healing," he whispered softly into the humming. "Human healing."

Juniper's emotional intensity made him feel faint. He looked toward the cavern's dark ceiling. He needed to be healed, he knew. The moment Father had told him Sheena was his mother he had felt a festering sore forcing him to resent his father, mother, and his life.

The realization he needed healing startled him. He had never been injured in any way, but standing beneath Simalucroix's immensity, his self-awareness was expanding. He felt almost the same as he had when Lily had first kissed him, driving away the loneliness he had always felt. He felt the deep sting of his mother's abandonment of him and the scars of having lived in wilderness away from town while those who might have been his friends lived different lives.

He would not ask to be healed. Asking would be too selfish, too short-sighted.

"You could relieve my mother of her madness," he said hesitantly. "You could give my father back his life?"

Simalucroix was silent for a long, long moment. Eyes glittered at Juniper as the humming grew louder and louder.

"Dragons have paths out of the caverns," he said. "Our ancestors found their way to this, the greatest of caverns. We can find our way outside like you have found your way here and back home."

"You're coming outside?" The amazement, fear, and doubt Juniper felt was in his voice. "There are armies now, not knights in armor. Airplanes.Tanks."

"There are caverns to retreat to and live in," Simalucroix said enigmatically. "More dragons to find great dragon strength instead of living as lizards in the earth's caverns."

"But why?" Juniper asked.

"Our secret is out," Simalucroix said. "Your friends know. There are miracles to work in the way of the old dragons. Your mother waits, your father waits, your friends wait."

"A miracle?" Juniper asked again.

"For humans," Simalucroix answered. "For you."

"For me?" Juniper asked, feeling dumb. He could not grasp what was happening.

"On Christmas night," Simalucroix said. "When dragons come out from their caves and test wings against December winds and a moon's silver light."

The dragon humming vibrated in Juniper's bones and flesh. Sparklets of fire rose, glittered, and danced like Simalucroix's eyes were glittering.

"Christmas night?" Juniper said, not believing what he was hearing.

"Near the house that sails amidst the stars," Simalucroix answered. "Near Four Windows Cave below the pinyon where you have hidden to watch your mother for all these years. You, your father, Lily, her grandmother, her grandfather, Sam, and your mother."

"This is unreal," Juniper said. "Am I dreaming?"

"Go back to the surface," Simalucroix answered.

Juniper could not take his eyes off Simalucroix and his wings' weaving. A small puff of fire snorted from the great dragon's nostrils.

"Go," he said.

Juniper felt forced backward even though he was trying to not move. Reluctantly, feeling Simalucroix's dragon will, he turned and walked toward the ledge. He moved as if a strong wind was at his back.

About to enter the blowhole to climb to where Lily waited, he turned and saw that Simalucroix had followed him. How had he not noticed?

"You'll need to gather your humans together," the great dragon said. "Dragons cannot heal over distance."

Then Juniper was climbing, Simalucroix's voice ringing in his head.

Surprisingly, the climb upward, unlike the last time in the confusion and fear of finding dragons and feeling the pain of shredded hands and knees, seemed short and painless. The humming behind him made the blowhole's walls vibrate with music. He was in the dark, and then light filtered down black walls, motivating him to move even faster.

When he came out of the blowhole, exhilarated, still seeing flickers of sparks rising up from the cavern in his mind, he smiled as Lily rushed to embrace him, holding him as if he had faced overwhelming danger.

"Whoa," he said. "Now that's a greeting!"

He was surprised she was crying.

"I wasn't sure I'd see you again," she said in a muffled voice. "I saw the white eagle carrying a white snake. I knew it was a sign, but wasn't sure what it meant. I thought I'd talked you into doing something dangerous and stupid."

Juniper held her away from him and looked into her eyes. His eyes were shining from seeing Simalucroix become a great dragon, growing larger as he spread his wings.

"It was magical," he said. "You were right in ways you cannot imagine."

"What?" Lily asked. "I saw the eagle and snake. Those are powerful signs."

"This is going to be a Christmas to remember," Juniper replied.

Lily looked puzzled, then smiled and hugged him again. Juniper felt like the luckiest teenager who had ever lived.

From the blowhole dragon voices echoed song into the lava fields' blackness. Juniper took Lily's hand and walked toward the Cairn Trail and the parking lot where Lily's brother Sammy would be waiting.

Chapter XI

On the way to school Monday morning Juniper told Sam about Simalucroix's transformation and the dragon conclave. Normally no one on the bus paid attention to them, but this morning Juniper could tell the Lowder twins, usually puffed up from their feats on the school's football field, were enmeshed in the story. Sam got increasingly excited when he heard about how Simalucroix had unfolded hidden wings and trumpeted triumph as puffs of sparks rose from the dragons, making the cavern as bright as a cloudy morning.

"God," he breathed. "What does it all mean?"

At school Lily was waiting for them with her grandmother. Juniper stepped off the school bus, and Lily and her grandmother slipped upstream from the crowds of students. Sam was just behind him.

"Juniper, Sam, this is Grandmother," Lily said.

She was more reserved than usual, her eyes bright as she looked at the woman beside her. Grandmother was even smaller than Lily and old. Silver hair floated like a cloud above her dark face. Her eyes were like Lily's, so alive and bright they lit up the morning.

"Good morning Juniper, Sam," she said, her voice so soft Juniper strained to hear what she was saying. She took Juniper's and Sam's arms and led them toward the school's double doors. "I've gotten us a place we can talk," she said. "I need to hear your story, Juniper. To see if it has meanings the way Lily thinks it does."

When Grandmother touched his arm, Juniper felt as if he was in the underground river's grip as it rushed down rapids squeezed into a torrent inside lava tubes. Lily smiled encouragement at both him and Sam, as if she knew what they were feeling and wanted to tell them it was all right.

Inside the school Grandmother did not hesitate, but walked to the principal's office where the receptionist, Mrs. Arviso, opened the conference room where the principal held meetings with parents and school staff.

After Grandmother had thanked Mrs. Arviso, she nodded toward the brown chairs, directing them to sit. She sat beside Juniper, with Lily on her other side and Sam across the table. She fixed her gaze on Juniper and made him squirm in the chair. Lily smiled reassuringly again. Seeing Lily smile, Grandmother smiled too.

"I want you to tell your story from the beginning," she told Juniper. "Since my granddaughter is involved, I need to know what is happening."

Juniper looked at the polished grain of the table's oak.

"What's the beginning?" he asked. He looked at Grandmother. "How do you know where the beginning is?"

Grandmother smiled, shaking her head slightly. "The beginning is where you think it is," she said in her soft voice. "There's really no beginning or end, just Ké[2], relationships with proper place and demeanor. Stars and earth dance through time like fine horses in a corral filled with their ancestors' spirits."

Juniper thought about what Grandmother was saying, but had trouble following it. Inside the room Sheena was standing in a Douglas fir, looking at her son, denying he was her son, denying who she was while concentrating moonlight, as lava wilderness wrapped blackness and fire into the spirit of who she, Juniper, and Father were as human beings.

"It starts with Sheena, my mother," Juniper said suddenly, startling himself… "and my father's strange relationship with his wife and my not knowing that El Malpais' spirit woman was Father's wife and my mother…"

The story went on and on. Juniper was surprised at its length. Grandmother, Sam, and Lily sat silent and mesmerized as the power of story-telling came into him and blocked out the conference room and the school's noises.

---

[2] A Navajo word that is central to a traditional philosophy of life.

He told about how Sheena haunted El Malpais on nights of a full moon by standing in low branches of Douglas firs and about the treehouse and how Father had built it when he had found where she had disappeared after running away from the hospital and medicines that were supposed to help her control her dark feelings about herself. He told about his flight down the lava tube and his discovery of the dragons and Father's revelation about Sheena and Lily. He told of the white eagle and elk and his dreams and ravens dancing in the sky as they braided invisible songs of relationship while soaring higher and higher. When he finished, at last, he kept his eyes on the table's oak grain. Silence was so powerful it seemed to never end.

At last Lily's grandmother sighed.

"The dragon, Simalucroix," she said. "He said to gather on Christmas night?"

"Gather for what?" Sam asked. "I didn't understand that part."

Juniper shook his head. Simalucroix's demand in the cavern had not made sense to him either. Could a dragon heal a human? And what kind of healing could it affect? A broken arm? A terrible wound? Cancer? A heart attack?

"It's about healing," Lily said. "We have relationships, Juniper and his father and Sheena, me, Grandmother, and Grandfather, Sam and his parents, and they're not right. The eagle and dragons are white, healing's color."

Grandmother looked thoughtful, her eyes still on Juniper.

"Perhaps," she said. "But why Christmas night? The white man's Christ child was not born on Christmas, December 25th. Christmas really came from Romans, their Sun God, and winter solstice celebrations. There's only speculation about when the Christ child was born. The lava fields are outside of time, frozen fire worn down by the weathering and creation of Earth, our mother." She got up from her chair, moving slowly as if her thoughts were too heavy to carry. She looked troubled.

"I must think on this," she said. "Until Lily told me of white dragons, I had never heard of them, not in the legends of Navajo or Pueblo."

She softly touched Juniper's shoulder.

"Thank you for your story, young vision-seeker," she said. "You make me happy even if your story puzzles me. You are good for my granddaughter even though you are white and do not resonate with our people's good ways."

Juniper glanced at Lily, his breath catching at hearing the word white in Grandmother's words. Lily smiled encouragement at him.

"You young people need to go to school," Grandmother said. "I need to pray and try to see what this means. Lily is right. Powerful meanings are rising from the black-fire lands."

Abruptly she turned and walked out of the conference room. Sam shook his head. "This is so interesting," he said.

"Grandmother will tell us what is right," Lily asserted.

Juniper remained silent, still feeling his story's spell, wondering where he had found the words and emotions that had formed it. Thinking about how he felt, he decided he was changing. Although he still had doubts about himself, Father, and his life, he felt confident, able to confront dragons, a white eagle, and fall in love with a beautiful girl who was also the smartest girl at school. He had lost his feelings of aloneness as he, Sam, and Lily had started facing the world together.

Mrs. Arviso came into the conference room looking stern.

She handed Juniper, Lily, and Sam excused absence slips.

"You need to get to class," she said. "This is a school, not where you waste the day talking."

Juniper got to his feet and the three of them left the room.

In the cafeteria at lunch Sam joined Juniper and Lily, deciding, for a change, to eat the bland food.

"What a day!" he exclaimed as he sat down with his tray. "I don't think I've ever been this excited. I can't wait until I see dragons!" His face fell as a thought occurred to him. "I will get to see them, won't I?" he asked. "I don't think I could stand not seeing them after hearing all this."

Juniper laughed, joined by Lily.

"You're expected," Juniper said. "All three of us are part of what's happening. I'm not sure why, but Simalucroix has mentioned you, Lily, Father, and Sheena."

"Great!" Sam said, rubbing hands above his macaroni and cheese. "Great!"

"Your Grandmother's powerful," Juniper told Lily. "I think she could lead us to a cliff and tell us to jump, and we'd jump."

"I know," Lily agreed. "She makes me feel like that too. The only one who avoids that feeling, I think, is Grandfather, and I think he feels it when he's sober."

"The only question I have," Sam volunteered. "Is, when on Christmas night are the dragons going to appear? And where are they going to come out from underground?"

Lily looked steadily into Juniper's eyes. "Simalucroix will tell Juniper," she said. "The question I have is, what's going to happen after the dragons appear? Simalucroix said dragons know how to heal humans and that Juniper is supposed to gather his humans. I've seen signs no human can expect to see, and Juniper has seen even more powerful signs. I don't think those signs are appearing just so we can heal ourselves, or even our families. There's more to the signs than that."

A chill crept through Juniper. "What do you mean?" he asked Lily. "I'm not sure I get what Simalucroix means when he talks of healing."

"You haven't told your father about the dragons," Lily said, her face serious and voice sober. "Why not?"

Juniper took a deep sigh. He had not told Father. He'd really only told Lily and Sam and now Lily's Grandmother.

"I don't know," he said after thinking about Lily's question. "When I came out of the blowhole into moonlight, I was so happy to see Father it didn't occur to me to tell him. I was alive, and he was alive, and Sheena was somewhere else. Later on I remembered what Simalucroix had told me to never reveal the dragons' existence, and so I never told him. It seemed wrong to tell him."

"But you told us," Lily pointed out. "Me and Sam."

"Thank God!" Sam chimed in. "I feel good not being depressed. I don't think I need to be healed anymore. Just knowing about the dragons has healed me. It's so exciting I'm looking forward to seeing every new day."

"That's strange, isn't it?" Juniper responded. "I mean, Father has been everything to me since I was born, and this is the most unusual experience I've ever had, and I don't tell him. What does that say about me as his son?"

"I don't think you want to face implications Simalucroix is hinting at," Lily said. "I don't think I'm up to the implications. What if Sheena was truly healed and able to join you and Father's lives? What if I could get Grandfather to where the dragons are Christmas night? What would his healing mean to my life?"

Juniper looked at the macaroni left on his plate. What would happen if Sheena were healed and really became his mother and came to live in Ramah with him and Father? he asked himself. His heart-beat hammered in his ears. He looked in wonderment at Lily. How had she known what was in his heart when he had not known? Was he up to the aftermath of healing? Or was he locked into a lifetime of living life as it was, not growing the way he had been growing, but crippled by being afraid of what he might face if his life changed? Did he really want Christmas day to come?

Now both Lily and Sam were looking at him. "What?" he asked them.

"You're thinking," Lily answered. "I've been asking myself questions since I told Grandmother about the dragons, and she swept me up and forced Sammy to take us to school and wait in the car. I've been excited about the signs you saw and those I was seeing, but until that moment, waiting in the car, I hadn't thought about what the signs might lead to in my life."

Juniper nodded. Was he ready for changes he had set into motion? The bell rang, but he hardly heard the bell. He knew he had to get to Algebra, but why was Algebra important when he, Lily, Sam, and maybe their families, were wrapped up in an adventure that seemed to be getting bigger and bigger?

"This is too much for me," Sam said, getting up to go to class. He stalked off to the front of the cafeteria with his tray.

Lily did not move, but continued looking at Juniper, dark eyes deep with the long thoughts that had attracted him to her. She always probed beneath the surface and tried to understand forces moving stars and galaxies in eternity-long orbits.

"I don't know if I'm up to all of this," Juniper said at last. "How would I feel if Sheena became my mother?"

Lily smiled. "What if Grandfather stopped drinking, and Grandmother and I went to live with him again?" she asked. "What does it mean to the two of us that we are confronting this together?"

"I love you," Juniper whispered.

The bell rang a second time.

Lily looked so intensely at him he blinked and felt as if he was in the black lava tube's timelessness, climbing toward the earth's center.

Chapter XII

On the way home from school Sam could not stop talking about Simalucroix and the coming of the dragons on Christmas day.

"I'm going to see a dragon!" he exclaimed loudly. "I can't believe it!" Juniper wanted to keep him quiet, but did not want to hurt his feelings. He put his hand on Sam's shoulder and tried to communicate without words that people were listening. Hearing Sam's excitement, he could understand how foolish the idea of dragons in the Twenty-first century sounded. We're like characters in a fantasy book, he thought, going on and on about creatures that could not be, but are.

In the seat behind them the Lowder twins, blue eyes bright with mischief, snickered when Sam said he was going to see a dragon. Juniper ignored them, but at last Bill Lowder, in a sarcastic, mean voice, howled. "Dragon twins!" he laughed. "Glittering eyes and fiery mouths!"

His brother Carson lifted his arms in the air like a zombie and moaned, "Ooooooohhhhh," as even first graders, sitting behind the bus driver, turned to look at Sam and Juniper and laughed.

Sam, sitting, as usual, by the window, sank into his seat. Animation that had enlivened him for weeks died. The bus was alive with kids imitating Carson and laughing at Juniper and Sam.

Sam looked out the window as if he had disappeared and left the hulk of who he was in his place. His excitement had disappeared so fast its absence scared Juniper.

He touched Sam's arm and said, "Sam?" But Sam would not look at him. He stared at junipers, pinyons, and mounds of passing black lava as the bus climbed up and down Chain of Craters Road's hills.

"It's okay," Juniper said, feeling desperate. "What the Lowder twins or anybody else thinks doesn't count. It's us, you, I, and Lily, that have something special."

A black feeling swept Juniper. Sam stared out the window, refusing to respond. Juniper felt like he had so many times during his years at school: Alone, without a chance of belonging. He tried to think of Lily and how she had become central to his life. She had kissed him more than once! He suddenly felt abandoned, left without a hope of friendship.

"Sam," he whispered. "Sam." But Sam did not respond. His face was blank. He had run from the bus's tumult and noise to some darkness, or hopelessness, inside his mind. When they finally came to Sam's stop, he got up as Juniper moved to let him slip past. He seemed oblivious to Bill's raucous call, "Hey dragon boy!" He quickly climbed down the bus steps and walked the dirt road toward home.

When Bill called out, "Hey dragon boy!" Juniper turned in his seat. "Why don't you shut up, Bill!" he said. "You're croaking like a raven finding a dead rat!"

Old Mr. Williams, the bus driver, sensed tension as Carson half stood in his seat, eyes dark with anger.

"Pipe down back there!" Mr. Williams said loudly.

Bill smirked at Carson's reaction and the anger on Juniper's face.

"The boy who sees dragons," he said softly. Carson, controlling himself, sat back down, smiling. "Maybe I'll wait to smash your face," he told Juniper, smiling like his brother. "Maybe I'll ride past our stop." Carson giggled. The bus lurched slightly as Mr. Williams shifted into gear.

"Then you'd have a mile hike home," Bill said. "I know how you'd like that," he laughed. "I can see Mom's joy after she finds out you came home late so you could beat up Juniper!"

Carson hummphed. "We can work Mom around, and you know it," he said.

Juniper turned around. He'd been ignoring the Lowders for years. He did not feel good, though. He had not felt good since leaving Lily at school and started trying to get Sam to stop talking about dragons. What if people did learn about the dragons in the caverns?

But now he was worried about Sam. He'd been so alive and far from depression as possible, then so depressed he could hardly move. He'd looked like an old man walking the road to his house, feet shuffling and shoulders bent; life sucked out of him. How was such transformation possible?

He thought about Simalucroix's transformation in the cavern and the triumph of his roar as he became a great dragon. He thought about Christmas day and what Simalucroix intended by asking Juniper to gather those in his life who needed healing together. He wondered how he could get Sam to come to the lava fields if his depression sank deep and took away his will to live.

At home Father was working furiously, sanding his sixth chair. He'd moved outside into the fifty-five degree sun, although, as the sun began to set, a biting cold was creeping into the air. Juniper put his backpack by his bed and came outside to watch. Father smiled, but concentrated on etching flying geese into the chair's oblong top. Unlike furniture in the house, the new chairs were beautiful. As beautiful as Sheena's treehouse, Juniper thought. As beautiful as his mother's face.

"Why do people get depressed?" Juniper asked Father after a long silence. "I mean, why do some people get depressed and other people don't?"

Father did not stop working. His eyes bored into the chair's wood. He finished gouging out the flaring wing of the lead Canadian goose.

"Sam depressed again?" he asked gently.

"The Lowder twins," Juniper answered. "He was okay. Then they teased him. He changed so fast it was crazy. One minute he was talking and excited. The next minute he was looking out the bus window and didn't seem like he knew where he was."

Father looked at the ground.

"I don't know how to answer your question," he said. "I've tried to understand what caused Sheena's problems for years." He gestured at the collapse's steep walls around them. "But the truth is, I don't understand. I want to understand, but…"

"Sam and Lily have made my life fuller," Juniper said.

Father smiled. "I know, and I'm glad."

He got up from the rickety chair he'd been sitting on and picked up the elegant chair he'd finished sanding.

"Let's fix something to eat," he said. "It's almost dark."

Juniper hesitated and thought about telling Father of the dragons and the signs he and Lily had been seeing, but before he could make up his mind to tell the story, Father was walking inside, the sixth chair under his arm.

"I'll start the table tomorrow," he told Juniper. He sighed. "I can't imagine leaving Sheena here alone," he said. "But you've got to learn how to live in the world. Not here."

Juniper shook his head. He thought about the dragons in their caverns, hiding from knights in shining armor. Now they were going to join the world again. Where was that joining going to lead? Why wasn't he telling Father, the person closest to him, about the white eagle and the dragons and what Lily said about them, the elk and white eagle and white snake? Why wasn't he telling Father about Lily's Grandmother, who knew things about Juniper Father did not know?

Sunset blazed crimson into the Western horizon's clouds. Inside the cave Father had built a fire in the stove. Father had to be at the gathering on Christmas day, Juniper thought. He had to tell Father what was happening even if he thought Juniper was showing signs of Sheena's mental illness.

Life had been satisfying ever since Lily had talked to him at his locker, but nothing had gotten simpler. Just better.

Father started whistling, the beautiful, rounded sound soaring into melody. "I'm Dreaming of a White Christmas" floated from the cave into the collapse's darkening bowl.

The next morning Sam did not get on the bus. The Lowder brothers were subdued, unlike the afternoon before. They looked like feral cats hunting a jack rabbit, but when the bus drove past Sam's stop, Carson hit Juniper on the shoulder so hard his shoulder stung.

"Your friend can't take the heat, can he?" he said.

Juniper didn't answer, but stared out the bus window, thinking that he was probably looking like Sam did when he was depressed.

Lily was waiting when he finally got to school. She had a red Navajo jacket dancing with black designs depicting the Zuni Mountains' abstract silhouettes.

"Where's Sam?" she asked brightly as Juniper walked up to her.

Juniper shook his head. "He's depressed again," he said. "He kept talking about Simalucroix and dragons on the bus yesterday. The Lowders started teasing him, calling him Dragon Boy. That drove him over the edge. He stared out the bus window, as if he'd left me, you, the universe, and life."

Lily frowned. "He's pretty fragile, isn't he?" she asked.

Anger welled in Juniper from deep inside. He closed his eyes and stopped moving. Lily touched his arm.

"Juniper?" she asked. "You all right?"

Juniper forced himself to calm down. He took a deep breath and forced the anger from his voice.

"You would think what's about to happen would be good," he said. "But it's scary. Sam getting depressed like that, Father working on his table and chairs so we can move to Ramah, the dragons…"

"I know," Lily said. "Grandmother hardly talked to me last night. She fixed supper, went to her bed, and started praying again. I think she spent from when she saw us until I got home praying. She doesn't know what to make of dragons or the signs we've seen. I asked her about finding a medicine man, but she shook her head and kept praying. I thought that if we kept looking we'd understand, and everything would happen the way it should, but now, I don't know." The school bell rang. "Sam will be all right, won't he?" she asked, her voice abrupt, as if the implications of what Juniper had told her had just made sense.

Juniper shook his head.

Mrs. Larson, the journalism teacher, was looking at them.

"Juniper, Lily," she called, her voice stern.

"I don't know," Juniper said. He and Lily walked toward the steps.

Mrs. Larson smiled at them. "Hurry," she said.

Lily started to say something. She opened her mouth, closed it, then grabbed his hand and skipped forward, dragging him behind her.

At lunch Lily was waiting for Juniper. Her dark eyes were troubled, and she looked sad as he got his tray and came to where she was sitting.

"Do you think we should do what Simalucroix wants us to do?" she asked as he sat down.

Juniper shook his head.

"I don't know," he answered. "I don't know where this is going. Father doesn't understand Sheena. You and I don't understand Sam. What's happening seems wonderful and magical one minute, but then it doesn't make sense."

"Do you think dragons can heal people?" Lily asked.

Juniper looked at her thoughtfully.

"I don't know what to think," he said at last. "The dragons scared me when I first saw them. Then, at the conclave, with all those eyes and huge bodies, and Simalucroix suddenly growing wings... I could swear he changed his body shape. Last night I woke in the middle of the night and wondered if Sheena's disease is starting to affect me, but then I felt Simalucroix in my head again, comforting me, and I fell asleep."

Lily looked at the cafeteria, people talking and gesturing, living lives only they understood. Half the people in the cafeteria were failing classes, she knew. On the reservations life was wonderful, filled with families and clans, but desperate too. There were not enough jobs or money. Some, like her Grandfather, drank when things got out of hand.

The whole world needed healing, she thought. Not just Juniper's family and friends, but ice caps in Greenland and Antarctica where polar bears, looking for food, swam with cubs into the ocean, hoping to find ice where they could hunt seals, but finding only waves and winds and death by drowning; the Amazon where forests burned in great fires that changed the world's weather patterns…

"I saw a white eagle and white snake," she said defiantly. "Those were as real as the bull elk on the lava ridge and the two ravens braiding flight into sunshine."

She reached over her tray and took Juniper's hand as he held his out to her.

"Whatever is going to happen, it's going to be real."

"We're going to get people together on Christmas day?" Juniper asked.

Her dark eyes locked with his eyes. "Yes," she whispered.

"But how are we going to get them to come?" he asked

Lily looked away. "It doesn't matter," she said. "Those close to us needing healing will be there whether we gather them or not. There's never been so many powerful signs given to two people. Something powerful is happening, and it's happening to us."

The bell rang. Lily continued to look into Juniper's eyes. I love you, he thought to himself for the hundredth time. Lily let go of his hand, and they both got up to go to class.

Chapter XIII

Sheena woke from a dream where she was a white swan flying in a half moon's light. The treehouse was creaking, but the creaking had not woken her. She was not good at sleeping anyway. Her dreams often made her gasp for air, her legs kicking blankets off the bed. A deep, rich humming floated through the night air. She got out of bed and went to the front window. The Milky Way glittered above the treehouse's roof.

The humming was as beautiful as it was strange. She felt more rationale than she had since the night she had stood above Juniper on the stairs leading into the collapse. She knew who and where she was. Waking bird dreams and haunting calls leading her into tree branches were gone. She was a woman filled with sadness and a sense of loss, standing in a treehouse her husband had built, listening to songs rising out of the lava surrounding her.

Why couldn't she get control of her life? she asked herself. She had visions of chasing after Rory with an axe, raging with storms that gave her feet wings as she ran across aa and pahoehoe lava.

The humming grew louder and even more beautiful. She sat on one of her living room's elegant handmade chairs. Rory's skill with wood furniture was amazing, she thought. She wondered if her son had a similar skill. She closed her eyes and listened to the music as it settled into her spirit and made her long for normalcy.

I've been in El Malpais long enough, she thought to herself. What a strange experience!

After a while November's chill got to her. She went back to bed, praying, though she never prayed anymore, that the music would go on forever. In bed she closed her eyes and drifted into sleep without dreams, without restlessness.

Father startled out of sleep, troubled. At first he failed to hear the humming, but when he did notice it, separating it from other night sounds, he felt strange, out of sorts. He got up and pulled the quilt back from Juniper's corner to look at his son. Juniper was sleeping peacefully.

So young and such a good boy, Father thought.

He dropped the quilt and went outside. Stars over the collapse's bowl smeared silver toward the southern horizon. The cold was sharp enough to make him shiver. The humming he was hearing was barely audible, more a disturbance of silence than sound.

He turned back to the cave he'd made from lumber bought from the well digger and water seller by the wayside on Highway 117. He must have been as crazy as his wife, he thought. Finding a cave and building a shack of a house while waiting for Sheena to come to her senses.

What he'd longed for with a fierceness that seemed a part of breathing had not worked out the way he'd hoped. Now, here he was, forty-one years old with a fifteen-going-on-sixteen year old son, a man who hunted out of season, always on the verge of being arrested, filled with regrets for the choices he'd made.

He wondered if Sheena was awake or asleep, if she heard humming in the earth. He wondered what was making the song. It seemed natural, as if it was being sung rather than drawn out of wind whistling through blowholes.

In a way Sheena was as capable as any human could be. Alone in the wilderness, crazy, she still got enough food and water to maintain a life that would have killed most people. He provided for her the best way he could, but she provided more for herself than he provided for her. She was still so beautiful she took his breath away.

He rubbed hands over cold arms and went back inside. He looked in on Juniper again. He felt his love so strongly, looking at the young face, he felt like he had to sit down. Instead, he dropped the quilt's edge and went to his bed. The humming was stronger, but he did not notice. He crawled beneath covers layered against cold, wondering if the stars were singing as he closed his eyes and fell into sleep as dreamless as Sheena's sleep.

    Juniper was troubled when he woke. He was surprised Father was still sleeping. He went outside into the collapse and saw the bright flash of bluebird wings in brush beside the western wall's Ponderosa grove. He could not concentrate enough to figure out what was bothering him, but then it came to him in a rush.

    Sam! Sam had retreated back into himself. The Lowder brothers had stung him with their words. Then Sam was gone, both intellectually and physically, turned inward to where Juniper could not communicate with him.

    Juniper wondered if he was as fragile as Sam. He thought he was stronger. Lowders' words were wind that blew through the bus and dissipated. But to Sam their words were emotional spears driven into his spirit, leaving him wounded and alone even sitting beside his best friend.

    Juniper could imagine what Sam was thinking and feeling. When Father had first told him Sheena was his mother, all he'd been able to think about was his reaction to unwanted information that went to the core of who he was. He'd felt like he was in the midst of a ferocious storm that drove him toward dark thoughts about himself and his life.

    Lily had brought him out of the storm by touching his bandaged hand beside his locker. In the end he'd found his way out of thoughts about how worthless he was. He rejected the thought that life, Father, and Sheena had cut him off from the life he could have had. He had not been like Sam, caught in an emotional vortex, swirling in a downward spiral.

    Behind him, in the house, Father had gotten up and built a fire. Juniper wrenched out of his thoughts, wondering if Sam would be on the bus. Maybe Sam's Dad would walk him to the bus stop. That had happened before when Sam had been especially bad.

"Morning," Father said as Juniper walked into the house.

Juniper smiled. "Good morning," he answered. "You seem good today."

A strange look flitted over Father's face.

"I slept good last night," he said. "I had the best sleep I remember. I woke up, but went back to bed and slept without a worry."

Juniper heard the strange wonder in his father's voice.

"That's good," he said. "I slept good too, although…"

"What?" Father asked.

Juniper sat on one of the new, elegant chairs his father had been making. Father had heard Simalucroix and the dragons! He had no idea how he knew, but the way his father was holding himself, filled with wonder forgotten when he had grown out of childhood, told him as surely as if Father had sang the dragon's song out-loud.

"Simalucroix," Juniper whispered.

"What?" Father asked, a strange look on his face.

"You heard dragons singing last night," Juniper answered.

Father looked puzzled. "Dragons?"

Juniper took a deep breath. He closed his eyes and envisioned Simalucroix with new wings outspread, sparks coming out of his nostrils into caverns lit by sparks from the nostrils of all the conclave's dragons.

"In the blowhole the night when Sheena chased me, before I knew she was my mother," Juniper said. "Simalucroix, the dragon's leader, showed me how to get to the surface."

"Simalucroix? Dragons?" his father repeated blankly.

He looked at Juniper, panic in his eyes. Juniper could see, as if he could read Father's thoughts, that he was afraid Juniper had inherited his mother's illness.

"I'm not crazy like Sheena," Juniper said sullenly.

Father's eyes fixed on Juniper's eyes with a terrible urgency.

"You're not?" he asked blankly, as if he could not force himself to consider what he was thinking.

Juniper shook his head. "I went back underground to see," Juniper said. "The day Lily visited us. I should have told you the night when I found my way to the surface, but I was so relieved and happy to see you and breathe fresh air…" He paused. "Simalucroix asked me to never tell anyone they were there."

"Dragons are found in storybooks," Father said, an edge to his voice.

Juniper closed his eyes. Anger was bubbling like lava stirred by a volcano's heaving fires. Sheena, Lily's grandfather, Sam, and all the emotional turmoil they were causing surged through him. He took one deep breath, then another, trying to calm down. I've come a long way from the loneliness I once felt, he told himself. I have Lily, Father, and Sam… He opened his eyes and looked at Father.

"I need to get to school," he said quietly.

The deer sausage Father had been cooking was smoking. Father turned to the black frying pan.

"Burnt breakfast again!" he exclaimed, looking at Juniper, stricken. "You can't go to school without breakfast. I've fixed breakfast every morning I've been here since you were a baby." He frowned. "I burned the crib I made for you years ago."

"Simalucroix says we need healing," Juniper blurted out. "We're to gather Christmas night at Sheena's treehouse, and the dragons will heal us."

The pain on Father's face made him look as if he was about to cry out with anguish born the night Sheena had fled the hospital. He had felt so alone with Juniper and the mystery of where his wife had gone.

"You'll be okay," he told Juniper. "We'll get through this."

Juniper felt sick to his stomach. He'd made a mistake telling Father about Simalucroix. He could see Father was terrified, but Juniper was angry too, angry beyond reason.

He felt Simalucroix in his head.

"Calm down," the familiar voice said. "Christmas night is coming."

"He thinks I'm crazy like Sheena," Juniper answered out-loud.

Father's face crumbled at the words. He could not hear Simalucroix, only Juniper, and Juniper seemed to be talking to voices that did not exist.

"Juniper?" Father whispered.

"Dragons have become dragons again," Simalucroix said.

"My father thinks I'm crazy," Juniper thought. "He does not believe you exist."

Simalucroix rumbled with laughter. The laughter startled Juniper. He had never imagined dragons could laugh.

"He will be surprised," Simalucroix said. "We have made a promise."

"What's wrong Juniper?" Father asked urgently. "What's going on? You look like you've gone somewhere else."

"I'm okay," Juniper said out-loud to his father. "How am I going to get those who need to be healed to the treehouse if they don't believe you exist?" he asked Simalucroix in his head.

"You're not acting right," Father said. "What can I do to help?"

"Peace little one," Simalucroix said. "Go to school and wait. Let time unwind to significance."

"I'm all right," Juniper told Father. He looked at his father's worried eyes. They were still bright like they had been when Juniper had first greeted him. He looked healthy, alive, in spite of his worry.

Simalucroix left Juniper's mind.

"I've got to get ready for school," Juniper told Father.

Father shook his head. "You need to rest. You haven't had breakfast."

Juniper smiled, moved toward Father, reached out and touched him gently.

"I'm okay," he said. "I am. I'm not crazy."

He moved past Father to his corner. He had not even gone to the spring to clean up yet, he thought to himself. If he was not careful, he'd be late and miss the bus.

He hurried through his morning routine. Father sat on one of his new chairs and watched him, but then made up his mind and started frying a fresh batch of deer sausage. When Juniper finished getting ready, Father handed him two sausage patties.

"Eat," he said. "You need energy to do well at school."

Juniper paused, looked into Father's eyes, and smiled. Father was still worried, but was reaching for normality.

Chapter XIV

Sam was not on the bus, but found Juniper after first period. He looked tired and shuffled coming down the hall. Lily hurried past them on the way to her Algebra II class. She hesitated when she saw Sam and Juniper, but thought better of her impulse to stop and waved discreetly at Juniper.

"I don't know what's wrong with me," Sam told Juniper. His voice was so soft Juniper had to strain to hear. "One minute depression is in the past. The next minute empty words by idiots send me reeling."

Juniper searched his friend's face, trying to choose the right words, but gave up the effort. He had no idea what the right words were.

"You're a good person, Sam," he said. "When you missed yesterday I was worried."

"I'm okay," Sam answered. "Just tired." Sam kept looking at Juniper as if he wanted to say something more, but was afraid of what consequences might flow from his thought. Juniper waited until the silence was becoming uncomfortable. "Simalucroix and the dragons are coming Christmas day, aren't they?" Sam asked at last. "I thought I'd healed myself, but…" His voice faded out, and he looked confused.

Juniper thought about how Father had reacted when he had told him about Simalucroix, how he'd made Juniper's cavern experiences seem unreal and unsettling. Now Sam was desperate to believe in those experiences, reaching out with a hope necessary for him to keep hold of his self. Suddenly the hallway's noise and daylight were gone:

Sheena, eyes glittering and intense, was standing in the Douglas fir near the Cairn Trail, long hair shining faintly from moonlight. The wilderness's immense silence surrounded him and Sam. Faint wind song rustled through tree branches. The image's intensity made Juniper dizzy until the school, hallway, and students moving past him and Sam came back, and he was again in his everyday world.

"They'll be where they told me they'll be," he said.

Sam had watched Juniper's daytime vision sweep over his face. He could not see what Juniper was seeing, but knew Juniper had left the hall and was someplace else. His pulse quickened. Dark fears that Juniper was as ill as his mother dissipated, and Sam felt the excitement he'd felt on the bus before the Lowders had driven him into the fog that had wasted too much of his life. Dragons! He was going to see dragons, he thought. He was going to live an experience humans had not had for so long the great beasts had become myths.

"Then I'd better get myself up to greeting them," he told Juniper. "I'm not going to be lost in myself when they come."

Juniper smiled and put his hand on Sam's shoulder. "Class time," he said.

Sam nodded. They walked together toward their separate classes.

At lunch Sam, Lily, and Juniper sat down together. Sam was subdued, but he had met Lily outside his class and walked with her to join Juniper. They had just sat down when the Lowders came into the cafeteria and made a beeline for where the three of them were sitting. Two tables away Bill took off his jacket and waved it over his head, getting everybody to look his way.

"The dragon clan is here!" he exclaimed excitedly. "The folks who talk, walk, and fart with dragons flitting and flying inside their fairy-little minds!"

Carson laughed as loudly as he could, swooped down on the table, and, before Juniper or Lily could react, grabbed Lily's purse and book bag and waved them in the air.

"Lookee what I got!" he shouted. His eyes were bright, dilated, nervous.

"Give me that back!" Lily shouted at him.

Juniper got to his feet and grabbed Bill's arm. Mrs. Larson, near the cafeteria's door, was moving toward them. People at the nearest tables were standing too. Bill swung and smashed his fist into Juniper's face.

"Stop!" Lily screeched.

Juniper's face felt numb where he'd been hit. He felt disassociated from what was happening. He let go of Bill and balled up his fists.

"Serves you right, dragon rat," Bill sneered at him.

"Sam, help!" Lily shouted.

Sam was out of his chair and moving toward Carson. Carson had unzipped Lily's purse and flung it toward Mrs. Larson, laughing as lipstick, coins, a blue comb, Kleenex, ear rings, and other stuff fell out.

"The lady dragon cometh!" he said.

Juniper swung at Bill, but Bill deftly moved out of his way. Juniper felt foolish when his fist failed to hit anything.

"Your turn," the sneering Bill yelled at Carson.

Carson still had Lily's book bag dangling from his hand. He pushed Lily to the ground and came toward Juniper. Lily was crying.

"Stop! Carson Lowder!" Mrs. Larson called in a panicked voice. "Juniper! Stop this madness right now!"

"Sure thing, dragon boy," Carson said to Juniper.

Bill moved behind Juniper and looked at Carson's menace. He pushed Juniper toward his weirdly smiling brother. Surprised, Juniper turned his head to see who was behind him. Carson swung the book bag at Juniper's head, swinging as hard as he could. Juniper felt, more than saw, the bag coming. He hunched his shoulders as the books slammed into his head. The world blackened as he fell to the ground.

She knew they had found her lair, the cold ice cave that made her sluggish most of the time. She had seen the old man with his long beard and heavy coats spot her when she had gone to hunt mountain goats that ran over edges of cliffs and bounded from one small ledge to another. She could almost hear them gathering in the village miles below, telling stories of her terrible fire breathing, ignoring the fact that several owed her their lives since she had healed them of diseases or fractures or one of the million disasters that beset human beings.

They were fragile, but she knew she was vulnerable to the way they gathered and came up with complex plans that inevitably led to a knight clinking in armor, carrying a sharp sword that would pierce her flesh again and again until, at last, breathing rage and fire, she would die.

She was glad when the word came. A place for them had been found where there were no humans. There were so few dragons now. Two sentient species were left on the planet. The dragons, slower, less social, not as quick to war, had slowly disappeared as humans bred at alarming rates and spread out from Africa, dispersing through Asia and Europe into Siberia's bitter cold and the variable weathers of North and South America. Soon dragons would be a memory.

Early in the evening the village below her cave gathered, scurrying like ants as they prepared to hunt her. She could feel their fear and exhilaration on cold summer winds.

Eat before flight, Grilgax had said. The flight will be exhausting. She did not bother to wait for darkness to hunt even though she knew it would excite the villagers when they saw her boldness. She came to her cold cave's lip and leapt into the air, spreading great wings with a joy and feeling of power that made mountain winds sing through her. She soared outward to where the villagers could not miss seeing her flight and veered into the heart of the great mountains.

She saw two snow leopards padding along a path they had made long ago, searching for goats, snow rabbits, mice, or other prey. They moved silently and swiftly across the ice. Then she saw a lone female goat a mile from the leopards on a high ridge. She made no sound, but folded her great wings and plummeted, flaring wings as her talons reached out and snatched the bleating goat as she soared upward once again. After she had eaten she began flying toward the high Himalaya valley where she was to meet the dragons that still lived after centuries of slowly declining toward extinction.

She flew for two days to the high valley. Her two great hearts labored as she strove to fly as high as possible so humans with their poor eyesight could not see her.

Not far from the valley she began to see an occasional dragon. None seemed to be young. Too few young were being born. Fewer still survived to maturity. She came to the valley in daylight and joined the others in a field surrounded by peaks that soared into airs so thin breathing was difficult.

Grilgax, old, great, glittering eyes dimming, greeted her.

"You've come," he said in his great voice.

His voice still thrilled her even after all these years. She acknowledged his greeting and looked around at the clutch of dragons that had gathered.

"So few?" she asked, her voice plaintive.

"We must leave where humans are," Grilgax said, sadness in his voice. "We must forsake our wings for survival."

"Humans are everywhere," Brandon, an ancient dragon said bitterly.

"Not where we are going," Simsilee, a younger dragon answered.

"We have to survive the flight first," Brandon replied.

"How many of us are left?" she asked.

"Under fifty, that's all," Grilgax said. "No more. I have scoured the earth."

Great sighs and keening greeted the statement. In the small field there seemed to be so many of them. Their huge bodies and intelligent eyes seemed to fill the world, but in truth all of them together were tiny compared to the immense, jagged peaks soaring above them.

"At sunset," Grilgax said. "We fly at sunset across the peaks of the mountains toward the ocean, then across the ocean, over islands, to North America, then over the land into small mountains where volcanoes still breathe sulfur in caverns carved by lava flows cooled by time. For survival we will give up our wings," he said. "For the sake of clutches of blue eggs and the birth of baby dragons we will live sightless in the earth's darkness."

Hearing the great king's words, feeling the immensity of his sadness, she settled wings and crouched to snow covered earth and waited for sunset.

When sunset finally came, and forty-seven dragons lifted wings in unison, the whooshing sound was exhilarating. They lifted from earth and began the forever flight across mountains and land. For hours and days they flew, wings getting heavy and harder to beat against air currents.

They stopped only once, in moonlit darkness, on North America's rocky shores where the wind was as cold as the icy depths of the cave she had left, without regret, behind. They rested for less than a day, afraid humans would find them, then lifted wings and labored through more days and nights.

A full moon was shining when they came to El Malpais. She was one of the first that landed before a large collapse of jumbled boulders with a great cave at its heart. As she looked at dragons silhouetted dark against the moon's round silver, wings outspread and necks elongated in flight, her sadness was so intense it tore at her hearts. To leave the joy of flight forever? To live in the dark of endless caverns?

Dragons did not weep like humans, but she felt as if she could weep if only she knew how humans brought tears to their eyes. After they had landed on the rough lava fields, Grilgax, without speaking, turned and glided the short hop into the collapse and walked into the cave. She held back as dragons started filing into darkness.

She took wild night air into her great lungs and filled her chest. Then, like others around her, breathed fire into the darkness, lighting up the night. When her breath was exhausted, she sighed and followed the others into the dark passages of their new home.

At least there are no humans, she thought. Not so deep in the darkness.

A bright light woke Juniper. He seemed to be inside a long, dark tunnel with light in the distance. He felt so sad it seemed as if he'd lost contact with the world. A strange woman, dressed in a white coat, was standing over him, shining a light in his eyes.

"He's awake," the woman said.

Father took Juniper's hand and squeezed it.

"Juniper?" he asked, his voice worried.

What was Father doing in town? Juniper wondered. He tried to tell Father he was okay, but felt the pain in his head and groaned instead.

"Take it easy, son," Father said. "You've been beat up pretty bad."

"Waking up is good," the woman said. "But you need rest."

The doctor gave him a shot in his arm. He twisted in the bed and looked up into his father's worried face. He tried to talk, though he was not sure what he wanted to say, but could not find his voice.

When he woke again Father was sitting by his hospital bed reading. Juniper looked at him for a moment, trying to understand where he was.

"Hi," he said weakly.

Father put the magazine down and abruptly stood up.

"You're awake again," he said, sounding cheerful.

"Yes," Juniper answered.

"You're going to be okay," Father said as if he was trying to convince himself.

"In the hospital?" Juniper asked.

"The Lowders beat you up pretty bad," Father answered. "Mrs. Larson was here too for a couple of days. They broke her nose. They're in jail now. They got ahold of meth before school. I don't think they even knew what they were doing."

"Meth? Really?" Juniper asked. He was suddenly afraid. A lot of the kids at school were into drugs, but meth? "Lily? Sam?"

"Lily's been here with her grandmother every day," Father answered. "They'll be here during visiting hours." He paused. "No one has seen Sam since you were hurt."

Juniper was having trouble staying awake.

"He was hurt?" he asked.

Father shook his head. "No, not physically, not badly," he said.

As sleep forced him to close his eyes, Juniper saw the great female dragon as she went into the entrance of Four Windows Cave. He tried to concentrate on Sam and what was going on with Sam, but another fear nagged at his thoughts.

The dragons were going to come out into a world where kids he'd known all the years he'd gone to school could buy meth, go crazy, and beat him to a pulp. There were twenty-four hour news channels, helicopters, and missiles so fast no dragon could evade them. Humans had driven dragons to extinction with spears and swords. What would happen to dragons in the modern world?

Simalucroix, he cried in his sleep. Simalucroix!

But there was no answer. Only silence and troubled dreams.

Chapter XV

Lily was beside his bed when he woke. His chest hurt. He looked at the IV in his arm that led, with clear tubes, to bottles half filled with liquid above his bed. He knew he needed the IV, tubes, and bottles, but being hooked to them felt weird. Lily was staring into space as if she was not where she was.

"Lily?" he asked, his voice soft.

Lily's face lit up. "Juniper!" she said, suddenly looking at him. "You're awake!" She was smiling. "Your father said you were awake!"

He forced himself to smile. "I'm okay," he said.

Tears pooled into Lily's eyes.

"Those boys were crazy," she said. "I should have let them have my purse and forgot about it."

"Father said they were on meth," Juniper said. "At fifteen! They're our age."

"Some of the rez kids are on meth," Lily answered. "You've got to stay away from them. That stuff doesn't let you go. How are you feeling? You've been here three days, and you haven't been awake once while I've been here."

Three days? He tried to remember anything from those days, but all he could recall was Father and the doctor…from when? Yesterday? Today?

"I don't remember," he said softly. "I saw Father, but before that all I remember was Carson swinging your backpack and thinking I couldn't let your books hit me in the head."

Lily started crying without making a sound.

"They kicked you over and over again. Carson started chanting, 'Juniper's dead! Juniper's dead!' Mrs. Larson screamed for them to stop, but Carson laughed and swung my bag at her. He caught her nose and broke it. She screamed from the pain. Then four wrestlers from the school team grabbed Bill and Carson and wrestled them to the ground."

Lily looked like she had lost touch with the hospital room and was reliving every moment of their nightmare.

"I'm okay," Juniper said again. "I hurt a little, but I'll survive." He paused and looked around. "It's strange being in here. I haven't been in a hospital before."

Lily shook her head. "This is wrong," she said, her voice serious. "The signs we've been seeing are of healing and power, but you, Sam, Mrs. Larson, even Carson and Bill are hurting. I hope I didn't bring this on by talking you into pursuing the signs' meaning. Grandmother says they're not evil signs, but I've been wondering."

Juniper winced when he shook his head. He could not seem to move without pain. He wondered how many times the Lowders had kicked him. It seemed as if they'd pummeled every part of his body. He lifted his hand toward his face, but put it down when pain jolted through his arm.

"Is my face okay?" he asked Lily, even though it seemed like a foolish question.

Lily smiled, wiping tears from her right cheek. "It's beautiful," she said. "For a while you looked so pale I was afraid."

"You said Sam was hurt," Juniper said. "I asked Father, but he said Sam was okay physically."

Lily looked distressed.

"None of us have seen Sam," she said. "He tried to stop the Lowders from kicking you after you were down, but Bill shoved him so hard he slid over the table and fell to the floor. He got up and started for Bill, but Ronnie Williams and the wrestlers were moving by then, and they got to the Lowders before Sam. Sam hurt his back when he slid off the table, but I think your father's right. I don't think he was hurt bad physically, but he was crying by the time the principal and teachers got to us. He had a strange look on his face. I don't know for sure, but I don't think he's in good shape."

Juniper looked at Lily so steadily she averted her eyes.

"This is a mess, isn't it?" he asked.

She looked back at him and nodded.

"The question is, what now?" he said. "I've been dreaming about the dragons. They shouldn't come to the surface. They can survive hidden, but it'll be a horror movie if people learn about them. We'd be lucky if the Governor didn't call out the National Guard. I was wrong to find them, and even more wrong to tell you and Sam."

Lily searched his face. She was silent for a long moment. "What are we going to do?" she asked at last.

Lily's Grandmother, looking tired and old, had come into the room. She looked first at her granddaughter, then at Juniper.

"You're awake and better," she said in her strong, soft voice. She walked to Lily's side and touched Juniper's hand. "They are as intelligent as you are, grandson," she said softly. "You must let them know how you feel and let them decide. Perhaps they believe they cannot hide in the dark any longer."

"Grandmother," Juniper said and smiled. He was happy to see the older woman. He carefully shook his head. "I've tried to talk to them from here," he said. "But Simalucroix doesn't answer."

He suddenly felt so tired and heavy he was distant from Lily. The thought panicked him.

"You're tired," Grandmother said firmly. "Lily, we need Juniper to sleep."

Lily grasped his hand and squeezed. He squeezed back. He wanted her to stay, to be with him for the rest of his life.

"Yes Grandmother," she said. "I'll be back," she told Juniper. "Don't worry," she whispered. She bent over and kissed his forehead. "I'll be here for you."

She let go of his hand and let Grandmother lead her out of the room. Alone again, feeling still more distant, Juniper tried to contact Simalucroix again. No dragon voice came into his head. He drifted in and out of sleep, struggling to stay awake. He wanted to talk to Father about Simalucroix and the dragons. He wondered if Father had gone home to check on Sheena.

Sheena's beautiful face smiled at him from a Douglas fir's highest branches. Juniper shook his head. She was his mother, but not his mother. He drifted into lava fields and bent down to look at purple lichens. Deep in Bandera Volcano, beneath the great cinder mound in the crater's center, lava drove volcanic gasses through layers of stone and rock. On the surface cinder smoked for the first time in thousands of years.

When he woke again the hospital room was dark. Father had a white hospital blanket over him and was sleeping in the corner chair. In the outside street lamp's light, he looked old and worn out. The hospital hummed from electronic devices and machines.

Looking at his father, Juniper wondered how he had ever felt as lonely as he had before Lily and Sam had become his friends. He had always had Father, who hunted, washed dishes, fixed meals, cut and chopped wood, read books to his son, taught with a patience greater than that of his teachers, carved wooden toys, celebrated holidays, and was always there, year after year. Love rose like a rising tide, making Juniper forget the throbbing pain that had woken him.

Without thinking, he removed the hospital sheet and blanket from his legs. The pain, as he forced himself to sit up, made him gasp. If I don't force myself, he thought, I'll vegetate in a hospital bed.

Father was instantly awake. "Juniper?" he said.

Juniper closed his eyes as waves of colors rolled in front of his eyes. He ground his teeth as he forced pain in his back, legs, and chest to recede.

"They really did me in," he mumbled.

Father was out of his chair and beside Juniper, strong hands and arms supporting his sitting up.

"Sheena didn't like hospital rooms," Juniper said. "I understand why."

"You'll get through this," Father said. "We need to be patient."

Juniper forced his eyes open. He'd caught colds before, and he'd hurt himself in the blowhole fleeing Sheena, but he'd never really been sick. How was he supposed to act after getting beaten up so badly? He did not want to whine. He looked up at Father.

"I've got to get strong enough to get out of here," he said. "I need to go home."

Father looked away from him at the street light outside.

"That's a problem," he said softly. "To get home you've got to walk the Cairn Trail. Getting home's going to take time."

"I can make it," Juniper mumbled through clinched teeth.

"I got us a place in Ramah," Father said. "This is going to take time."

"In Ramah?" Juniper asked, his heart sinking. He had to talk to Simalucroix. Christmas was less than a week away. Lily had told him he'd been in the hospital three days already.

Dragons had to continue living in their caverns. Lily's grandmother had said they were as smart as he was and that he had to let them make their own decisions, but he could not let them come out into the wilderness, frightening idiots like the Lowders, and end up massacred. He had to get out of the hospital, get Father to take him home, and talk with Simalucroix.

"I don't want to stay in Ramah," he said. "I want to go home."

Father leaned back and looked into Juniper's eyes.

"Home is a shack built into a cave," he said slowly. "It's not a home. You don't know what regular life is like because I've never given you the chance to experience one."

"The Lowders could have hurt me on the bus or the Cairn Trail," Juniper said. "I've got to go home. I don't want to stay in Ramah. Home is a shack in a cave at the bottom of a collapse. When I was a kid I dreamed about being normal and living in a house, but I'm not a kid anymore. Not after this."

Father closed his eyes, the insanity of what Juniper was saying making him feel uncomfortable. Why had he never allowed his son a normal life?

"The dragons are coming on Christmas day," Juniper said softly. Father's face with salt and pepper beard and blue eyes came in and out of focus. "I want to go home," Juniper said.

"Dragons are phantoms," Father said softly. "You were scared. Your mind made them up until you found the surface."

"You think I'm like Sheena. It scares you."

Father closed his eyes and sighed a deep, despairing sigh.

"No," he said. "No. You're Juniper, my son."

Juniper closed his eyes again.

When the great female dragon reached the huge cavern, she stopped. Like the others she opened her great wings, clawing cold earth. She had lived in caves her entire life, but always she could go out on a ledge, spread wings, and soar into open skies, exhilarated by her power. Her wings were useless now, she realized. She could spread them and lift herself off the ground, but the ceilings of even the great cavern were too close. Neither she nor the others could fly.

Several of the great dragons, especially the young, were humming in their chests, mourning the loss of light. The great female looked around at darkness. This would be her sons' and daughters', grandsons' and granddaughters' home. She did not hum in mourning, but felt the loss they would feel with a physical weakness in her wings and legs.

"This is a terrible choice," Grilgax had said in their minds. "But we are intelligent. We will adjust. Our race and children and grandchildren will have a tomorrow. Our breath will bring light to darkness. Our spirits are great enough to turn darkness into our homes."

"I miss the moon and stars," a young male dragon said. "I flew beneath them and through days of sun. I feel like we've chosen extinction rather than life."

"Courage," Grilgax said, his words' strength echoing through them, deep into their spirits. "We must have the courage of life and safety until humankind murders itself on its fields of glory and gore, or humans evolve into beings intelligent enough to accept our intelligence. We can clutch eggs and cherish our young even in darkness."

The great female folded wings against her back and dropped to all fours. Walking would be strength in such close spaces. Hunting would be different. She would have to find small animals. Dragons would no longer feel the excitement of hurtling toward a goat leaping from ledge to ledge in the mountains. She and the others would have to work at building their forelegs' strength.

Sadness grew into her being. Without thinking she moved away from the others and began looking for a lair she could call her own. She felt eggs growing inside her. This would be their world. Courage, she told herself. Peace. Hope. Love. She reached out and touched Grilgax's mind. He did not shy away, but sent feelings of comfort toward her.

"Our kind will see the stars again," he said. "The stars and moon. We'll feel the rush of winds beneath our wings."

She did not respond, but kept searching until she found the underground river. She found a ledge and a huge lava tube above the river's bank. She leapt to her new lair and settled in for the long darkness to come.

In his sleep Juniper twitched. Father had gone back to his chair and covered himself with a blanket, but stayed awake, thinking about all the choices he had made since Sheena had gotten sick. He wondered if he had been sane since the day Sheena had fled the hospital and left him alone with his young son.

Chapter XVI

Juniper woke as dawn's first light filtered through the hospital window. He did not seem as foggy as he had before. For the first time he wondered where he was. He was not in Ramah. Ramah did not have a hospital as large as the one he was in, but how had Father gotten to Grants? How had Father found out he was hurt? How had Lily gotten to Grants? Grants was almost an hour's drive from Ramah.

He looked around the room, but he was alone. He steeled himself and carefully sat up, maneuvering around the needle and tubes taped to his arm.

Father came into the room with a styrofoam cup of coffee. Juniper stared at him. They made Navajo tea in the morning. Coffee cost money and a trip to town. Father sometimes hitched a ride on the bus for supplies, but the sight of him drinking coffee seemed as strange as the idea that they were in Grants, not Ramah.

Father smiled at Juniper as he walked through the door.

"You're up," he said, sounding satisfied. "You're getting better."

Juniper felt his body before he replied. He was sore, but his head felt clearer, and he was more in control of himself.

"I'm ready to leave and go home," he said at last.

"How are you going to hike the Cairn Trail when you can't walk?" Father asked. "How about the stairs into the collapse? I heard what you said last night, but we have to be realistic. You've been hurt. Bad."

Juniper thought about what Father was saying. He did not feel steady. How could he walk the Cairn Trail with aa lava underfoot and hills that seemed as daunting as mountains? The realization of why he could not talk to Simalucroix hit him. He was in Grants, a long way from the caverns.

"We're in Grants?" he asked Father. "We have to be."

Father nodded.

"An ambulance brought you and Mrs. Larson from school. Donald Sharp picked me up and brought me down. He hiked out to the shack. We've been here a time, but in addition to watching you, I've made good use of being here. I've sold the table and chairs. I've got to finish the table, but we've got money to make a new start. I contracted to do two other sets. I can still make a living."

The satisfaction in his voice grew stronger as he talked. Juniper looked at the man who had been his only friend for years.

"What about Sheena?" he asked. "Mother?"

He slid carefully over the bed's edge and touched his feet to the floor. Father put his coffee on the window sill and hurried to Juniper's side.

"Easy, son," he said. "Easy. There's time."

He had tears in his eyes. Juniper could hardly believe Father was crying. Dizziness made him sag, but he forced himself to stand on his own. He'd been in bed long enough.

"I'm okay," he said, forcing himself to sound calm, not hysterical. He took a deep breath and let Father help him back to bed. He felt like he'd been in a battle that had taken all his strength.

"What about Sheena?" he asked again. "We need to go home. We can't leave her alone. Not after you've been faithful all these years."

Father looked shocked by Juniper's words.

"You're as important as Sheena's ever been," he said after a silence. "I love your mother, but I can't do anything for her. I've tried to take care of her all these years, but now I've got to take care of you. I can't let my love for her endanger a son I'd give my life for."

"How are we going to get home?" Juniper asked. "We don't have a car."

"Lily's grandmother will take us," Father said. "Her grandfather's been driving them down here every day. With the table and chair money we can rent an apartment until you're ready for the trek into El Malpais. Maybe we'll stay in Ramah. I can visit Sheena from there. When you're well enough you can come to the lava fields with me. We can have where you grew up without living there."

"Lily's grandfather?" Juniper asked, a shock running through him.

If by getting hurt he'd forced Lily, her grandmother and grandfather back together, the results from the Lowders' beating was worse than he'd thought. He closed his eyes. "We've got to go home," he said. "Soon."

Father's strong hands gently patted his shoulders. Father was looking better in the daylight, Juniper thought. Not so gray.

"The doctors have to tell me you're okay to travel to Ramah," he said. "I'm not risking losing you."

I'm going to go back to sleep, Juniper realized. Whether I want to or not.

"I'm going to walk today," he said softly. "I don't care how much it hurts."

"One day at a time," Father said.

The humming woke Sheena again. She was in the treehouse sleeping more soundly than she ever slept. It rose out of black lava, a symphony of volcanic fire cooled into stone. Why did she keep hearing it? She could feel the strangeness inside her, changing her. Reluctantly, since the night was cold, she put aside the warm quilts Rory had put on her bed years ago and got up.

She felt lost and lonely. She went to the treehouse's deck and put her arms in the air and started to dance to the humming. She was a ballerina on a night of a waxing half-moon, a river of moonlight that flowed into the night. But the dance did not seem right. She waved arms in the air and moved, but the humming was too constant. It bothered her, moved in counterpoint to her movement, made her aware of cold and her shift's thinness as she danced.

She could not match, or even feel, its rhythm, though she could sense rhythm beneath non-rhythm, molding, shaping her in ways that confused her. She tried to get angry, but the humming defeated even that.

What was she doing in a treehouse in El Malpais? she asked herself. Where was Rory? Her son Juniper? She was never aware of them, never aware of the food Rory left, or the gifts of blankets or clothes or furniture. How did she know her son was her son?

She tried to rise like an eagle and screech at the sky. She tried to spread wings and fly over lava, an avenging spirit that could rain destruction on the earth. She tried to turn into a black mountain lion padding down trails no human could see.

The humming nagged her. It would not let her disappear into herself. She knew Rory and Juniper had left El Malpais. After all these years, why had they left her alone? Where was the humming coming from? Why was it rising out of earth, interrupting the flow of who she was?

She tried to screech at the night sky, at wilderness's stillness, but the humming interrupted the screech in her throat. She turned in her effort to dance, but did not dance.

Leave me alone, she told the humming. Leave me alone. Where was Rory when she needed him? Where was her son? The ungrateful son who ran from her and disappeared into earth?

What was wrong with her? she asked herself. She put hands to her ears and tried to block out the humming, but the humming vibrated her bones. She was tired. She turned away from the deck and walked back inside. Rory was a great builder. The treehouse was warmer inside than outside. She went back to bed, put layers of quilts over her body, and closed her eyes.

How could she sleep with infernal humming everywhere around her? Rest, a voice said that was not her voice. Sleep. Sleep.

She had thought about Rory before she had run away from the hospital. He had been so worried. He had hovered by her side so persistently it had frightened her. No one should have cared for her that much.

When he had gone home to take care of one year old Juniper, she'd gotten out of the bed a nurse had propped up with pillows and turned into a white owl and whooshed out the window and spread speckled wings in moonlight as she fled toward dead volcanoes that would keep her warm forever.

But she had not flown out the window. The night had been warm, and the nurse had left the window open. No one had expected her to run away. She had been so filled with lassitude she did not have the energy to breathe. How could they have known she intended to slip out the window, climb down the brick wall with jutting ledges to the ground, and hitchhike with a trucker bemused by this crazy woman in a pink robe and slippers who wanted him to drop her off outside Ramah at Chain of Craters Road.

He had been an old guy who had seen too much of living and mostly did not want to be bothered, but he'd been going to Ramah anyway, from there to Zuni, so he let her sit silently inside his cab as the big semi roared out of the truck-stop and took her to where she wanted to go.

She had flown, but not as an owl. Even her sanity had gone. She knew she needed help, that she should stay with her husband and child, but her unborn daughter was gone! The movement in her belly she'd felt for months was gone, and she could not stand the pain.

God, how she had loved Juniper the night he had been born! But she could not stand herself, nor the idea that her parents were dead after a lifetime of treating her like she was less than dirt beneath their shoes, nor even the idea that Rory loved her more than she loved herself. She had flown to El Malpais and tried to die, running to places where tourists sometimes did die.

If you got lost in El Malpais, every tree and bush looked alive. Ground was treacherous, rising, falling, twisting into bizarre shapes and holes. But Rory had found her and fed her and built her treehouse. She tossed and turned in sleep. Rory still loves me, she mumbled. He still loves me, she said.

The humming kept singing through lava into night. She did not wake. She slept.

Another day passed. Juniper got out of bed and walked, holding onto Father's arm for support. He did not talk much. Father seemed preoccupied, but quickly moved when he saw Juniper was awake. Pain was hot and fierce, but he persevered, wondering when Lily would come. After the day's last walk, taken after he had eaten solid food for the first time, he drifted off to sleep, disappointed Lily had not shown up.

In the morning, as Father helped him get out of bed, Lily and Grandmother opened the room's door. Lily's face lit up when she saw him standing beside Father. He smiled at her, filled with resolve. He left the bed's safety and walked to her. Both Father and Grandmother smiled at them.

Later, after Father and Grandmother had left for coffee, Juniper took Lily's hands and clasped them as she stood beside the bed.

"I've got to get out of here," he said.

"You've got to get well," Lily answered firmly.

"I can't wait to get well," he said. "I'm well enough now."

"Juniper…" Lily's voice trailed off.

"The dragons," he said. "Sunday is the start of Christmas week."

Realization grew in Lily's eyes. "They can heal you," she said.

Juniper's frustration tugged at him. He tamped it down.

"Think about what happened to us," he said. "Simalucroix and the dragons didn't want to be found, but I found them. They're getting ready to come out of caverns into the modern world. They couldn't survive knights in rusty armor," his voice pleaded. "What are the Lowders going to do when they find out dragons are real? The dragons have no idea about our world."

"The Lowders are in jail," Lily said, her voice hesitant.

"I'm not talking about the Lowders," Juniper said. "I'm talking about how the Lowders with their bullying and whining would react. How many Lowders are there at school? In Ramah or Grants or Albuquerque? Afraid of themselves, but determined to show they're afraid of nothing?"

Lily opened her mouth and shut it. "Oh," she said. She thought for a minuteand then shook her head. "But the signs," she objected. "If the dragons don't come out, what do the signs mean?"

Juniper shifted in bed.

"I don't know," he said. "But I don't think the world is ready for dragons. They've been gone from human reality for a long time."

Grandmother and Father walked back into the room. Grandmother looked first at Lily, then at Juniper.

"What's wrong?" she asked. "You were happy. Now you're both frowning."

"Juniper has to leave the hospital today," Lily said. "He can't communicate with Simalucroix from Grants. He's afraid the dragons will come out of the caverns, and people like the Lowders will go nuts if they hear about live dragons."

"Dragons again," Father snorted. "Hallucination from the lava tubes. Now you're afraid they're going to be destroyed."

Grandmother looked calmly at Father, deciding what kind of man he was.

"Lily and Juniper have seen signs," she said. "The signs are more powerful than any I've heard of. If Juniper says he has met dragons, he has met dragons."

Grandmother's voice gave Juniper strength. Confirmation of dragons was a confirmation of who he was. He smiled at Lily. Her eyes gleamed with pride. Father looked steadily into Grandmother's dark eyes. He seemed confused, but then his face relaxed.

"I'm being a white man again," he said gently. "I'm back in Grants. I've forgotten wildness, haven't I? I've forgotten the power in Navajo and Zuni mysteries and stories."

"We've never heard of dragons," Grandmother said. "They're white man myths, but I know my granddaughter and your son, and I trust them. If they tell me Juniper has to leave the hospital, you should consider letting him leave."

Father was suddenly panicked. "But he can hardly move," he objected. "He can't walk the Cairn Trail and get to the house. The terrain's difficult enough for a healthy boy with good legs and lungs."

"He can stay with us at the Hogan," Lily said quickly. "He'll have to walk, but it's mostly flat ground."

Father shook his head.

"I have money," he said. "I've rented an apartment in Ramah, but Juniper has to heal. He can't be like Sheena. He can't slip into El Malpais and lose himself."

Juniper had stopped breathing. His father looked lost. He was remembering coming into a Grants Hospital room to see his wife and finding an empty bed. He was feeling how he had felt when Sheena had disappeared. He was afraid Juniper's dragon hallucination was the start of the sickness that had led to his wife's madness.

Juniper closed his eyes. He had to keep Simalucroix from leaving the caverns, but God knew how much healing he and his family needed.

"The dragons are not a hallucination," he said, his voice soft. "I've seen them twice. Once could have been hallucination, but not twice. I saw Simalucroix in the cavern by the underground river discover his wings. They need me to tell them not to come to the surface."

"Juniper has not been the only one to seeing signs," Grandmother said. "Lily saw a white eagle rising with a white snake in its talons. These are not everyday sights, but the spirits speaking."

"And afterward two ravens dancing over the lava fields," Lily added.

"It can't be true," Father said softly. "Dragons are creatures from storybooks, not life."

"Grandfather will take us," Grandmother declared. She looked fiercely at Lily. "He'd better not have decided Grants is a good place to get liquor."

"He was willing to drive us," Lily said. "Sammy had to work."

Grandmother's face softened.

"He has been a good husband in many ways," she said. "Just not in one way."

Juniper put his legs to the bed's edge and sat up. Movement was getting easier, he thought. Both Father and Lily moved to help him. Seeing both concerned about him made tears come to his eyes. Love flowed out of him like a river turned into golden light.

"I'm ready to go," he said as he sat up.

"Are you sure?" Lily asked. "Christmas week doesn't start until tomorrow. One more day can't hurt, can it?"

Juniper sighed, the sigh making him wince. Tomorrow?

"Sammy can bring us tomorrow morning," Grandmother said.

Father looked desperate. He was afraid, Juniper thought. The thought troubled him. He had once believed his father invincible, but since telling Juniper about Sheena, he seemed more like Juniper or any other normal human being.

"I've got to get home," Juniper said.

"Tomorrow will be okay," Lily said. "The man I love isn't so stupid he'd kill himself just to get his way."

Juniper laughed and winced again. Damned chest, he thought to himself. Father sighed the way Juniper had when pain had debilitated him.

"Tomorrow," Father said.

"I'll get a good night's sleep," Juniper agreed.

"I love you," Lily said to him, moving her lips without speaking.

He nodded, wrinkling his forehead.

"How's Sam?" he asked Lily. "Have you heard from him?"

Grandmother answered, surprising him. "He's not good," she said. "Lily kept after me until I had Grandfather take me to see his parents yesterday. They brought Sam out of his room and had him sit at the kitchen table. He knew me, but wouldn't talk."

Father's eyes fixed on Grandmothers beautiful, aged face. She was luminous even in the hospital room's harsh light.

"Sam's always had a hard time," he said. "I wish it wasn't true, but it's true."

"Sam's too sensitive," Lily said. "He's good, but words are arrows shot bloody into his heart." She closed her eyes. "He needs to be healed," he said.

The dragons, Simalucroix, could heal him, Juniper thought, but by healing him the dragon race could be destroyed. What Grilgax had bought them by moving to El Malpais and the caverns could be eliminated by rage stirred by fears wrapped in myths.

He winced again, not from pain, but from his dilemma. To save Sam he would have to put Simalucroix and the dragons at risk. He made sure he kept his breath shallow and slowly lay back on the bed.

He had to talk to Simalucroix, he thought. The dragon leader was wise.

Chapter XVII

The grandmother dragons gathered in a small cavern far from the underground river's great cavern. They were 150 years old and older, and they were troubled. Most had rejoiced when young Simalucroix had become dragon leader. They had lived under Windfall's cautious leadership for over sixty years and had believed the time had come for someone younger and more energetic, but now they were disconcerted.

The young human's discovery of them and their children was troubling enough, but now five dragons, led by Simalucroix, had unfurled wings and were preparing to venture outside, an event that had not happened for over a thousand years. What good could come of such an event? they asked themselves. Had Grilgax led them to dark caverns and blind lives in order to allow a young male leader to endanger dragonkind?

Every day dragons had gathered at the river cavern and sang ancient songs that entered lava tubes and porous lava and filtered upward into the world above.

The oldest grandmother dragons remembered stories the oldest dragons told when they were just out-of-the-egg. In those days Smilgamashé, the oldest dragon then living, head broad and eyes bright, front legs still powerful, led the grandmothers in telling frightening tales of humans stalking through fogs with bright swords to plunge cold metal into dragon hearts. She told of how dragons had once dominated earth with tongues of fire, speed in flight, and powerful jaws.

The nightmare of dragons had driven deep into the human spirit and, when dragons were ready for peace and wise enough to realize their numbers were dwindling, humans could not still fright and rage and continued the ancient war, forcing Grilgax to forsake his kingdoms in the Far East, Europe, and the highest mountains of Asia for the darkness of El Malpais caverns.

"Beware, little ones!" Smilgamashé had told them. "Beware of those who would leave the caverns for light, who want to gain glittering eyes and wings. Humans, puny in their selves, are powerful beings that would spill dragon blood even here, even now, if they knew where you little ones are hiding!"

But in the time of the grandmothers, fewer and fewer nightmares were dredged from dragon consciousness by grandmother and grandfather stories. Now, in the small, dark cavern, thoughts flew from one grandmother to another:

"Juniper has told other humans we live!"

"The human child has found us!"

"Have human hearts and spirits changed? Are they still powerful?"

"Simalucroix, Winnigan, Fruchault, Jennfer, and Straaglon have uncovered their wings! They can fly."

"What will humans do when they see a dragon in the skies?"

"What should the grandmothers do?"

"What should the grandfathers do?"

"Simalucroix is the leader, but is too reckless to be the leader."

"He is ensorcelled by the boy."

"Can we stop what is happening?"

"Simalucroix says Juniper is a sign. His ability to talk to Juniper over distance is a sign."

"Simalucroix says Juniper is seeing signs too."

"During songs we feel Juniper's mother's flitting spirit."

"She is crazy with grief and fear."

"Simalucroix is going to cure Juniper's family and other human families."

"Can we stop him? Simalucroix, Winnigan, Fruchault, Jennfer, and Straaglon have wings. They can go to the surface and fly!"

The talk went on for hours, then for days. The grandmothers were worried. What could they do? They consulted grandfathers whose sightless eyes saw the humans' great cities shining and moving all day and all night, never sleeping. They saw the size of the armies and told the grandmothers,

"The humans are invincible. They have made machines that fly!"

The grandmothers listened and talked, but what could they do? What could the grandfather dragons do?

Simalucroix paced through caverns. In places where he could, he unfurled his wings. He fed energy into daily conclaves. The young dragons were excited, longing to separate wings from the skin on their backs. Grandmothers and grandfathers worried in endless circles, trying to tell him to slow down and consider the long-term fate of dragons. What was he going to do when the humans saw him, Winnigan, Fruchault, Jennfer, and Straaglon and ran in terror, stirring ancient fears, awakening aggressions that could lead to spilled dragon blood?

How could days in a dragon's life seem so long? Simalucroix asked himself. When would Christmas day come? When could his anticipation and fear end? Why had he decided, so powerfully he knew he was right, not to go to the surface the moment he found his wings in the conclave? How could he blind Juniper and his friends to dragons beneath the earth?

His nervousness had increased when he had felt intense pain from Juniper and then days of silence. He cast his voice all over El Malpais and even tried to reach into human homes, but all he could hear was Sheena's endless movements. Even Juniper's Father was gone from the lava fields.

He paced through caverns, his energy overflowing, listening to grandmothers, seeing visions of the modern human world the grandfathers were seeing, the armies, cities, the human hive of energy multiplied and multiplied since Grilgax had led dragons into darkness.

Why has Juniper's mind gone silent? he asked himself. Has he died? When he thought about the possibility of Juniper's death, sadness surprised him. Why should a dragon care about a human? Juniper was a sign, not a dragon. Why should the leader of dragons, Simalucroix, son of Wwhhitrapeau and Sarooon, great great great great great grandson of Gilgamax, care? What would he do when Christmas came and winter sun faded into night?

His great eyes glittered in facets as he imagined the outside, but he heard the voices of grandmothers, saw the visions of grandfathers. He was a leader, but he did not know what he was going to do. Keep his promise to Juniper? Or try to hide dragonkind from humans for more centuries? But the people who knew: Juniper, Lily, Sam, kids on the bus, Lily's Grandmother, Juniper's Father, Sam's parents, what could he do about them? What enmity did dragonkind, after all these centuries, have against humans?

Sheena started out of deep sleep again. Snow had dusted lava fields. The wind was cold. She shivered like she always shivered in winter. She had not seen Rory for days, and the small services he provided, meals, split firewood, were missing. She had her axe, and she could find dead trees. She could snare rabbits. She would be okay, but the humming was more powerful than ever. It made her nose's bridge bone sing, and, she thought, startled she could think rationally, she missed her husband and son.

She got out of bed and went to the bedroom's closet. During moments of lucidity she cleaned and organized the treehouse, making sure she lived like a human rather than a wild animal. After shrugging on the elk-skin coat Rory had made for her, she went outside. Standing on the treehouse's porch she waited for visions—for words that went round and round in her head like a toy train around a magically lit Christmas tree. She felt like she had the night she had walked to the shack where Rory and Juniper lived and saw Juniper and recognized him, grown-up, as her son.

She walked slowly down the treehouse stairs, wincing as wind slapped her, and started making her way across lava fields to Rory's. When her feet touched lava the humming changed into a powerful rhythm pulsing with emotion. She shook her head. She could almost hear the words making the rhythm. Was Bandera Volcano about to erupt again after all these centuries? Was that the meaning of the humming song?

Less than an hour later she was standing on the top stair above where her husband and son lived. Wind moaned through El Malpais' pinyon, juniper, Douglas fir, and ponderosa, swirling into caves, collapses, and lava tubes, whistling, chuckling…

Juniper did not appear like he had the last time she had come to the collapse. The night was weird, as haunted as she usually felt. She expected her wild father to appear in front of her, laughing as he reached toward where she was standing, his fist clenched. She climbed down the long, snow-slicked staircase.

At the cave's door she stopped. She had no idea how long she had spent lost in dreams, visions, and word riddles, but she had never climbed down to where her husband and son lived. The small cave structure, with its sturdy wooden door, felt empty. She closed her eyes, expecting visions to swirl around her, but all she could feel was the wonderful humming.

She pushed the door open and went inside. A red and pink lantern was on the kitchen table. Without thinking, as if she belonged where she was, she picked up the blue and red Diamond match box on the table, turned the small, sharp-edged brass dial, and lit the lantern. She went to the small square firebox, took split wood from the wood bin, and lit a fire, putting her hands toward open flame in the black stove.

Then she looked at the east corner draped with a large blanket. Dozens of small hand-carved animals, trucks, buildings, and trees had been placed on wooden shelves stacked from eye-level to the ceiling. The sight of perfectly carved animals, looking almost alive, sank into her chest and formed a lump in her heart. She dropped the blanket, saying to herself that this was where Juniper slept, and went to the cave's west corner.

Rory's bed was so narrow she wondered how he slept in it. She slipped into the small sleeping area, sat on Rory's bed, and, surprising herself again, laid down where her husband spent his nights. Lying in his bed she wondered what had happened. She had been so happy when Juniper had been born. Her husband had been gentle and kind, unlike her beast of a father whose tongue whipped wife and daughter when he was at home rather than at flea markets trying to swing a deal that bought liquor, but little else.

Rory Window had come into her life and swept her into a wonderful reality where days had a predictable regularity. Her mother, with her sly whining and petty cruelties taken out on Sheena because she did not dare confront her husband, kept away from her daughter.

Their courtship had been perfect, Rory bringing flowers and telling her she was beautiful and wonderful, and making furniture, animal toys, and other clever carvings for her. One was of Adam and Eve, both nude, in the Garden of Eden standing below the apple tree before the serpent came. Another had been her portrait in wood, so lifelike it had enchanted her, her skirts whirling upward as she spun in dance.

The humming went on and on. Her heart beat with the rhythm singing through lava and the warm, silent, lantern lit house. What had happened to her when her mother and father, both people she despised, had died? What had changed inside her because of her miscarriage?

She had hated the hospital. She had decided she had to escape antiseptic smells, fluorescent lights, and her feelings of confinement. But then…? She tried to remember, but could not.

In her head she was flying above earth, craning her great neck as she looked at swamplands below. She longed toward the escape in her head. She felt sad and relieved. She could escape memories! But then she felt stranger than she had ever felt, stranger than when she stood in a Douglas fir baying at the full moon, trying to match the howls of distant Mexican wolves.

She was not the one flying. She was living a dragon's memory. She was not Sheena, but a great female dragon pushing powerful wings downward as she rose into daytime skies. She closed her eyes, feeling her great body's mass.

She turned in bed toward the plain gray wall. She wondered why Rory, with his huge talent, waited in El Malpais. She loved him. She had always loved him. And her son? What of Juniper living in wilderness instead of town? Why had she missed the magic of his growing up? Guilt gnawed her with a familiar, powerful uneasiness. The lava field song grew louder, more powerful. She suddenly realized she was laying in her husband's bed weeping.

The cabin's warmth made her feel safe for the first time since she had collapsed when told her parents had burned to death in a car accident. Why had she collapsed? Her reaction had been so strange.

The lava song slowed, calming her, making her sleepy. Where was Rory? she asked herself. Juniper? In sleep she traveled, for the first time in years of hard, desperate living, into the love she had for her husband and son.

The great female dragon landed at Four Windows Cave and keened as she followed other dragons into darkness. Why? She mourned. Why cannot humans and dragons live on the same earth?

In the cabin's darkness the dragon song hummed into corners, into the firebox's closed-door fire, through light from the red and pink lantern with its brass wheel gauge.

Sam sat in front of his Macintosh computer and stared over the monitor through his window. He could not seem to put two thoughts together. He knew Juniper was badly hurt in the hospital. The Lowders had always been bullies. They had picked on Sam and Juniper since kindergarten. What Sam had done most of the time was to let them bang around as if they did not exist, but he had gotten excited about dragons, that most likely were not real, and woken violence lurking in the twins. How could he have been so foolish?

If he had his way he would take up causes of peace and justice and crusade his way to becoming a great man, but he could not crusade by sitting behind his computer, looking out his bedroom window at rocks and hills of Chain of Craters Road, circling around and around a self that had proven nothing, done nothing, realized nothing in spite of big dreams.

Why wasn't he more like Juniper? Able to climb down a lava tube to discover a cavern with a river where dragons lived? Why wasn't he more like Lily? Excited about who she and Juniper were and determined to understand what the signs she and Juniper had seen meant?

He groaned out-loud. In the kitchen his Mom heard him.

"Sam?" she asked. "Are you all right?"

He stared out the window over the Macintosh. He ought to try to get out of his misery, the pain burning his body. He had to do something that would make him feel better. He put his head in his hands and closed his eyes. He felt nothing, he thought to himself. Nothing.

His Mom came to the door and looked in at him. The bedroom felt oppressive. She shook her head, started to speak, thought better of her impulse, and turned back to the kitchen. Why can't Sam get better? she prayed under her breath. What could she do to help him feel better about himself?

Near the road, close to the house, a mound of volcanic rock hummed dragon song into late afternoon light.

Chapter XVIII

Pre-dawn light filtered into the hospital room and woke Juniper. Today! he thought. I'll go home. He was tired even though he'd just woken, but the dream he had been having made him restless, uneasy.

In the dream a towering Simalucroix had been walking across lava fields when he came upon Sam wandering with a lost look on his face. When Sam saw Simalucroix his face lit up. He had turned and reached out toward the huge dragon. Simalucroix had smiled and reached out his enormous right foreleg with long, sharp claws, but the foreleg turned into a human hand. He shook Sam's hand as if he was a human being.

The image of Simalucroix with a human hand made Juniper want to scream, warning his friend that Sam, he, Lily, Grandmother, and Father might reach out hands in friendship to dragons, but the world had more Lowder twins than Sams. To the Lowders dragon claws did not turn into human hands.

Father was sleeping in the brown chair. His face twitched as he huddled beneath two yellow hospital blankets. Juniper put legs over the bed's edge and sat up. Although pain, especially in his ribs, burned as he moved, the pain was not as intense as it had been. He could deal with the pain, he thought.

As he put his feet into brown hospital slippers so that he could walk, an older woman in a doctor's coat opened the door. When she saw he was getting up, she moved to his side, waking Father.

"Whoa there young man," she said. "You're still recovering."

"Dr. Laila?" Father asked sleepily. He shrugged off the blankets.

Dr. Laila smiled. "None other," she said, talking to Father but looking at Juniper. "Glad to meet you, Juniper."

Juniper said nothing, but finished the effort to stand. Dr. Laila's hand firmly gripped his arm, helping to support his weight.

"You are anxious to go home," Dr. Laila said.

"Dr. Laila's taking care of you," Father said from his chair. "She has to release you if you're going to get out of here today."

Juniper took one step, then another.

"I've got to get home," he said. "I've been here long enough. When Lily and her grandmother come, I'm leaving."

Dr. Laila let go of Juniper's arm and watched him as he made his way to the window sill. A dusting of snow glittered in morning light.

"Will you rest if I sign release papers?" Dr. Laila asked him. "Not overdo it, or are you going to break everything I've stitched together inside you?"

Juniper looked at her. She looked serious, concerned. He was being rude to the person who had maybe saved his life. He grimaced.

"Sorry," he said. "I should be thanking you."

Father smiled. "That's better," he said. "I still claim you as my son."

Dr. Laila smiled too. "You didn't answer my question," she said. "You're a wonderful young man, but I'm a tough, old doctor."

"I want to go home," Juniper said carefully. "Home is not easy to get to, but it's important I get home."

Dr. Laila frowned. "That doesn't make much sense to me," she said. "Your father has told me where you live, and frankly, Juniper, you're going to be so tired after riding in a car to Ramah you're not going to be able to move. Your father's rented an apartment in Ramah. If you leave the hospital today, you're going to Ramah, not home. I can't keep you here against your father's will, and he might give in to you, but I won't sign the release papers. Then your father, not the school's insurance, will be responsible for your medical bills."

Juniper looked at the doctor. Could Simalucroix speak to him in Ramah? Could Juniper convince the great dragon to stay underground? He glanced at Father who was looking at him as steadily as the doctor was. Would Father let him walk out the hospital doors without the doctor's release? Would Grandmother over-rule what Lily wanted if she was worried about bad consequences if he did not have the release?

"I'm tired and hurt," he said out-loud. "But I need to go home."

"You can't go home," Father said. "Such as home is."

Juniper felt grateful Father had not mentioned the dragons. Father did not believe Simalucroix existed, but he would not betray Juniper.

"I'll stay in Ramah," Juniper said. "But I'm getting stronger. I want to be home for Christmas."

The doctor looked toward the door as it opened. Lily walked into the room. Lily? Already? So early? Juniper felt triumphant. Behind Lily, Grandmother and Sammy crowded into the room.

The doctor smiled and shook her head.

"You're a stubborn young man," she told Juniper. "But I'm not going to ruin Christmas for you. I have no doubt your father will carry you, if he needs to, to get you home. I just don't want you breaking anything open that's stitched together. I know the lava tube area. I don't understand how anybody can live there. So the question is, how are you going to walk miles into wilderness when you can barely walk across a room?"

Grandmother touched Lily's shoulder.

"We'd better wait for the doctor," she told Lily. Sammy had already backed out the door. Lily's eyes were fastened on Juniper's face.

"We'll be outside waiting to take you home, Juniper," she said.

Juniper smiled. Lily and Grandmother turned and left the room. Juniper looked back at Dr. Laila.

"I don't know," he said. "But I'm going to heal at home faster than in Ramah. If it takes me all day to make my way over the Cairn Trail, it takes all day."

The doctor frowned. "That's the best I'm going to get, isn't it?" she said. She looked at Father. "I'm going to let him go," she said. "I don't like it much, and I want you to make sure he doesn't overdue it."

Father sighed. "I'll try," he said. "But Juniper's tough as well as stubborn. I'll make him go slow, and there are places where a travois might make sense, but if he's as determined as he sounds, we'll try the Cairn Trail."

Dr. Laila looked back at Juniper.

"I'm going to sign papers, young man," she said. "But your body's had multiple shocks. You need to understand that. If you don't you'll be back here tomorrow afternoon, and I won't be so easy to deal with the next time around."

Juniper smiled. "Thank you," he said. "I'll go slow."

Dr. Laila looked at Father. "I'll send an orderly with a wheelchair," she said.

She looked at Juniper. "You can get dressed. You can sleep in the car." She shook her head, looked about to say something more, then turned and left the room.

Juniper looked at Father. "We can go?" he asked.

Father smiled. "I'll tell Grandmother, Lily, and Sammy," he said. "I don't know how you're going to sleep. The car's going to be crowded." He shook his head. "I've been away from civilization so long I can't rent a car." He paused, still looking at Juniper. "The truth is," he added. "I want to go home too. I miss Sheena even though she's never around."

After Juniper had dressed and gotten out of the hospital gown, a nurse showed up with a wheel chair. He protested and said he could walk, but she just stared at him.

Christmas was omnipresent once he left his room. Hospital hallways had long ribbons of green tinsel with lights and cutouts of Santa Claus, reindeer, and snowflakes attached. Father went to the checkout at a lobby window. Minutes later Sammy was driving with Father riding shotgun and Lily and Grandmother sitting in the back with Juniper.

Juniper fell asleep as they drove into San Rafael before the rise into the Zuni Mountains. When he woke they had passed El Malpais Visitor Center, Cinder Hill, and Cimarron Rose Bed and Breakfast and were passing Inscription Rock Trading Post and Coffee Company, the Ancient Way Café, and Old School Gallery.

Lily and her grandmother were talking quietly beside him. Father and Sammy were discussing elk trails crisscrossing lava fields. Juniper ached over every inch of his body.

When they finally drove into Ramah, Sammy did not hesitate, but drove to a small house on the side of town closest to Zuni. Father glanced back and saw Juniper was awake, but not looking good.

"We're here," he announced.

The car had been warm, but when Juniper got out of the car with Father's assistance, he was surprised at how cold it felt. No snow was on the ground, but the ground was frozen and hard. He could hardly think through his pain, so he let Father support him without protest. Juniper failed to think of Simalucroix until he was in the house sitting on a large brown couch in a living room with a television set.

As soon as he was seated, Lily sat beside him and took his hand.

"You're almost home," she whispered.

"Almost," Juniper agreed softly.

Father went into the kitchen and came back with a glass of water and a pain pill. Juniper looked at Lily.

"Can you hear Simalucroix here?" Lily asked, understanding what he was thinking.

Juniper tried to use his mind to listen. He knew any chance of touching Simalucroix's mind would be gone when he swallowed the pinkish white pill, but his ribs, head, and left side hurt so much he knew he'd have to take the pill to keep from passing out.

"Not now," he told Lily. She touched his arm.

"Take the pill," she said. "Sleep. You've got to get better. Christmas is three days away."

"Lily's right," Father said. "If you're going to talk to dragons, you need to rest."

"Dragons?" Sammy asked. "You say dragons, Rory?"

Juniper groaned. The secret kept spreading even while he worked at keeping it limited to those who already knew.

Lily hhmmphed. "He's not talking about you, Sammy," she said to her brother. "You're too accommodating to Grandmother and me to be a dragon."

"Besides," Grandmother added. "Juniper needs rest. Every bump in the road jolted him. We've got to go home and fix supper."

"You don't want to talk about dragons," Sammy said.

"Guess not," Father answered, looking strangely at Juniper.

He got up from the pink rocking chair across from the couch and held his hand out to Sammy.

"Thanks," he said. "You sure you don't want gas money?"

Grandmother looked sternly at Sammy.

"You're family," Sammy told Father. "Grandmother says so, and Grandmother rules."

"Oohhh!" Grandmother said in mock exasperation.

Sammy and Lily, then Father, laughed.

All this way, Juniper thought to himself, talking his way out of the hospital, riding in the car, and he still could not contact Simalucroix.

Lily let go of this hand and kissed his cheek. "Tomorrow," she promised. She got up and followed Grandmother and Sammy out the front door.

After they had gone Father looked at Juniper. "Let's get you into bed," he said.

Juniper nodded. Father half lifted him from the couch. He kept silent even as chest pain shot through him. There were two single beds in the bedroom, both covered with elegant woolen blankets with Navajo storm designs. Father led Juniper to the bed beneath the room's lone window and eased him onto the mattress and beneath the covers.

"I shouldn't have mentioned dragons?" he asked.

"Humans will slaughter the dragons if they come up from the caves," Juniper answered. "I need to tell Simalucroix to stay underground. Humans can't be trusted."

"Not all humans," Father said softly. He smiled.

Juniper closed his eyes. He felt lightheaded, out of sorts. Then he was asleep.

Chapter XIX

Sheena stood over a beautifully hand-carved oak cradle, looking at a small baby boy looking up at her. She was peaceful, her green eyes shining contentment. The baby laughed, and the laughter thrilled into Sheena's body. She stood still as her face changed into the beaked feather face of a silver raven. Wings grew on her back as her body changed, her skin parting as wings unfolded. Hands and legs disappeared as her body morphed into a bird.

Shocked, Juniper realized he was the baby. He reached toward his mother, but his mother was flapping wings, hovering above him as moonlight called to her. Yellow raven-eyes blinked, and she was gone. Juniper cried in his crib, screaming for his mother… He woke in the small Ramah apartment's bedroom.

His body trembled from the dream. He did not think he was as weak as he had been. He felt stronger, but ached all over. He got out of bed and tried to think. He had to make it to El Malpais and the lava fields. If he could not climb the Cairn Trail, he would have to sit on black lava and try to communicate with Simalucroix. If he could talk to the great dragon and tell him his fears and what had happened in the school's cafeteria, maybe the tragedy the dragons faced could be avoided.

Father was in the small kitchen off the living room getting coffee. When Father saw Juniper he stopped pouring and smiled.

"Getting used to civilization is easy," he said, nodding at the coffee pot. "I'd forgotten how much I like coffee." He stretched and yawned. "Donald Sharp is coming over in a while," he said. "You'd better get dressed. Donald's driving us to the Cairn Trail. I'm going to check on Sheena while you stay by the parking lot. I don't want you to try the trail yet. We'll do that Christmas Eve, but I don't feel right not checking on Sheena to see how she's doing."

Juniper's relief allowed him to smile. "Good," he said. "I'll get ready."

When Donald Sharp showed up, Juniper realized he knew the old man. Donald traded in Zuni fetishes, small animals and symbols carved in stone, and traveled around the West and Midwest selling them after buying from craftspeople lined up outside his Ramah house on weekends. When Juniper had been in grade school he and Father had visited Donald on one of their rare trips to town.

As Donald drove his old Ford pickup down Chain of Craters Road, he and Father talked incessantly.

"About time you considered joining civilization again," Donald told Father. "You've been in El Malpais long enough."

Father frowned. "I've got a dilemma," he said. "I want to do right by Juniper while not forgetting Sheena."

"You could try the medical establishment again," Donald said.

Father shook his head. "Last time was a nightmare," he said.

Juniper said nothing as the truck rattled over ruts and wash boarding, jolting every hurt in his body. The closer he got to the Cairn Trail turnoff, the more excited he got. He kept listening for some indication Simalucroix knew he was back, but the truck's rattling was the only sound in his head.

When they passed Sam's bus stop Juniper could almost feel Sam's sadness washing over hills into the huge, black lava boulders beside the road. When they turned toward the Cairn Trail, coming up on the lava wall, Juniper closed his eyes and concentrated on searching through a silence he forced into himself. At the parking lot Donald pulled the truck in front of the railroad ties.

"Thanks," Father said. "You'll wait while I try to find Sheena?" He looked at Juniper. "Juniper shouldn't strain himself this soon after the hospital."

Donald grinned and winked at Juniper. "We'll be okay," he said.

Father got out of the truck and headed up the trail. Juniper slid off the cracked brown seat. Donald came around the truck as they watched Father climb the trail, then veer off toward the treehouse.

"What now?" Donald asked as Father disappeared into a depression.

Juniper shook his head. "I don't know," he said vaguely. What should I do? he asked himself. How do I contact Simalucroix? "Can I climb up the trail just a little?" he asked Donald.

Donald smiled. "Don't know that I could or should stop you," he answered. "I'll stay here. Just listen to your father and stay close. If you hurt yourself you'll be slow mending."

Juniper breathed deeply. "Thanks," he said, then slowly climbed the trail, watching his feet as he made his way over sharp aa lava.

I've never had to be this careful before, he thought to himself. As soon as he'd reached a big boulder, he stopped and leaned back on the rock. He felt tired. He closed his eyes and tried to feel the wilderness around him. He'd lost the wilderness in the hospital and Ramah. He felt his way into twisting and turning lava fields, the gnarled toughness of pinyon, juniper, and Douglas fir, the sound of wind as it sang over stone, trees, and brush.

As he reached outward from the rock, he could feel dragons moving as they hunted fish, bats, insects, and rodents and remembered when Grilgax was king.

At the treehouse Father stopped beside the pinyon on the hill and stared at a structure that looked as if it had been empty for days.

"Sheena?" he called, dreading what he would face if she heard him, but there was no response.

He made his way down the hill to the Douglas fir. He climbed to the deck. The only sound was wind in the tree's branches. He walked inside. Sheena had not been there for a while. The bedroom and kitchen/living room not only felt empty, but dust was everywhere, unlike when Sheena was at home.

He felt sick in the pit of his stomach. What had gone wrong? Sheena stayed overnight in the wilderness, but he had never known a time when she had not come back to the treehouse the next morning to sleep and recover. She had not been in the house since he had left for town when Donald had come and got him with the news that Juniper had been badly hurt at school.

Where should he look for her? He had no idea. The only thing he could do was wander the wilderness. He had done that enough times over the years, looking for Sheena, but this was the first time in a long time that he had felt panicked. How long could he be gone? Juniper needed to get back to the apartment and rest.

He left the treehouse and walked toward the cave. He would not find Sheena at the shack, but he could check things out and move on to the blowholes. She might be there. Then he would work toward the Ice Cave. After that he would have to give up and go back. He could stay overnight at home if he could talk Juniper into going with Donald and staying alone in the apartment. The treehouse's emptiness raged inside him.

At the top of the collapse's stairs he stopped so suddenly he jarred his right knee. Sheena was climbing the stairs. She saw him appear above her and stopped. She did not look as wild as she normally looked, but tremendously sad. Tears streaked down her face. Father could see the tears even from where he was standing.

"Rory?" she asked. "My love?"

Her voice was calm, normal, the way it had been when they had first been married before Juniper's birth.

"Sheena?" he asked hesitantly.

"I'm ill, aren't I?" she asked, panic entering her voice. She sat down on the steps. "I've been ill a long time."

A fierce feeling of hope and fear spiked into Rory. What was going on? How could Sheena be talking so normally? Could their long nightmare end? How should he answer her?

He slowly sat on the top step and looked at his wife. She was not as beautiful as she looked traversing lava flats or standing on a Douglas fir's branches in moonlight. Her face sagged under the weight of what she was thinking and feeling. But to Rory she was more beautiful than she had ever been.

She looked up at him. "Where's Juniper?" she asked. "He's not in the cave."

Rory swallowed. "He's been hurt," he said softly. "At school. Badly."

Sheena stood up. "My baby?" she asked.

"Your young man," Father answered.

Panic grew in her face, growing wilder and wilder as Rory sat and watched and tried to know what to do, how to stop the madness animating the way she was standing below him.

"I want the moon," she said. "The beauty."

She moved off the stairs and climbed over the collapse's boulders. Rory stood up, but she was past him, heading toward the treehouse. She stopped and turned toward him.

"I've been sleeping in your bed," she said. "It's nicer than my bed. In the treehouse they keep singing. I don't know that I want them to sing!"

They? Singing? What was she talking about? Rory felt Sheena's panic transferring out of her tense body into him.

"Wait!" Rory said, but she turned and was gone.

Rory started to follow her, but stopped. Chasing after Sheena had never done any good. He could keep up if he pushed hard enough, but she would run and run, always keeping him away.

What had just happened? Was there hope beyond his fleeting hopes? What was she talking about when she talked about them singing? He sat back down on the top step and stared into winter blue sky.

"Juniper!" the great voice reverberated in his head. Juniper started, but kept his face expressionless so Donald could not see Simalucroix had spoken to him.

"Simalucroix," he said in his head, relieved to have finally made contact.

"I lost you," the dragon said. "You went to school and did not come back."

"You have to rethink coming out of the caverns," Juniper answered urgently. "Humans are dangerous. I should have done as you asked and kept silent. I want you to be safe."

Simalucroix was silent. Juniper tried to look into the cavern's darkness with his eyes closed. He tried to relive the moment Carson Lowder had swung Lily's bag of books, sending pain and blackness ringing through his head. You have to see, Simalucroix, he told himself. You have to understand.

"You are hurt badly," Simalucroix said. "You should not walk the wild lands."

"The Lowders were on drugs," Juniper explained. "They were crazy with rage stoked by hallucinations."

"We will heal you," Simalucroix answered. "We remember how."

"No!" Juniper said in his head. "No! It's too dangerous! If anything happened to you or the dragons, the world would be wrong. Humans are too dangerous."

Simalucroix seemed amused.

"I understand," he said. "But we've made our decision. We understand human hearts and spirits, their weaknesses and strengths. I understand dragon hearts and spirits and our weaknesses and strengths. The time has come for dragon hearts to be strong again, to face turbulence and danger that has to be faced if humans and dragons are to both inhabit the world."

"You have to stay in the caverns," Juniper said desperately. "Father, I, Sam, Lily, and Lily's grandmother will keep the secret."

"Nothing can ever be hidden from humans," Simalucroix said. "Not forever. Your kind pokes, prods, and explores every phenomenon it suspects exists. I and the others with wings have been exploring. Your world is frightening, with more humans than I imagined, but hiding will not make you fewer or more peaceful. Sooner or later we'll be found. The grandmother and grandfather dragons are not pleased, but I am winged and the leader. I will not hide in darkness any longer."

"But there are tanks and helicopters!" Juniper objected. "Laser beams that can explode a rocket in mid-flight. If you're found you're not going to have a chance!"

"We have sentience," the dragon said. "We have free will. I am deciding to come out of darkness. Others have found their wings and will come with me."

He was silent. "On Christmas," he continued. "We will meet you in the Christmas moon's light. We'll heal you, your father, Sheena, who will come to the sound of our singing, Lily, her grandparents, and Sam and his parents. You and Lily must gather all of you outside Four Windows Cave."

Juniper cast around for arguments to change Simalucroix's mind, but he could feel the dragon's resolve in his voice. This is impossible, he thought. Wrong.

"You need to rest," Simalucroix said. "Your father is coming. We will make you stronger, especially on Christmas day, but you need to rest."

The great dragon was out of Juniper's mind. Wind sang across the earth's surface. Juniper looked around him. What could he do? He ached so badly he could barely stand the pain. He was in no shape to crawl down a blowhole to the caverns.

Father was walking toward him over the Cairn Trail from the direction of the cave and home. How could Simalucroix be so reckless as to come to the earth's surface? he asked himself. How could he have been so foolish as to let others know about the dragons? He sat still as Father approached.

Chapter XX

Juniper sat down on the small brown couch and, stunned, stared at Lily.

"They're out of jail?" he asked disbelievingly. "How can they be out of jail?"

Lily looked scared. "Their uncle's a judge. He arranged with Judge Luhan to offer them bail. The family came up with bail money."

"That's not right. Not after what they did to you, me, and Sam."

Outside Father and Donald were quietly talking over the news with Lily's grandfather who had driven her over to the apartment.

"Do you think they're still dangerous?" Juniper asked. His heart sank. "Sam lives less than a half mile from them. Does he know? Did the drugs make them crazy? They've always been scary."

His thoughts ran one way and another without focus.

Father and Lily's grandfather came in the front door. Donald was driving out of the driveway.

"You kids will be okay," Father said. "Mr. Maryboy and I will take care of this."

"It's Christmas Eve," Lily's grandfather said. "The Lowders aren't bad people. Not like some families. They'll be having Christmas in spite of the troubles those hellions have brought home."

"They're not going to get meth again?" Lily asked. Her voice was on-edge. "Meth users always get meth."

Grandfather went over to his granddaughter and touched her arm so gently Juniper could hardly believe how tender he was. This was the man who had forced Lily and her grandmother to move to the canyon away from his drunken violence. When he had seen Lily drive up with her grandfather after he, Father, and

Donald Sharp had gotten back from El Malpais, outrage had run through him like a lightning strike.

What were people all about? he asked himself. Were the Lowder twins like Lily's grandfather? Filled with love and caring one minute and crazy violent the next?

Father was not like that. Even Sheena, wild and scary as she could be, was predictable. You needed to stay away from her. . . But then again, he thought about the night she had stood above him talking rationally about him and Father. He shook his head.

"I'd feel safer in El Malpais," he said. "Especially if Lily was there."

Lily smiled at him. Father shook his head.

"The Lowder boys know the lava fields," he said. "Not as well as we know them, but they can make their way around. They don't live that far away, and they know where we live."

"Christmas day I'm going home," Juniper said. He tried to put finality in his voice that could not be disputed.

"And I'm going to be with Juniper," Lily said, her voice soft. She looked at her grandfather. "And Grandfather, Grandmother, and Sammy."

"Those boys don't know where Lily lives," Mr. Maryboy said. "We'd all be safer going to the canyon for Christmas. I know Lucille would be happy to have us. I can hunt up a couple of turkeys for the Christmas meal."

Lily looked at her Grandfather, her eyes so bright they seemed to pierce him.

"Grandmother will agree with me," she said. "We'll be at Juniper's in the collapse. Sammy'll be there too."

Mr. Maryboy's face folded into a frown. He looked at his granddaughter's eyes, then looked away.

"If my family's there, I'll be there," he mumbled. "Guess I've got to face that what's going to be is going to be." He sounded bitter, as if he was swallowing something rankling him deep inside.

"Juniper's not in any shape to make it home," Father said gently. "Home's where you ought to be on Christmas day, but this year this apartment is home."

Juniper closed his eyes. "I'll rest tomorrow," he said. He felt tired. The day's events had worn him out. "On Christmas morning I'll make it home one way or another."

"Sammy will take us," Lily said, looking at Father. "Grandmother and I will be here early. Then we'll go."

Juniper looked at Lily and felt like he had risen above earth and fallen into light. Lily looked into his eyes and smiled as if she knew what he was feeling.

"I thought you were going to talk your dragons out of coming to the surface," Father said.

Mr. Maryboy looked warily at Father, as if he was afraid Father was losing his sanity.

Juniper shook his head. "I tried," he said softly.

Father shrugged in resignation. "If necessary, I'll carry you," he said. "If we need to be home for Christmas, that's where we'll be."

At home Sam was at the kitchen table. He felt heavy and fat, as if the anti-depressant medicine was weighing him down. He was not as upset as he had been. For days he had not been able to think about Juniper and Lily or the dragons. All he could think about was how he had shrank back when Bill had grabbed Lily's purse and started swinging it around. He had gotten up and gone after Carson, but Carson had been too much. Then the disaster Juniper had faced as enraged Lowder brothers ganged up on him and pummeled him, first with fists, then with legs and feet after he had fallen to the cafeteria floor.

And what had Sam done as his best friend was beaten to a pulp? Bill had knocked him to the ground; he had hit his head against the table where he, Lily, and Juniper had been sitting. He had heard Mrs. Larson screaming at Carson and saw Bill kick Juniper with a wild look in white eyes, but Sam's head had been ringing so loudly he was paralyzed. He had not moved, but watched as members of the wrestling team and Mr. Rickshaw had moved in and taken Bill and Carson to the ground. They had struggled and yelled at the top of their lungs and cursed as other people came over to see how Sam and Juniper were. Sam kept telling them he was okay and kept trying to see how Juniper was, but then the police were there, and Juniper and Lily had disappeared as Juniper was hurried to an ambulance.

When they came with a stretcher for Sam, he had seen Juniper's blood pooled on the cafeteria's black and white floor tiles. He had felt so sick to his stomach self-hatred had welled inside him, attacking who he was.

He had been afraid, he kept telling himself over and over again. His weakness had overwhelmed him and turned him into an ineffective fool who cowered under the cafeteria table as Juniper had tried to fight two bullies. He could do nothing, was nothing, and would never be anything. He was a coward and a fool.

But now, at the kitchen table with sunset red on the horizon, he felt calmer, more at peace with himself. He could almost see Simalucroix in deep caverns by the dark river rising up before Juniper, spreading enormous white wings and speaking about healing and humans in a sibilant, deep voice ringing with the wisdom of deep earth. Juniper was whole, unhurt, filled with the courage that had led him to take on Carson. Around Juniper thousands of dragons rumbled a song of becoming, of possibilities taken away centuries ago.

Without thinking, Sam got up from his chair and went outside into the glorious evening. What did he have to fear from the Lowder brothers? he thought. He'd known them his whole life. They'd played together as toddlers.

His feet seemed to have a mind of their own. He climbed the hill between his family's house and the Lowder's. What had caused Carson and Bill to grow so mean? Their parents were decent, hard-working people. Their father worked construction and was gone a lot, but their mother was normal enough, a waitress at different cafes in Grants or Ramah, a large woman with a soft smile and careful manners. She looked sad a lot of the time, but had always treated Sam, when he played with her sons, with respect and kindness.

At the hill's top he looked through pinyon and juniper at the Lowder house, a forest-green A-frame in the woods. Bill and Carson were standing outside by the Ford pickup their father drove. Sam stood stupidly, trying to remember why the two of them at home was not right--was grossly wrong. He almost called out to them, but fear kicked in and bent him to the ground. How had they managed to get out of jail? What would they do if they saw him?

He searched for what he thought Simalucroix looked like, huge, white, with wings spanning dozens of feet when spread for flight. He forced himself to slowly straighten up. A humming sang in his head. The humming vibrated his bones, making him tingle all over. He would not be afraid, he told himself.

He thought about walking down the hill to a house he had spent so many hours visiting when he was young and confronting the Lowders, asking them what had gotten into them. Instead, he turned away, listening to the imaginary humming, wondering if he was imagining what it was like to hear the dragon conclave sing.

He did not have to confront the Lowders to defeat his fear, he thought to himself. Confronting them would be stupid and serve no purpose. The Lowders were the Lowders' problem. Their father had gotten them out of jail. If they came over the hill to Sam's house, he would have to deal with them, but he knew they would not be that foolish. Their jail cell experience would be too immediate. Their father and mother would be home too, watching them, making sure they stayed home and kept out of trouble. Later they would be dangerous, but not right now.

Unexpectedly, Sam smiled to himself. He had gotten himself out of his room. He could move again, act, be more than a lump inside the house. On Christmas day he would hike to Juniper's house. He would see Simalucroix and the other dragons. He would not tell his parents, but leave them a note so they would not worry. He would act and try to become more than a depresser, a fool, a lost soul. The dragons would help him. The dragons, Juniper, and Lily would help if he started trying to heal himself. He smiled as he walked into the kitchen door. His mother saw him smiling and looked puzzled.

"Sam?" she asked. "Is that you?"

"It's me, Mom," he said. "I'm trying to get out of my funk."

His mother put the dish towel she'd been holding down and sat on a kitchen chair.

"Really?" she said, hesitantly smiling.

"Really," Sam answered, sitting in a chair beside his mother.

He did not have to be depressed, he told himself. Heaviness weighed down every step he made, but his mother and father loved him. He could find reasons to live a good life. He had friends, Juniper and Lily. He did not have to be spectacular for a good life.

He was going to see Simalucroix and the dragons.

Chapter XXI

That night Juniper had a dream that seemed more real and alive than his other dragon dreams. The dream started before he was even asleep, vivid with color and sounds heard beneath earth in the great cavern by the dark river:

The ancient female dragon stalked dark cavern corridors. Grilgax had long been dead, and she no longer had his comforting presence to tamp down ancient fires in her two hearts. She despised the darkness. She longed to wind through dark caverns until she could climb to the stain of silver stars in the night sky. She despised the thought of puny humans who had driven the few remaining dragons into perpetual darkness beneath the earth's surface, breathing sulfur-tinged air.

Why had humans been so endless? So rapacious? Buying and selling? Swirling about like a disease upon earth? Sometimes, in this endless end-time of life, her rage grew so great she thoughtlessly snorted fire, bringing huge shadows alive along cavern walls, lighting, for a moment, in sharp relief, contours of walls in smaller caverns.

The young dragons were adjusting to their new world without the rage and anxiety she felt. Sometimes, when she had managed to control her emotions, she was proud to see what she, Grilgax, and the three dozen surviving dragons had accomplished. Dragons were no longer a dying race.

The young dragons were smaller than she and Thrundun, the only surviving dragons from those who had entered the caverns. Unused wings had welded to backs beneath smooth skin. They still had wings beneath their hides, but a thin membrane had pressed wings to bodies. The young were paler too. Not one had the multi-jeweled skin of Grilgax or the other great males. Some were a pale green, but, born away from light, none had the dark, rich, gleaming green of her own thick hide, or the dark yellow and brown of Thrundun's hide. The youngest cavern dragons were losing their sight as sight became less important than smell, the sense of the dark landscape, and movement.

What surprised her most was how the young seemed to be thriving in the dark. They relished catching bats and scurrying small mammals. They concocted great adventures as they explored this cavern and that cave, sometimes getting caught in a blowhole's narrowness as they squirmed into places that put them at risk.

They talked endlessly, chattering about spots where bats were plentiful or rodents or fish could be found, or about their dark world, teasing each other, and laughing in a way she could not remember laughing when she was young. She could not adjust to the darkness. Not ever. But children of her eggs seemed to be adjusting better than she could have imagined.

Their adjustment should have made her glad. That had been Grilgax's dream when they had gathered in the high meadow before the forever flight to El Malpais. Survival of dragonkind had driven them to give up lives they loved for a different existence that might allow dragons to continue to think and converse as their numbers spread out of the sight and minds of humankind, the ancient enemy.

The idea that intelligent beings could adjust to endless darkness had seemed far-fetched as they walked into Big Skylight Cave and wove out of humanity's awareness. But the truth was that the young dragons were doing well. They had made cavern darkness their home.

She stopped pacing, feeling faint and slightly ill from her exertion. She was no longer middle aged. She was not even old. She had lived for over two hundred and fifty years in mountain heights and far below the earth's surface. She had flown to the Himalayas from the Alps, then across ocean and continents with only brief rest periods. She was weary, ancient, and tired of rage that should not infect young dragons if they were to perpetuate dragonkind's existence. How had Grilgax got them to give up all they loved for a dream?

Gray light filtered to where she was standing. Wrapped in her thought's maze she had climbed through the tortured bewilderment of passages that led from where the river flowed cold and massive into volcanic fires steaming and spitting into a wall of ancient volcanic stone. Ahead was Four Windows Cave and daylight. She had not seen light for so long the dim grayness hurt her eyes as they swirled with dark colors, a kaleidoscope moving so fast the movement blurred the rainbow of who she was.

I cannot stay here, she thought. Humans will find their way much deeper into the earth than this. She stared at gray light with a longing that made her two hearts thrum in opposition to each other. Her body felt so huge and heavy she could not believe she had dragged it so far upward.

She roared in her mind the way she had once roared in her cave high in the Alps as she launched into skies so clogged with falling snow and howling winds that only an insane creature or a dragon would have dared to confront the storm. How could anyone as large as she, or Grilgax, fly?

They would drag her great body in the funeral procession to the cliff's lip above the volcanic fires, she knew. Dragons would keen ancient songs into the dark canyon by the even darker river and rejoice that she had lived and made the great journey that had saved dragons from extinction.

Then, after singing, they would, as they had with Grilgax, throw her carcass, bereft of intelligence and being, into the river which would take it over the precipice into fires that burned forever.

Forever passed, and still she dragged herself downward. She saw earth below her as she flew and flew: Mountains, hills, plains, rivers, lakes, marshes, flocks of birds, herds of animals, humans with bows and spears running after game…

Dragons did not belong in the deep caverns, she thought to herself. They deserved a full moon's light in a starry night. She sang the funeral songs they would sing about her to herself. She dragged herself downward, feeling heavier and heavier, until she happened upon a young adventurer who startled into her presence. He yelped out-loud when he saw her. She sighed, breathing a great gust of fire that lit tunnel's stone into sharp relief.

"Peace little one," she said to the young male.

She closed her eyes, felt winds sweep over her body with gale force, sang of life's glories on earth to the young male, and then, sad, deep, deep in her bones, died.

Every dragon in the caverns heard her final song and felt the anguish of her passing.

Juniper woke up with the vision of dragons in the great cavern, the great female dragon's body carried upon the backs of nine dragons. He could not shake the dream from his head. He threw covers back and sat up on the bed's side. What was that all about? he asked himself. What did it mean? Were the dragons supposed to remain hidden? Were they supposed to come out of the caverns and live in light again?

He felt as heavy as the female dragon as she dragged downward through caverns and tunnels to where she had finally met the young male. Had the dream been a dream? Like other dreams he had dreamed of the great female, it had not felt like a dream.

He laid back down and closed his eyes again. He did not think he could sleep, even though the night was still dark, but within minutes he had drifted off into deep, dreamless sleep.

In the caverns the older dragons' opposition to Simalucroix and his Christmas plans had been growing. One of the oldest female dragons, Ssissensin, remembered the generation after the generation of the three dozen had died and the fear instilled by her father, mother, uncles, and cousins.

Her fear was acute and made her rage at younger dragons foolish enough to reach toward the surface and endanger generations of dragons yet to be born. Shrillness, energy, and largeness gave her power over the others.

"We have to stop them," she hissed to three dozen dragons gathered in the small cavern miles from where Simalucroix was holding yet another conclave, allowing more dragons to slough off skin that had long imprisoned wings.

The elders had carefully sealed their speaking off from the minds of those who might be listening. The elders moved uncomfortably hearing the malice in Ssissensin's voice.

"We are not more powerful than they are," Creleigh, an old male said. "I am not in favor of what Simalucroix is doing. It's dangerous, but talk of stopping them is not going anywhere. Our hope is reason and teaching, not anger."

"They will not listen," one of Ssissensin's chief allies, Syllabrie, said. "We have tried to talk reason, but they are caught up in memories our parent's parent's parents suppressed in themselves and tried to kill. They feel new wings and wind beneath them even though none of them have felt a breath of wind."

"There is no way to stop them without reason," Creleigh said. "There are thousands of dragons now. Most are young. We are old, and like all old creatures, our strength is in our youth."

"There is a way if we have courage," Syllabrie answered. "Tell them Ssissensin."

Ssissensin moved sinuously as she faced the elders. Surprisingly, her eyes whirled as she prepared to speak, sparking with rainbow colors long bleached out of dragon eyes. Her white eyelids flickered with the colors. Her eyes did not open the way Simalucroix's eyes had opened, but there was a change in them.

"I have been exploring," she announced carefully. "Making my way toward the surface. I've found two narrow places in the path upward. Only one dragon can fit through either passage. I am surprised our ancestors, who were larger than we are, could move through them. If we make our stand we can stop movement upward. We can force our will on the conclave."

The entire group, except for Ssissensin and Syllabrie, gasped. The cold strength in Ssissensin's voice made several elders recoil from what the great female was saying.

Creleigh stepped forward and shook his huge head. His eyes too glittered behind his eyelids. Dragonkind is changing again, he told himself. The young have found wings, and our eyes glitter as we transform ourselves from members of dragonkind into individuals who feel their power.

"You suggest war," he told Ssissensin calmly.

"An action, not war," Ssissensin replied.

"Even the young human that brought this misfortune is afraid that if dragonkind shows itself in light again humankind will dredge up old insecurities and fears and react by destroying us," Syllabrie said.

"This is fools talk," a voice toward the back of the cavern said. "I will not go so far against my sons and daughters," a male, Old Brighton, said.

Ssissensin and Syllabrie both swayed back and forth, their eyelids glittering.

"You do not have the courage to stop those courageous enough to stand in the narrow passageways and block Simalucroix and winged ones," Ssissensin declared. "You will not stop us from doing what our ancestors would have had us do."

Old Brighton and Creleigh rose on their hind legs, hearing the threat in Ssissensin's voice as she crouched as if about to launch herself at them.

"You will not stop us," Syllabrie said defiantly.

Creleigh stared at her, calculating, fearful, enraged.

"You think I will not fight a war to keep war from happening?" he roared. "No, old female. Think again."

Syllabrie whimpered; then, finding her courage, laughed, although the laugh was nearly a whimper as she looked up at the huge males.

"The grandmothers have courage," she said. "We will stand in the passageway."

"We will stand and be strong for dragon survival," Ssissensin said. "You cannot stop us unless you decide to fight us."

Slowly, her eyes whirling, the two great females stood on their hind legs.

Old Brighton slowly lowered himself to the ground.

"I don't want to fight," he said, his voice quiet. "We must face this threat without fighting among ourselves and frightening the young ones."

"Ssissensin?" Creleigh roared.

Ssissensin laughed as she lowered back to four legs.

"You can't stop us," she said to Creleigh. "Too many grandmothers agree with me for you to stop me. What is going to happen is set and in motion."

Then she and Syllabrie turned toward the small cavern's entrance and walked away from the two males confronting them. Of the thirty-six old dragons in the cavern, sixteen filed around Creleigh and followed Ssissensin and Syllabrie into the cavern maze.

"The young ones will not accept Ssissensin's leadership," Creleigh said.

"Simalucroix may be as great a leader as Grilgax," Old Brighton agreed.

"This is turning into a troubling time," Framwing, one of the oldest males said.

"I am afraid of tragedy," Creleigh answered, falling to four legs.

"We must keep our heads and try to keep tragedy from happening," Kassandrae, one of the younger grandmothers who had stayed in the cavern, said.

"How do we keep Ssissensin from fulfilling her plans?" Creleigh said. "If she moves into those narrow passageways on Christmas and tries to hold her position with her followers' help, blood will be spilled where bloodshed has not been seen since dragons came."

The fourteen dragons left in the cavern looked apprehensively at each other. Most did not want to confront Ssissensin. None wanted Simalucroix and his clutch of newly winged dragons to follow caverns and tunnels to the surface. Stomachs roiled with stress. Silence was so intense it echoed outward into the darkness of their home's cavern, tunnel, and blowhole maze.

Chapter XXII

Juniper got out of bed feeling groggy. The dream about the great female dragon was still with him. It seemed so real he felt as if he had lived inside the dragon's head. But how could that be? He had been born thousands of years after she had lived and died inside her fierce regret in the caverns.

Christmas Eve. Could he make it home today? The need to go to the small cave with handmade furniture inside the collapse was so strong it made him ill. He felt better than he had when he had first woken in the hospital and better than when he had walked through pain to get Father, Lily, and Lily's grandmother to take him to Ramah, but his ribs and legs hurt. He knew he would suffer if he climbed the Cairn Trail and made his way to the cabin.

Why was he so determined to make it home? At first he had realized the danger Simalucroix and the other dragons were in if they came from the caverns and were discovered by humankind. But now he knew, deep inside, that Simalucroix was not going to listen.

The dream told Juniper why. He thought about the great female wandering in confusion toward light and the world she had once known. Dragons were creatures of earth and air, not darkness. They had disciplined themselves to darkness to save their species, but inside, where they did not look, ancestral dreams nagged them to feel wind beneath their wings, light in their eyes.

They were no longer endangered. Juniper had seen hundreds, if not a thousand or more, at the conclave. Instincts were driving them to the surface as creatures of light. If Juniper's motivation was to keep dragons from humankind, he had failed. If he could not achieve that, why was he so determined to walk through pain so he could greet Simalucroix when dragons walked out of Four Windows Cave on Christmas night and claimed their right to live above ground again?

Juniper got up and went into the apartment's small kitchen where Father was brewing coffee. When Father saw Juniper he smiled and picked up a Teflon frying pan.

"Bacon, eggs, and toast?" he asked. "This isn't like the cave. Civilized home cooking."

Juniper smiled. "But in some ways not as good," he said. "I mean, the food is better, but it's not home."

Father's face grew serious.

"You're a young man," he said. "You have a future ahead of you. I don't know what that future will bring, but it's not going to be living in El Malpais with your crazy father and even crazier mother. We have to take steps to make sure whatever future you're going to live comes about."

Father peeled bacon out of its package and put it on the frying pan. Juniper sat on an aluminum chair with a plastic white back and watched his father, bemused.

"There's truth in El Malpais," he said at last. "Or maybe truths," he amended. "The kids at school are okay. They're wrapped in who they are and what they want to do and have no idea what seeing Sheena by moonlight standing on a Douglas fir's black branches while wind sighs, whistling through caves and collapses, is like. Those sights and sounds mean more than store-bought bacon and eggs.

"They let me know that other intelligences than mine exist, that their intelligence is as valuable as mine. I don't want a future launched from civilization, but one launched from wilderness where living is hard and wind haunts your spirit beneath a waning moon."

Father looked at him, away from the frying bacon. He had grown somber at the mention of Sheena.

"People are important," he said quietly.

"I know," Juniper answered. "You are important. Lily is important. Sheena is important. Sam is important. People at school are important. But there's more to the universe than people. It's when the *more* touches us that we find our potential."

Father took bacon out of the pan and put it on a small blue saucer. He cracked four eggs and scrambled them. "How did you ever get so deep?" he asked, lifting a forkful of eggs to his mouth.

Juniper smiled. "Who's raised me all these years?" he asked.

"I don't understand why you're homesick," Father said. "When you were young you couldn't understand why you and I had to live in wilderness when that made you different from everybody else. You wanted to live in a nice house and drive around in a nice car."

Lily knocked at the door. "Come in!" Father shouted before Juniper could move. Lily opened the door, and she and Sammy came into the apartment.

"Breakfast?" Father asked before Juniper could say anything.

"No thanks," Sammy said. "Grandmother fed us blue corn mush at the Hogan."

Lily sat across from Juniper. "Finish eating," she said, looking at Father. Juniper felt as if her smile banished every hurt in his body.

"Hmmph!" Sammy said. "Two fifteen year olds and you'd think they were twenty-two and married already. You won't find me settling down that fast."

"Juniper and Lily have found something special," Father said gently. "It shouldn't happen so young, and it might not last, but it might keep on until they're older than Grandmother is and their days have passed in knowing rich as sunshine." He smiled. "I'm hoping for that," he said.

"Have you heard any more about the Lowders?" Lily asked. She sounded nervous. "I'm afraid of them and what they might do."

"They're not going to come to town," Sammy said. "Too many cops around. They're outlaws. Outlaws keep themselves where they won't be seen. At least until they're ready to rob a bank."

"They might go into El Malpais," Father said. "No police are there, and they might be looking to spread their wings. I don't think so, but when we go home we're going to be careful."

"When are we going home?" Juniper asked, looking first at Lily, then at Father. Father looked back at him. "How do you feel?" he asked.

Juniper looked at Lily. "I want to go home today," he said.

Lily smiled. "I'm going with you," she said. "I'm sure we can be proper according to Grandmother's rules, and I can stay all night." She paused. "Sammy, Grandmother, and Grandfather can come to the Cairn Trail tomorrow. I'll go to the parking lot and bring them to the house."

"Sam's coming Christmas day," Sammy said. "He called last night and said to let Juniper and Lily know. Lily was out with Grandmother collecting greens for the Christmas feast. He said to tell you he had to get out of himself and start living life."

Lily, Sammy, and Juniper looked at Father. The mention of Sam and his determination to come to the cave on Christmas made Juniper even stronger in his determination to go home.

Father seemed hesitant. "Today?" he asked. "Christmas Eve?"

"Please Father," Juniper pleaded. "I'll be able to walk the trail."

"Your presents are at home," Father said slowly. "I've got presents for Lily and Sam too, but I don't know… You were hurt pretty bad, son. You're trying to hide it, but you aren't healed. Not close."

Juniper turned to Sammy. "Will you take us, Sammy?" he asked.

Sammy threw his hands up and sat back in his chair.

"Whoa," he said. "This isn't my deal. This is between you, your Dad, and Lily… And Grandmother," he added. "She seems to be on your side. I don't understand what's going on, but she believes there are dragons and that all of us, including Sam and his family, need to be in El Malpais when they come out of the underground and greet humans again."

Juniper looked quickly at Father.

"I know the Navajo believe in spirits," Father said slowly. "But dragons? When dragons aren't part of Navajo stories? Grandmother's told me what she thinks, but I hardly believe she believes what she believes. Dragons in the twenty-first century?"

Sammy smiled. "Grandmother is a powerful woman with powerful understanding," he said. "I never argue with her. Lily and Grandfather do, but not me."

"I'm nervous about the Lowders too," Father said. "Even as kids those two were wild. They'll be okay if they don't get meth, but what if they do?" He paused, shaking his head. "Dragons aren't going to cure meth," he continued. "Nothing cures meth."

"Are you going to let us go, Father?" Lily asked.

Father blinked to hear Lily address him as Father, as if she had become his child as much as Juniper was.

"On Christmas Eve I fix a special meal for Sheena," Father said sadly. "After Juniper goes to bed I take it to her and leave it on the treehouse's porch and wait until she finds it to make sure no animals come along. I never talk to her. I tried early on, but never in recent years. I'm always worried about what she's getting to eat and how she's getting along. I can't imagine not being there with a meal. I've been trying to imagine that, but I can't."

"We can go?" Juniper asked, hope and nervousness intermingled in his voice.

"We can go," Father said quietly. "If Sammy will drive us. If you get too tired, son," he said, looking at Juniper, "I'm going to carry you."

Lily smiled and reached across the table to Juniper. Juniper high-fived her and whooped.

"We're going home!" he said. "Home! Christmas Eve at home! With Lily," he added, smiling. "Lily and Father."

"And Sheena," Lily added. "No boyfriend of mine is forgetting his mother."

Juniper sobered. "And my mother," he said. He wondered why he no longer shivered every time he thought about her. "I can't go to her, but this year I'm going to help fix the meal Father takes to her."

Father looked into Juniper's eyes.

"She loves you, Juniper," he said. "She showed you when she came to the stairs that night and talked to you. I've given up hope she'll return to the way she was, but that doesn't make our responsibility to her any less."

He got up from the table and started gathering dirty dishes. "We'll pack," he said. "Then, if Sammy will take us, we'll go."

Sammy laughed. "If little sister says I'm taking you, I'm taking you," he said. "I learned a long time ago her tongue's sharper than she is."

Lily yelped, turned toward Sammy, and hit him on the shoulder.

"Let's go home and get some overnight stuff," she said as he flinched and hollered dramatically when her fist brushed him. "We'll be back," she told Juniper. "We'll spend Christmas Eve and Christmas together."

Chapter XXIII

Carson looked at Bill sitting on a cedar stump and shook his head.

"I feel like shit," he said.

Bill nodded. "We need meth," he said. "Hell, the trees look washed out and half dead even though my mind tells me they're like they've always been."

"Dad's watching us like we're criminals," Carson complained. "Either he or Mom's got eyes on us every time we move."

"We are criminals," Bill grinned. "We beat Juniper half to death, smacked Sam up, and scared the shit out of Lily Smallhand. We're big, bad boys, just like we've always been."

Carson grinned back. "Yeah," he said. "God I felt good that day, like I was floating in paradise and lording it over everything."

"Don't feel like paradise today," Bill said. "Feel more like Juniper did when we kicked in his ribs." He got up from the stump and jammed his hands into his jean's pockets. "We got to score drugs," he said, restlessness making him twitchy and out-of-sync.

"If we take off Dad'll bring us back," Carson said matter-of-factly.

"They're going to decorate the tree tonight," Bill sneered. "Jesus Christ and the season's joy." He laughed. "Maybe we ought to blow our brains out. That'd make this a Christmas to remember. Maybe better than jail anyway, and that's where we're heading. Dear Uncle Jasper, judge of the universe, making sure we could have one last Christmas at home before his best friend, Judge Lucius Luhan, sentences us to hell."

"Dad talked him into it," Carson said. "Uncle Jasper has no truck with criminals, and you can bet he sees us as criminals big time."

"I feel like shit," Bill said, repeating what Carson had said earlier.

Carson smiled. "What we ought to do," he said. "Is wait until tomorrow morning after we open presents. We can act all happy. Mom's going to fix Christmas dinner. Dad, sure as shit, is gonna help her, just like every year. They'll be happy everything's going well. We'll slip outside when they go into the kitchen, then find some real celebration."

"How we doing that?" Bill asked. "I hate to point out the obvious, but no way are we gonna get car keys. If we ask for them Dad's likely to lock us into our room. Mom doesn't have keys in her purse. I already looked. I think Dad's got both their keys in his pocket."

Carson smiled maliciously. "So we can't score meth," he said. "It's too far to town, but by now Juniper's home. He, Sam, and Lily will be waiting with baited breath for great and terrible dragons to surface tomorrow. The way I feel right now, beating the hell out of Juniper again might make a day half bearable… It might mean more jail time," he added. "But what the hell. We're going to jail anyway. Uncle Jasper's not gonna keep that from happening."

"We could get probation," Bill said, his voice doubtful.

"We damned near killed Juniper," Carson said. "They're gonna forget that?"

"It felt good, didn't it?" Bill asked. He paused. "Maybe we ought to use the plan Christmas morning, but get away. Fuck, I didn't enjoy myself in that jail cell at all."

"How do we do that?" Carson asked. "No car. No cash." He shrugged.

"We could hike to Ancient Way Café and knock it and the Inscription Rock place off. That'd give us cash. Then we could find Snuffy and score meth."

Carson shook his head. "You think they won't know what we're up to?" he asked. "Hell, we'd get to Ancient Way and walk right into the arms of cops."

"So we go ahead and kick the shit out of Juniper and Sam?" Bill asked. "Maybe we could get it on with Lily. Hell, I wouldn't mind that."

He rubbed his crotch and smiled maliciously.

"Better than feeling like shit until they take us to court," Carson said. "I'm tired of feeling like shit. Maybe we can get our jollies before the curtain comes down."

"You sure we won't get probation?" Bill asked, trying to keep his voice neutral.

He did not want to send Carson into a rage. He could feel how close Carson was to going nuts and slashing out at Bill, Dad, or Mom and the hell with consequences.

"You chicken?" Carson goaded. "Want an easy life with probation? Want to get off drugs and live the good citizen's life?"

"We might kill Juniper this time," Bill said. "He'll be hurting pretty bad."

Carson shrugged. "What the hell," he said, looking disdainfully at Bill.

He stalked toward the house, leaving Bill standing alone.

I feel like shit, Bill thought to himself. His mouth had a dry, sour taste that made him feel like puking. His head buzzed with a dullness that made him feel only half alive. He really, really needed a hit to lift his spirits.

He took three swift steps toward a grandfather pinyon behind the stump and slammed his fist into its bark. He cried out, but the pain made him feel alive for the first time since the first morning he and Carson had woke up in the jail cell.

The living room screen door slammed. He turned and saw his mother, looking worried, staring at him.

"Bill?" she asked, her voice concerned.

"I'm okay," he said, masking the pain in his hand.

He forced himself to smile and walked toward his mother. She did not take her eyes off him.

When Sheena woke it was late morning. She opened her eyes and looked around the treehouse. Snug corners and solid walls with windows looked outward over the Douglas fir's branches into the dark twisting of lava fields. The humming never seemed to end. It buzzed in her head as if bees were in her brain and dancing and singing a ceremonial. Sometimes she felt as if she could not stand the noise. At other times the sounds were beautiful and soothing, a master song bringing out her inside beauty.

She got out of bed, dressed in one of the long dresses she wore, and walked out on the treehouse deck. She felt like two people, one in touch with everyday life, who knew she was not really sane, and the other who felt she was flying over El Malpais' dark tangle of volcanic stone, a beautiful spirit who sometimes sailed with stars during nights when a full moon poured brilliant silver into the sky.

The sanity she felt was new. She could not remember experiencing it since the day her parents had died. She thought about Rory and her son and her confrontations with them: Juniper when he had been at the bottom of the collapse and Rory when he had found her on the collapse's stairs.

She was immensely sad that Juniper had grown into a young man without knowing the mother who had given him birth. She knew she had not been that mother for a long time. She had been the beautiful witch who swam among stars. She had listened to music of the spheres and laughed as she floated from Douglas fir to Douglas fir secure in her powerful magic.

She wondered that she had not killed her son and husband. The witch did not care. She was not aware her son and husband had any relationship with her. She only cared about beauty emanating from her powerful core.

She wondered when Rory and Juniper would return home. She visited the cave every day now, climbing down the collapse's stairs, walking into the small, warm structure, sometimes sleeping in Rory's bed.

Perhaps Rory had given up on her ever returning to sanity, but the thought did not seem right. Rory was steady in his commitments and would not shirk from what he believed was important. He and Juniper would be back. The question was, what would she do when they came back?

She climbed down the treehouse stairs and walked the trail that led past the pinyon on the rise. Snow had drifted into nooks and crannies of volcanic stone. Whiteness contrasted sharply with the rocks' shiny blackness. As she walked the deep earth humming started again.

Topping the collapse she stopped and thought about what she wanted to do. She could not remember when she had felt so stable and sane. She remembered the night in the hospital when she had decided to stop taking pills that made her feel dull and bloated and run to El Malpais next to where she had been raised as a child. She had lost her grip on sanity in the hospital. She had pretended to swallow pills the nurse had given her, but threw them away after the nurse had left.

She shook the memory out of her head and climbed down the stairs. She opened the door and went inside the cave. Like she had every time she had come to the cabin, she went and looked at Juniper's room and at Rory's carvings. Then she looked at Rory's room and bed and wondered why he was still missing. Then she looked into the cupboards, found dried elk jerky and chewed thoughtfully as she wondered what was happening to her.

Why did she seem saner now than at any time she could remember since walking up Chain of Craters Road and making a pine branch bed to start her new life in wilderness? How could she have failed to remember her husband and son even when lost in the flying dream? In the cabin where they lived in order to help her survive in madness, she could feel their goodness.

The humming in her head went on and on. Was that what was bringing her to sanity? The humming had to be a sign of insanity.

Normal people did not hear humming rising from volcanic rocks into their bones.

She sat in one of the old kitchen chairs beside the roughly made table and closed her eyes, trying to understand who she was. She had not wanted to see Rory for years. She had not wanted to see Juniper for years, but now she wanted to see them both and hug them and make them remember she was a wife and mother before she became the El Malpais' witch.

She wondered how they would react when they found out she sometimes escaped her powerful dreaming. Did both of them still love her? Rory most certainly did. What other reason would he have for living in a boxed-in cave? Juniper knew she was his mother. He had called her mother when she had stood at the top of the stairs, but what did he feel about a mother who had never been a mother to him?

She put her head down on the table. Tears streamed down her face. What had possessed her to leave her wonderful life behind for a cold, hard life in wilderness? How could she have left her baby and husband and forced them to follow her into a place only fit for someone not in their right mind?

Sobs wracked her chest and body. She could not stop crying.

Chapter XXIV

Grandfather was in a towering rage. Lily and Sammy heard him before they could see him as they walked up the canyon toward the Hogan.

"I'm gonna smash your face, old woman!" he screamed. "I'm tired of you and those kids! What are they doing with us when we're too old to take care of them? That worthless son of ours shouldn't have got in that car wreck and died! I'm gonna tear up the whole damned world and shove it down your throat!"

The minute Sammy heard Grandfather's voice he ran ahead of Lily. Lily ran after him, but he had a head start and was fast. By the time Lily got to the small hill in front of the Hogan, Sammy was less than a hundred feet from Grandfather, running like a hurtling cannon ball. Grandfather heard his grandson behind him and turned. He almost fell, so drunk he could hardly stand. Sammy stood in front of the old man with the long gray hair, face flushed. He was so angry he could hardly control himself.

"You leave Grandmother alone, old man," he said, his voice filled with menace. "I told you last time you beat up Lily that if you touched Grandmother or Lily again, I'd beat you to an inch of your life."

Grandfather leaned toward Sammy as if he was trying to see him.

"You call me Grandfather, boy, and show respect," he said. "I'm an elder with lots of cultural knowledge. You respect that. That's our people's ways."

Lily hurried over the rise and stopped. Sammy was tense, waiting to see what his grandfather was going to do.

"Our culture doesn't teach you to be a woman beater," he said. "When you're sober you deserve to be called Grandfather. When you're drunk you deserve to be called old man."

Grandmother had come out of the Hogan's door. She looked okay to Lily. Grandfather had not got to her with his fists yet.

"Go to hell," Grandfather told Sammy.

"Grandmother's coming with us," Lily said, forcing herself to sound brave.

Grandfather looked at his granddaughter with bloodshot eyes. He had been drinking all night and slept in his clothes. He was frowning so hard his lower face looked twisted.

"I ought to beat you too, little brat," he said. "You've had a tongue ever since your Dad and Mom died, and you came to live with us, ruining our lives."

Sammy balled his fists.

"You ready to get it on, old man?" he asked. "Or you going to get out of here?"

"I could of beat you when I was younger," the old man complained.

"You're an old fool of a man," Grandmother said. "Who can't hold his liquor."

Grandfather shook his head.

"Fuck you," he snarled. "Fuck all of you."

"Watch your language," Grandmother demanded. "You were raised better. If your mother was here and heard that language she'd take a broom after you."

The old man looked puzzled. "Mother? My mother?" he asked.

"You'd better leave until you sober up," Sammy said. "We're going to Juniper's and his father's place in El Malpais. If you're sober you can have Christmas dinner with us."

"El Malpais?" Grandfather asked. He did not seem to understand what was being said to him. "Juniper's place?"

"I'm not sure I want to see you there, old man," Grandmother said, walking up to stand beside Sammy and Lily. "You can be good, and you can be bad. I'm tired of your bad."

Grandfather looked at Grandmother.

"I ought to beat you, old woman," he snarled.

"You lay a hand on her, you're gonna be one sorry old man," Sammy said.

"I'm helping Sammy," Lily said, her voice fierce. "You're going to have to take on two of us. Neither Grandmother or I are going to take another beating from you. Not ever."

"Juniper and his father live in a collapse in lava cave country," Grandmother said. "You used to hunt there when you were young."

Grandfather looked at Lily, rheumy eyes unwavering. He looked as if he was about to say something, but shook his head.

"Hell with it," he mumbled. "Hell with it."

He walked around Lily, Sammy, and Grandmother and started off toward the road mumbling. Lily, Sammy, and Grandmother watched him top the hill.

"I wish whiskey hadn't gotten ahold of him," Grandmother said at last. "When he courted me he didn't touch the stuff. He was a handsome man, but then..." her voice trailed off.

Lily took Grandmother's arm and steered her toward the Hogan.

"You're coming with me to Juniper's tonight," she said. "I don't think Grandfather will come back, but you can't tell. We're not running the risk, especially while Sammy drives me. I'm not going to see you with another black eye."

"Dragons," Grandmother said. "You're going to see the dragons."

"Those aren't real," Sammy said, ducking his head as he went inside the Hogan. "I don't know a single story our people tell about dragons."

Inside the neat, rounded earthen walls, Grandmother shook her head.

"No," she said. "I don't know any stories either, but old Donald Sharp has an unbelievable Zuni stone carving. It's old too, not done by the younger carvers. The dragon has turquoise eyes and is hunching out of green stone. It's one of the most beautiful carvings I've ever seen. He showed it to me at Smith's Grocery. He said he was going to give it to Juniper for a present. Rory's been talking to him."

"Am I going to see them?" Sammy asked, his voice lighthearted and teasing.

"You're having Christmas dinner with us," Lily answered.

Sammy smiled and touched Lily's raven black hair.

"I'll be at Juniper's Christmas day," he said. "I'll bring Grandfather, and I'll make sure he's as sober as a judge in a Baptist Church."

"Grandfather ought to be sober all the time," Lily said. "I don't understand why he needs whiskey so bad. It turns him into a monster."

"He's always been big on disappointments," Grandmother answered. "When we were first married he thought he was going to be somebody big. He worked hard to make his dreams come true, but they never happened the way he wanted. Racism held him back; he couldn't win elections he tried for Council, so he found whiskey and the glory of forgetting. He's okay, but then starts brooding. Whiskey calls, and he can't resist the call."

Sammy stuffed presents Lily and Grandmother had made for Juniper and their family inside his green army duffel bag as Grandmother handed Lily her backpack.

"I love the old man," he said. "But I won't see him hurt either one of you. I didn't go to Afghanistan to fight Taliban to come back home and accept violence from my grandfather."

By the time the three of them got back to Rory and Juniper's apartment, noon had passed, and the sun had dispelled the morning's chill. Father had fixed sandwiches and hot tea for lunch. They ate before loading into Sammy's old Buick and heading toward Chain of Craters Road.

They had turned off County Road 42 when they heard the high trumpeting. Sammy, driving, looked back at Father.

"An elk?" he asked. "We can hear it with the windows rolled up?"

He reached toward the automatic window button. The elk trumpeted again, louder this time. The car turned around a crook in the road beside the black lava wall.

Lily and Juniper were both leaning against the front seat.

"The bull elk!" Lily exclaimed.

The massive animal, branches of horns shining in afternoon light, was standing where Lily and Juniper had last seen it.

Grandmother looked sober in the back seat beside Lily.

"The first sign," she said, as if she had expected to see and hear the bull elk.

Sammy stopped the Buick and leaned out the window. Father got out of the passenger's side door and put his hand on the car's roof.

"What a beautiful bull," he said. "Look at that rack!"

The bull trumpeted again, craning its neck toward the afternoon sun. Juniper felt chills running up and down his spine. After trumpeting the bull turned and disappeared. Juniper scanned the wall, looking for Sheena, but the wall's rim was empty except for brush and trees.

After the bull was gone Father got back in the car. Juniper kept listening for Simalucroix's voice, but heard nothing. After Sammy had parked, they unloaded backpacks and Sammy's duffel bag. Then Father led to the Cairn Trail toward home. As he came out of the parking lot's trees, he stopped and stared at the sky. Grandmother, Lily, Juniper, and Sammy hurried to catch up with him. Above their heads the white eagle circled lazily above lava fields.

"The second sign," Grandmother said softly. Father turned and looked at the older woman, a question in his eyes. "Lily's and Juniper's signs," Grandmother explained. "If we see them all, tomorrow will be more significant than any of us imagine."

"Lily saw a white snake in the eagle's talons," Juniper said. "The eagle doesn't have a white snake."

"Over there," Lily said. "On that rock."

She was pointing toward a swelling of black lava off the trail. A huge white bull snake, though it was winter, and it should have been hibernating, was coiled, soaking up afternoon sun. It looked asleep.

"The third sign," Grandmother said. "Now Sheena."

They stared at the snake, but when it did not move, went up the trail.

Juniper was sore and aching by the time they reached the collapse. He was not sure he could climb down the stairs. Father looked at him, concerned, and touched his shoulder.

"You going to make it, Juniper?" he asked.

Sammy smiled. "He'll make it," he said. "He can lean on me."

"You're not like you were the first time you dropped Lily off," Juniper said as Sammy took his arm and led him to the stairs. "You didn't seem to like me then."

Sammy laughed. "I didn't know you then," he said. "As strong and willful as Lily is, I wanted you to know you'd better be careful and treat my sister right."

Juniper put his right foot on the first stair. The others let him and Sammy go in front even though Juniper was moving ridiculously slowly. As he moved down the stairs both legs throbbed. He leaned on Sammy, wondering at how he had always run so easily up and down the stairs.

At the bottom he turned and looked at the others. Lily was first, followed by Grandmother. Sammy stood by him while he leaned against a boulder. After Lily was standing beside him, he took a deep breath and walked toward the house.

He paused at the cabin's door, but opened it. He gasped at seeing Sheena. Sheena looked like a deer paralyzed by headlights at night. She looked at him, then at Sammy standing over his shoulder, and then at Lily behind Sammy. She looked like she had been crying.

"Who are you people?" she asked, her voice panicked. "Where's Rory? Juniper?" she asked.

Juniper felt paralyzed. "Mother?" he asked. "Here?"

Sheena ventilated, her breathing increasingly uncontrolled.

"I can't stay," she said.

Father moved to stand beside Juniper as Sammy, Lily, and Grandmother quietly moved away from the door.

"Sheena?" he asked. "You're here again?" He paused, confused. "I…I'm overjoyed to see you," he said.

The minute Father stood beside Juniper Sheena got up from the chair. She looked from one to the other of them, and squeaked, so unlike the presence that had frightened Juniper into the blowhole she seemed unreal, "I love you. Both of you."

Then she was running between Juniper and Father. Father barely stepped aside as Sheena brushed her shoulder against Juniper. They watched as she climbed over boulders, disdaining the path, quickly reaching the collapse's rim and disappearing into the afternoon.

No one spoke. Grandmother, wonderment in her voice, said, "the fourth sign." Her voice sounded satisfied, filled with quiet excitement.

"I've never seen a white eagle before," Sammy said quietly, thinking about Grandmother's litany. "Or a white snake."

"The dragons are getting ready to come to the surface," Lily said. "Like Simalucroix told Juniper. When they come, the world will change."

Father was looking from one of them to the next, his forehead wrinkled.

"What's happening?" he asked Juniper. "What's that humming I hear?"

Juniper, startled, looked from Father into the cabin. The conclave's humming was making the cabin alive. He held his breath and closed his eyes.

"Simalucroix?" he asked in his head. "Simalucroix?"

The great dragon did not answer.

"What's happening to Sheena?" Father asked. "Is she getting better or worse? After years of avoiding us she's come to the house twice now."

Grandmother came into the house and sat in the chair where Sheena had been.

"I'm getting too old for miracles," she said quietly. "But good magic is afoot, and we have to be open to it."

"Magic?" Father asked. "Navajo magic?"

Grandmother shook her head.

"No," she said. She paused for a long time. "Maybe Mother Earth magic. That's really the only kind of magic there's ever been." She turned to Sammy. "Tomorrow before lunch. You and your grandfather," she ordered. "He has to be sober."

Juniper and Lily moved into the cabin and put their backpacks on the floor.

"We'll be here," Sammy promised.

Juniper felt the humming, the dragon song filling him with power he had never imagined having. It eased the pain in his chest and legs. He sat down with Lily standing beside him.

"Simalucroix shouldn't come out," he said. "It's not safe. There's too much going wrong: Sam, Lily's grandfather, the Lowders…"

Grandmother looked at him with kind eyes. "When spirits give us signs," she said. "We aren't in control. We flow where they want us and try to be the best humans we can be."

Sammy brought the duffel bag and Grandmother's backpack into the room, dropped them and turned to leave.

"There's sleeping bags," he said as he left. "The floor will be hard, but the bags will be warm."

He was out the door, walking down the path before anyone said anything. Father had still not moved from the open doorway.

"What's happening?" he asked again.

Grandmother smiled. "I've already told you, Rory," she said. "A miracle is happening. You need to be open to the impossible."

Chapter XXV

The appearance of five people at Rory and Juniper's cabin startled Sheena. She had heard them coming down the stairs, and her heart had started beating rapidly, but she had not realized anyone other than Rory and Juniper were coming.

She had been sitting by the door, wondering what to do, when she realized five people were walking to the cabin. Then she was staring into Juniper's startled face. She ran before she even knew she was running, climbing the collapse's boulders.

"Sheena!" Rory called out, but she did not acknowledge him or stop.

Above the collapse the humming started in her head again. The further from the cabin she got the louder the humming became. She tried to imagine she was a golden eagle flying over lava fields, but she could not lose herself, though she badly wanted to, in the dream that had helped her survive.

She headed toward her favorite Douglas fir, a tree whose branches spread so massively over lava fields it dominated the landscape. When she got to the tree the humming was so loud it drove her to distraction. She dropped to her knees on the sharp aa lava and put her hands over her ears.

What was happening to her? What was happening to her?

She wailed, her voice echoing over lava fields, grief for herself, her dead father and mother, her early life, her dead girl child, her abandonment of husband and son, her loss of a life she had loved vibrating, weaving into humming that had grown to such a pitch it seemed to be reorganizing and changing the structure of her mind and being.

Images of her father in a drunken rage, smashing furniture in their small house when she had been five years old—

of her mother screaming at her as she cowered in a closet, hiding from violence and drunken words cutting away at childhood, leaving it in tatters of whimpering, uncertainty, and avoidance—

of fear, anger, and hatred sweeping over her again and again when she had become a teenager and emotions ruled who she was—

of her partying with idiot boys who kept shoving alcohol and LSD and groping at her when all she wanted was to flee into darkness that would go on forever—

of the pain she had felt in her extended belly when she went into too early labor.

Her wailing ululated across sun-struck lava fields.

What am I living for? she asked herself. I'm a mad woman with no link to reality and those who love me. The words in her head were so powerful they stopped the wailing. She sobbed, gulping for air as sobs wracked her body.

Rory stood paralyzed as Sheena bolted from the cabin. He had been talking to Grandmother about Juniper's impossible visions when he saw his beautiful wife running as if pursued by the demon Grendel[3]. As she reached the collapse's rim he shouted, half screaming in his need to get her attention, to tell her that everything was all right, that she could join them for Christmas, that they could live as a family again, but she disappeared over the rim. He felt as if Juniper, Lily, Grandmother, and Sammy no longer existed. He felt alone, caught in emotions that had frozen time and flung him into a universe where breathing from moment to moment was bizarre.

"Father?" Juniper asked.

Rory looked at his son still weak from the beatings he'd taken. Rory looked away, shrugged out of his backpack, and took off after Sheena. He topped the stairs and looked wildly around, trying

---

[3]A reference to the monster in the ancient English epic poem, *Boewulf*.

to catch some glimpse of her as she ran across the lava fields. He ran toward the Douglas fir where he had most often seen her.

Sheena's voice wailed across the landscape, entering Rory with physical force. He did not break stride, but felt the panic he'd felt when Donald Sharp had found him to tell him Juniper had been beaten up bad and was in Grants Hospital, a place Rory had hoped he would never see again.

His life had been other-worldly since Sheena had fled her Grants hospital room, but now the other-worldliness had, in a single moment, become even stranger. A vaguely familiar humming started keeping time with his feet as he leaped and shuffled across the uneven, dangerous lava.

He had just topped the small rise above the Douglas fir's trunk when Sheena started sobbing. She was kneeling on sharp lava. Her body heaved as she gasped for breath. Rory stopped. What should he do? If he approached she might flee and disappear for days. He'd had that experience often enough, but he could not stand seeing the pain wracking her body. He stood paralyzed, fears and doubts about himself mixing into his panic. He took a deep breath and forced himself out of his thoughts.

"Sheena?" he asked without moving. "Sheena?"

Sheena did not respond. The uncontrollable sobbing continued, but she looked up at him, her face a mask of suffering. She did not look at all like the beautiful, unearthly woman standing in Douglas fir branches beneath a full moon. Her sobs subsided.

Then, as suddenly as she had bolted from the cabin, she got to her feet. She looked at the Douglas fir's trunk, then toward the treehouse. Unbelievably, she looked back at Rory. She opened her arms, embracing empty air, and stumbled toward him, eyes streaming tears.

"Rory," she said, her voice so soft he could hardly hear it.

He had not heard her say his name for fourteen years. He held his breath, but kept his eyes open even though he had an almost uncontrollable impulse to close them. Sheena came up the small rise, put her arms around him, and held him so fiercely it seemed as if she intended to hold him forever.

My God, he told himself. My God.

He felt relieved, elated, as if his world had suddenly turned a corner, and life was the way it should be, not the way it had been for so long. He let his arms clasp his wife to him. She stopped sobbing.

"Rory," she said again. "Rory."

Let this be the end of her illness, he thought. Let this be the end.

She tensed, becoming as stiff as a board in his arms. Oh no, he thought to himself, feeling her going away. She looked into his eyes, frightened, and stepped out of his embrace.

"Sheena?" he whispered, trying to hold on to her.

She shook her head, turned without saying a word, and ran toward the treehouse the way she had run from him dozens of times before, long, uncut hair flaring out behind her.

He took a step toward where she was running, but stopped. What should he do? he asked himself. Sheena seemed to be coming back into herself, finding what had been lost. Should he run after her and try to bring her home with him? Or was it better to be patient and wait? He took another step, but stopped. He stood paralyzed beside the great tree. Old sadness and fierce regret made him feel insignificant and weak.

Sheena could not believe she was holding Rory in her arms. Where had he come from? How had she found him? She felt as if she had not seen him for years, but also felt as if they had never been apart. What was she doing in the middle of El Malpais? Why was Rory there? Where was Juniper?

As she had walked toward Rory the humming in her head lessened. She hugged her husband as hard as she could. She relaxed into his embrace and felt as if she was waking from a nightmare that was finally ending.

But then she tensed. What was happening to her? Where were the moon and stars? Why was she not sailing through the sky? A jumble of thoughts and emotions made her want to flee, to get away from demons gnawing her bowels and intestines.

She stepped back from Rory and looked into his eyes. He was filled with hope, but frightened. She heard him whisper her name, but took a step backward. What was she doing next to Rory? Where was she? She had to run, to find a place where she could be herself.

The strange humming started again. It had disappeared while she had held Rory. But who was Rory? She felt confused, unsettled, afraid.

She moved as if she was wind and could fly without thinking about who she was. She ran toward the house that sailed through stars, toward songs and dances that let her live in a universe without meaning or time.

After Sheena disappeared Rory shook himself out of paralysis. He thought about Juniper's face as he had shrugged off his pack and ran toward the stairs. Juniper was still too hurt to even be in El Malpais. His son's face had been confused and frightened.

Rory tried to listen to the wilderness, to see if Sheena had gone back to the treehouse. A strange, deep voice spoke inside his head.

"Don't go after her," it said. "Wait. Miracles happen at Christmas."

The voice had to be his voice. It felt strange, alien. He forced it out of consciousness, hoping he was still sane and not slipping into Sheena's dream world life.

Juniper would be at home with Lily, Grandmother, and Sammy, wondering what was happening with his father and mother. He was still struggling with the idea that Sheena was his mother. Rory thought about the first Christmas with Juniper in El Malpais. He had thrown the cabin together after making Sheena's treehouse. Sheena had surprised him by finding the treehouse after he was finished and moving in without strategizing on his part. He had started the effort to keep his wife fed and safe, exhausting spirit, body, and mind.

Pam and John at Inscription Rock Trading and Coffee Company had helped out by taking care of Juniper while he built the treehouse and cabin. Neither he nor Juniper were ready for the years they would live in wilderness. At that point Juniper was just over one year old and endlessly busy. Rory could hardly keep up with his young son and still hunt and do the chores necessary to make it through winter until spring.

One of his biggest worries had been to figure out what to get Juniper for Christmas. He'd still had his old Ford pickup with its rusted-out sides, but he'd pretty much exhausted cash realized from selling craft furniture and needed what little they had left for supplies. The thought of not having a Christmas present, even though Juniper had no way of knowing when Christmas was, had made his gut ache.

Then he'd decided he'd make his son a carved wooden train. He'd worked on the train at night for weeks using kerosene lamp light. On the night of Christmas Eve, he'd finished and went out into the cold and snow and cut down a Christmas tree in the dark. The next morning Juniper had squealed with delight at tree, train, and colored candle light. Inside Juniper's delight Rory had found the ability to walk the path he'd fashioned for his son.

He could not make the world the way he wanted it to be. He could not conjure the past and turn it into the future, but he could make a life for Juniper and himself in the collapse and help Sheena survive her mental illness. He did not fool himself into thinking the path he'd set on was going to be easy, but he'd found his ability to survive inside Juniper's joy.

As he mused about that first El Malpais Christmas, he thought: Miracles have happened at Christmas. He started walking back to where Juniper and the others would be waiting.

Maybe Sheena would come back to him, he thought. Maybe a miracle, even after all these years, is possible. He could not help wondering if his wife was okay. She had survived for years without being aware of who she was, but she was changing.

Would the magic that had kept her alive keep working?

Chapter XXVI

In the caverns tensions were rising. Ssissensin's threat to block the newly winged dragons' passage to the surface burned through dragon talk like an out-of-control underground coal fire. The news stopped the conclave's gathering. No more dragons felt the pain and exhilaration of gaining wings. As soon as he heard of the elders' determination, Simalucroix left the great cavern. He stalked caverns and lava tubes like a dragon of ancient times, sparks puffing from great nostrils, his countenance dark with snarling storms.

The grandmothers and grandfathers still remembered stories of a time when dragons battled in skies above mountains. The stories had seemed unreal to generations of dragons. In the birthing caverns only the youngest out-of-the-egg dragons acted ferocious and tumbled and spitted in mock battle. Dragons had grown increasingly social through the generations, living carefully in the caverns' confinement and husbanding resources.

Until now the fears of Grilgax's generation--grim stories of how dragon after dragon had died from the cunning of puny humans; the description of blood running in rivulets on cave floors, or the sound of a grandmother dragon burning inside from metal sword blades and spear points thrust into flesh—had kept them beneath the earth, whitening tough hides as they adjusted to living without sunlight, moonlight, or starlight.

Their minds had changed too. Once ferociously proud and independent, gathering in conclaves only to settle issues that led to dragon wars, their ability to communicate from mind to mind had strengthened, forcing them to learn how to be private and individual. They had learned how to shield thoughts so that all dragonkind would not be aware of personal emotions or thoughts.

They worked together incessantly, finding food, encouraging the growth of fish in pools carved out from the river, making sure bats, rodents, underground lizards, edible lichen, and insects thrived and were not over-harvested, extending caverns by digging new caves, taking care of dragons just out-of-the-egg, teaching youngsters to avoid caverns that wound upward to the earth's surface, ensuring spelunkers exploring El Malpais' caves and caverns that stretched for hundreds of miles never saw a dragon or found clues about dragonkind's existence, and telling ancient stories to teach how to live in the present.

For generations no leader had been remotely like Simalucroix, willing to risk what Grilgax and his generation had gained by confronting the reality that human beings had spread like cancer over the earth's surface. The humans had grown increasingly sophisticated in their strange, communal intelligence, developing machines that could even take them through outer-space to walk on the silver moon's surface—machines imbued with an intelligence neither human nor dragon.

When young Simalucroix had been compliant, listening to old stories, he had reacted cautiously to social events with wisdom far beyond his years. He had explored caverns like all young dragons, always searching for a new cave, a new shape, or a new sound. But he had never gone beyond limits set by elders and had been assiduous, not bold, when humans descended with headlights, flashlights, ropes, and other gear into the caverns. He had worked harder than any other youngster to ensure no sound or sight would reveal the secret dragonkind had kept for so long.

But now? The most cautious of dragons, the one whom elders had, in their conclave held in a cavern where lava singed the brutal cold of deepest air and lapped orange and bubbling against black stone hardened into a shore dancing with twisted shapes, selected him as the dragon leader, was changing.

No one so young had been selected as leader since Grilgax. His selection had echoed through the caverns. Younger dragons had been excited. Older dragons had greeted his selection cautiously, hoping it was not a harbinger of change since no one could see how change could improve their existence in a universe where dragons did not belong.

As Simalucroix stormed through caverns, looking for Ssissensin and the elders supporting her so that they could talk face to face where he could see their reactions to his presence, dragons vacated where he would be before he could get to where they were. His thoughts and emotions were so turbulent they were painful to feel. He moved from one place to another, looking, listening intensely for a clue to where Ssissensin and those supporting her were hiding.

Ssissensin, Syllabrie, and the elders had no trouble avoiding him. As dragons quietly moved away from him, the elders shielded thoughts, sticking to the deeper caverns where fewer dragons lived, waiting for the confrontation they were determined to make inevitable.

Simalucroix frightened even Ssissensin. She had been with the conclave when Simalucroix had been selected. She had felt the strange coming together of minds that happened when a decision had been reached.

She had not thought Simalucroix would be selected. She had believed Creleigh would be chosen. He was the largest and most powerful male and would have been appropriate, but after the death of Sprangshorn, who had lived as long as any dragon had since the time of Thundrun and the mate of Grilgax, Smilgamashe, few had wanted to settle on the obvious choice. The conclave had wanted to feel that difference was still possible among dragons.

Inside the conclave minds had met, melded, separated, grew apart, and met again. Sometimes Ssissensin had felt so alone with her thoughts she could not sense the great bodies around her. Then the moment of coming together, when suddenly mind locked to mind, and the dragons had started humming, singing a song as old as dragonkind.

When the humming had started they all knew. Simalucroix, a young dragon Ssissensin did not know, was their leader. The conclave had chosen.

At first Simalucroix had acted even more cautiously than his reputation had suggested he would, consulting elders whenever disputes or decisions came before him. He seemed even more conservative than Thundrun, but his conservatism had passed, and he started consulting younger, as well as older, dragons. Since the generation after the founding generation, dragons had modified the caverns in small ways, making their dark universe more livable. The dragon population had grown steadily, ending Grilgax's great fear that dragonkind would become extinct.

The population had grown so much that during the last two generations, fearing ecological disaster beneath the earth, dragons had been forced to limit their population, keening with terrible grief when precious eggs were destroyed. Everyone understood such measures were necessary, but even that understanding was terrible to hold inside, and emotional storms swept back and forth through the caverns. Many regretted, with terrible ferocity, Grilgax's ancient decision while still holding fiercely to the idea that dragons had to stay hidden.

It was under this burden that Simalucroix embraced changes often considered, but always rejected, as too risky. Younger dragons, in small lava tubes scores of miles from the great cavern, began expanding the labyrinth's size. They used tools and claws to build new living spaces shored up with stone mined from other caverns and hidden behind false walls that protected against a spelunker's accidental discovery. He had started the process of expanding the dragons' universe.

Then he had allowed the largest change of all when Juniper had found them in the great cavern. The youngster had scrambled down the lava tube from the surface so fast dragons in the cavern had little time to hide.

Simalucroix had been in the cavern at that moment. If there had been an elder present, Ssessensin believed Simalucroix might have acted differently and preserved their ancient secret, but the young dragons, perceiving the young human too late, had frozen as Simalucroix searched for dreaded human eyes.

When he had found them he had not acted with ferocity and ended the danger, but had reached out to the young boy, drawing the young man's eyes to where dragons were strung along dark river banks, two hearts thundering beneath breast bones. He had spoken mind to mind to the human Juniper and led him to a small lava tube that led to the surface.

When the young human had decided to come back to the caverns, fear making him as spooky as a cottontail rabbit, Simalucroix had called a conclave. Not a conclave like those called when a leader died and a new one had to be found, but one unlike any other in the underground dragons' history.

The elders had come, but had hung back in lava tubes leading into the cavern, curious, frightened, wondering what insanity possessed the leader they had chosen. Later they had argued fiercely with Simalucroix, trying to convince him his path was wrong and could lead to extinction. But all Simalucroix would say was that "the time for change and courage has come."

In front of the human, the conclave had entered into power, and for the first time since Smilgamashé's death after dragging herself away from the surface, a dragon had wings. Eyes whirled with the ancient spirit of dragons, mesmerizing the boy and gathered dragons. The song of flying had begun, echoing, rising into volcanic stone and vibrating through stone and roots of trees to the surface where it sang into sunshine and moonlight and made dragons long to be on the earth's surface once more.

Fear had gripped the elders with a terrible anguish. Two, then three, five, then nine young dragons endured the angry pain of separating wings from hides, spilling dragon blood on the dark cavern's floor as bodies grew and whirling dragon eyes bloomed. The conclave's song unleashed dreams long suppressed, exciting even the most cautious of young dragons. They dreamed of dragon flight as wind sang across the earth's surface.

As Simalucroix moved from one cavern to the next, searching and searching, Ssessensin's rage at him grew. He seemed to be flying even though his claws touched ground in great strides as dragons fled from him.

The mythical dragon wars before humankind's slow ascendancy were said to have been terrible as dragons died excruciating deaths from burns, claws, and teeth. In some stories the wars had gone on for centuries as competing leaders tried to gain territory or hoarded treasure. For a conservative elder like Ssessensin or Syllabrie, or even Creleigh, the thought of fighting in the caverns and re-igniting a dragon war was anathema.

But as Ssessensin fumed and meditated, avoiding the rampaging Simalucroix, her eyes whirled with a kaleidoscope of colors and her hearts beat with rage. At last, turning on Syllabrie, who had stuck with her through all her fuming, Ssessensin let her mind echo through the underground.

"You are mad, Simalucroix," she roared. "We must stop your madness!"

Simalucroix stopped in the small cavern he was passing through.

"Ssessensin," he said, his mind-voice calm. "You're angry. We must talk this out face to face and come to a resolution."

"I will not allow you to endanger generations to come!" Ssessensin roared. "I and the elders will render you senseless unless you come to your senses!"

"Speak for yourself!" Creleigh declared from somewhere in the caverns. "I am an elder. You do not speak for me."

"We need to talk," Simalucroix said, his voice powerful, assured.

"You've enchanted yourself!" Ssessensin declared. "You've enchanted the conclave. You're risking lives with enchantment and dreams. You are not going to have the chance to enchant me! I, Syllabrie, and others will stop you. We're old, but still have strength in our breath, claws, and teeth!"

Dragonkind, frightened by Simalucroix, listened. The horror of newness and what Simalucroix was about to do swept through them.

"We are strong enough for light and are tired of darkness," Jennfer said, supporting Simalucroix.

"Dragons are intelligent beings," Winnigan said, his voice as powerful as Simalucroix's. "We can find a way to live in the world with humans. We run risks, but we are intelligent beings with the power of speech. Simalucroix has shown us how to communicate with humans."

Ssessensin felt Simalucroix, in a manner that seemed eerie, moving toward her even though he could not have any idea of where she was. Did the old dragons have the ability to hone on to the direction of voices? The thought frightened her. She saw Simalucroix growing as he stood over the human boy's smallness. What were the old dragons capable of? she asked herself. What did she have to fear?

"We will stop you!" she said again. "If it is time for dragon wars again, beware! We are elders, but we will stop you!"

Looking at Syllabrie, who was staring at her, she shielded her mind again. "We need to move quickly," she said.

Syllabrie nodded. They moved toward the great cavern. Simalucroix and the other winged dragons felt Ssessensin's mind shield go up. They felt sick and worried.

"She's gone," Jennfer said. "She's hiding," Straaglon said.

"It doesn't matter. She can't stop us," Winigan answered.

Simalucroix, alone, miles from the great cavern, let his mind travel toward the surface. Juniper, his rib cage hurting, was lying down in his cabin. Sheena was fleeing her husband, making her way toward her treehouse. He felt pain and restlessness from his searching and Ssessensin's rage.

How could a leader let a situation get so out of hand? he asked himself. "Because changes cannot be controlled," his mind answered. "Because the unknown is frightening."

He reached for the strength of the seven other winged dragons. Could they manage the transition from hiding to revelation? Or were they moving toward the extinction Grilgax and the dragons of his time had avoided? He shuddered. The seven dragons heard him, but their resolve did not bend.

"On Christmas night," they said in unison and anger. "We will see the light of the moon."

Chapter XXVII

By the time Father made it back to the cabin, Juniper, Grandmother, and Lily had collected wood, started a fire, and cooked supper. Father was volatile when he came back. He seemed excited, hopeful, scared, and upset as emotion after emotion flitted across his face. He did not say anything about what had happened with Sheena.

Juniper, sitting beside the small table, waited for Father to say something, especially after noticing Grandmother's dark eyes searching Father's face, but Father only shook his head and frowned. Juniper thought his father was afraid to tell them what had happened, afraid he would tip whatever was happening with Sheena toward a dark conclusion he feared, but expected.

Juniper felt, as talk with the Smallhands rattled in the cabin's small space, that Father's sense of a tipping point toward disaster had truth in it. He had not heard from Simalucroix since coming into El Malpais. Instead he felt, rather than heard, the dragon conclave's humming. He sensed turmoil not coming from the great dragon. Juniper had a sense enormous change was in progress, not only in his, his friends', family's, and dragons' lives, but in the fabric of what was now and would be in the future.

After supper was finished and cleaned up, Lily took Juniper's hand. They went outside, leaving Father and Grandmother talking quietly to each other. The collapse was dark; winter's cold biting. The Milky Way was faint with fused starlight, but immense, stretching across the collapse's rim's blackness.

"I hope Sammy'll be okay with your grandfather," Juniper said as they sat side by side on a boulder halfway between the cabin and stairs.

"I'm never worried about Sammy," Lily answered. "He's my big brother and can take care of himself." She paused and looked away from the sky into Juniper's eyes. "What's going to happen tomorrow, Juniper?" she asked. "Do you know?"

Juniper shook his head. "I haven't heard from Simalucroix," he said. "I thought he'd contact me like he did when we came to El Malpais before I could walk the trail. I feel turmoil when I try to contact him, but I have no idea about tomorrow. Simalucroix said they were going to come out near Four Windows Cave, close to where the treehouse is, after dark."

"Do you think they'll really come?" Lily asked. "That I'll get to see dragons?"

Juniper shook his head slowly.

"Sometimes what I experienced in the caverns seems a dream, as if Father's right about what I saw, heard, smelled, and felt there. It seems real only when Simalucroix's talking to me. But he said they're going to change centuries of dragon history, bringing the dragon's gift to human beings with them. The way I'm feeling right now, I don't know. Everything's unsettled, Father, Sheena, Simalucroix..."

Lily snuggled closer to him, forcing him to notice her slim body's warmth against his left side. He closed his eyes, letting deliciousness transport him out of conscious thought. He looked so seriously at Lily she smiled, as if she knew, and even approved of, what he was feeling. The night's unsettledness kept filtering into his mind, distracting him from his powerful feelings about Lily. Suddenly, smiling, she stood up.

"We'd better go in," she said softly. "Father and Grandmother will start to wonder."

He sighed. What was going to happen Christmas night? he asked himself. He took Lily's hand, and they walked back to the cabin.

Sam could not understand why, but he kept climbing the hill above the Lowder house, staring down at white Christmas lights in juniper trees and colored lights strung along the roof's rain gutters. Bill and Carson had not come outside since their mother had called them to supper, but bristled threats seemed to rise in waves from the house.

Why did he feel a threat? he asked himself. The Lowders were out of jail, but still in trouble. They were not stupid. If they chose to make trouble their troubles would multiply.

Dad had been forced to deliver LP gas even on Christmas Eve for years. Mom held off fixing their traditional Christmas Eve trout supper until she was sure Sam Sr. had finished his route. Too many families did not have money for fuel, so had to buy gas when they had money in their hands. More than a few Christmas presents promising money were opened early so the family could have a warm Christmas. The night was resplendent with stars and moonlight when Sam's Mom stepped out the back kitchen door and called him to supper.

His Dad was surprised when he saw how alert and well Sam looked. He laughed when Sam sat down at the table without urging and smiled at his mother, who usually looked worried.

When his illness had first started to affect Sam when he was ten, his Mom and Dad had started a long history of going to doctors who prescribed medicines that made him calmer, but took his sense of color and vibrancy away. The medicines helped him function most days, but too often their potency stopped working. He spent hours at his computer, pecking keys and ruminating about his failures. The computer, during those days, was his only link with the physical world outside his thoughts and emotions.

Whenever he managed to come out of his depressed periods, his Mom and Dad began to hope for the nightmare's end. They cheered up and began to do everything they could think of to help him find stability.

After a supper where he conversed happily with his Mom and Dad, making them gleam with pleased, hopeful feelings, he went outside and again climbed the hill. The Lowders were playing Christmas music about the wonderful Christ child.

As he stared down at the house that looked merry, but felt ominous, Sam wondered why he was the way he was. What combination of emotions, events, and thoughts had triggered an anesthesia leading to a life he despised? Was he fascinated with the Lowders because they had been part of what had entered his psyche and tortured him? Or had he interpreted his place in the universe in a way that led to the dark thoughts that controlled him?

In depression's depths he had no doubts: He was the problem. Other people, including his Mom and Dad, were phantoms dancing the macabre dance of living.

Thinking about depression, staring at the threatening house, Sam thought about Juniper and the dragons. He had not heard from Juniper since his release from the hospital. Even Lily had not called the house and given his Mom news. Was Juniper back in El Malpais? Would the dragons come out of the caverns and offer healing to those who came to greet them?

He tried to imagine what Simalucroix and the dragons looked like, but all he could conjure were two-dimensional pictures from children's books. He could not imagine how they would move, or what multi-faceted eyes looked like, or how their hide's whiteness looked. They could not be real, he thought. Bill and Carson kicking Juniper as Sam lay on the ground holding his stomach was real.

How could he believe he would meet creatures that existed only in storybooks and human imaginations? Had the Lowders acted in some mysterious correlation of events so that Sam, Lily, Grandmother, and Juniper's Father would never know for sure if dragons existed?

Sam stopped the chain of his thoughts. He recognized the pattern. One concern led to another, generating emotions he did not welcome and could not control. Depression set in, making the universe and people seem like stones floating through mucous liquid so thick it kept them from sinking toward a bottom where they naturally belonged.

Shaking himself, he turned away from the Lowders. Strange, he thought to himself. He was terrified of the twins, but all he could think about was himself, family, and friends.

He walked down the hill toward his well-lit house. He felt good moving toward the warmth he felt for his Mom and Dad. They were good people. Really good people.

Tomorrow afternoon, after presents and Christmas dinner, I'll get them to go with me to check on Juniper, he thought. I'll tell them I need to find out how he's doing. I want Juniper to heal, to be well enough to make Simalucroix alive.

The dream came out of complete blackness. Even asleep Juniper knew it was a dream, but could not shift on the cabin floor where he was sleeping in his down sleeping bag and force himself awake. Carson Lowder, smiling like he had smiled when smashing Juniper's face with Lily's book bag, was on the hill above the treehouse where Juniper watched Sheena. The sky was dark with clouds. A wind sang across lava fields behind Carson.

Suddenly, Simalucroix flew out of the night sky, his huge body erratic above twisted ground below him. Carson's look grew even more manic. He laughed as he took a rifle out from where he had hid it behind the pinyon tree Juniper always hid behind. Simalucroix twisted his body to look at Carson, eyes whirling. Simalucroix took a deep breath; fire spewed out of his throat.

Seeing Carson, Juniper tried to leap into the dream, clutching desperately for Carson's rifle, but he could not move. He lay paralyzed while Carson grinned and put his finger on the trigger.

"Stop!" Juniper cried. "No!"

Father was shaking his shoulder. The cabin was as dark as the dream night. Juniper looked wildly about him, trying to see where he was. He reached for Simalucroix in his mind to warn him to stay in the caverns, but he only found the roiled feeling he had felt earlier when he had tried to find the great dragon.

"Calm down, Juniper," Father whispered. "Grandmother Smallhand and Lily are asleep. You're having a nightmare."

Juniper tried to relax. He looked toward the room's corner where Lily was sleeping in his bed. The nightmare stalked him even though he had shaken it off. His body ached from sleeping on the floor.

"Yeah," he told Father. "Yeah. I'm all right."

"Merry Christmas," Father said quietly. "Another hour, and it'll be light."

"It's morning?" Juniper asked.

"Almost," Father answered.

"I dreamed Carson Lowder was on the hill above the treehouse with a gun," Juniper said.

Father's face fell.

"The treehouse?" Father asked softly.

"Where mother lives," Juniper answered.

Father was silent. He seemed to be thinking deeply. He shook off whatever he was thinking and smiled.

"I made three presents this year," he said. "One for you, one for Lily, and one for Sam."

"Really?" Juniper asked. "For Lily and Sam too?"

Then the realization struck him.

"I didn't get Lily anything," he yelped. "I've been so concentrated on getting home… What will she think? It's Christmas!"

Father chuckled. "You've been pretty beat up," he said. "You can give her the present I made and say it's from you." He acted like he never acted and impulsively hugged his son. "You're going to have to do better next year, though," he chuckled.

Juniper looked at him in the dark and could hardly speak. Father had always been there for both him and Sheena.

"Merry Christmas," he whispered.

He hugged his father back, holding him tight. His chest and arms hurt from the pressure he was putting on them.

Chapter XXVIII

On Christmas morning Sam woke giddy with excitement. Most Christmas mornings he woke feeling like he had to look excited when he really felt depressed. Christmas seemed more a burden than a joy even though he loved Christmas carols, especially "Silent Night", and the idea of the Christ child in the manger. The world, too often torn apart by violence, needed peace.

He never liked to see the strain on his parents' faces as they tried to make him feel the joy they had felt on Christmas mornings as kids. The idea he could not respond the way they deserved drained him more than his most depressed days.

But this morning was different. He got out of bed, put slippers his mother had given him last Christmas on, and walked into the living room smiling. Mom was in the kitchen brewing coffee and making the ice orange frosting and hot cinnamon rolls she made every Christmas morning. Dad was reaching behind the pine tree, turning on the colored Christmas lights.

"Hi Dad," Sam said cheerily.

Startled by his cheerful tone, his Dad looked out from the tree's branches. His Mom, wiping hands on her apron covered with cardinals and bluebirds, came out of the kitchen.

"This is going to be a real Christmas?" she asked.

Sam, smiling, turned toward her and laughed.

"This is a magic day," he said. "A magic Christmas."

Dad plugged in the lights, and the Christmas tree lit up. As he crawled out from the tree he picked up a package wrapped in red Christmas paper.

"Merry Christmas, Sam," he said. "Merry Christmas," his Mom whispered.

Sam cheerfully turned the package over and carefully slid his finger beneath clear cellophane tape. Inside was a huge, red, leather-bound book. He turned the book over, and his smile grew bigger: *A History of Dragons*. A huge dragon in mid-flight, scaly, horned head turned toward the reader, was on the cover.

He looked first at his Mom and then his Dad.

"How did you know?" he asked.

His Mom smiled. "Parents are supposed to know their sons," she answered enigmatically.

"We try hard to know what will make you feel good," his Dad said.

Sam sat on the floor, legs crossed, and slowly, as if the heavy book was fragile, opened the first page.

At Lily's grandfather's house, Sammy crawled out of bed and walked to the kitchen door and looked at the old man praying as the sun rose above red and purple clouds in the eastern sky. His grandfather looked peaceful. Sammy could not understand the change that happened when he started drinking and lost his spirituality.

After watching his grandfather for a moment, he turned back into the house and started the coffee pot bubbling. Then he started packing presents and food Lily and Grandmother had ordered him to bring, along with clothes they would need for the day.

When Grandfather finished he came into the kitchen. Surprisingly, he did not look as if his drunk the day before was affecting him.

"It's going to be a good Christmas," he told Sammy. "I can feel it!"

"You up to the morning hike?" Sammy asked. "The Cairn Trail's rough."

"Grandmother made it," Grandfather said. "I'm as agile as she is."

Sammy laughed. "You are," he said.

Grandfather grinned. "Coffee, then we'll go," he said.

At the cabin Father and Juniper built a fire and started cooking breakfast. Lily and Grandmother came from behind the blankets shielding the beds.

"Morning," Father said cheerfully.

"Morning," Grandmother answered.

Lily smiled shyly at Juniper. Juniper, tired from his restless night, smiled back. Then he flinched.

"Tonight," Simalucroix familiar voice said in his head. "Be ready when the moon has risen above the horizon. We will be safer if we fly after dark."

"Simalucroix," Juniper breathed.

Lily was looking at Juniper, aware something was happening in his head.

"Tonight," Simalucroix said again.

He sounded as if he had not slept for days. Could dragons get tired? What did he know about dragons? Juniper asked himself. He took Lily's hand and glanced at Grandmother and Father. Father was frying potatoes, and Grandmother was reaching to the cupboard above the stove for salt and pepper for strips of elk steak.

Juniper nodded toward the cabin door. He and Lily slipped outside.

"Simalucroix," he repeated again, out-loud this time.

Simalucroix did not answer. Lily stared at Juniper. The collapse's air was cold. A snow skiff had fallen during the night. The collapse's steps would be slick, she thought to herself. She tried to hear Simalucroix in her own head, but heard nothing.

"Simalucroix," Juniper said again.

"Breakfast is ready!" Father called out from the kitchen.

Juniper looked at Lily: First the dream, then this brief, fleeting communication. Something was wrong in the caverns.

"He's gone, isn't he?" Lily said softly.

Juniper nodded. "Something's wrong," he said.

"Breakfast," Grandmother called brightly. "Come on you two. The table's set."

"He kept saying, 'Tonight,'" Juniper told Lily.

She squeezed his hand. "We'd better go in," she said.

Juniper concentrated, trying to reach Simalucroix. What's going on? he thought. Where are we supposed to be tonight? Lily tugged him again. Grandmother was looking at them. Reluctantly, Juniper let Lily lead him toward Christmas breakfast.

Sheena woke feeling the universe was an anvil pressing against her. She could hardly move even though she was in the treehouse in her own bed. The humming was gone from her head, but was around her: In the floor's solid wooden planks, in the roof, in the Ponderosa, branches and needles singing vibrations not coming from wind.

Christmas morning, Sheena thought, surprising herself. She had not thought about Christmas for years. Inside the dream she had lived for so long, time meant nothing. She flew across earth from tree to tree, a beautiful human bird that could wave her hand and make the lava flat's twisted surface alive with moonlight or sunlight or music woven from winds allowing her to feel the earth's aliveness: From El Malpais to North and South poles' ice fields to the deep fjords of Norway where her great grandparents had been born.

What was she going to do? Pressure was building in the humming around her and in her head. She thought about getting out of bed and making her way to Rory and Juniper. The thought made the pressure in her head lessen. She could spend Christmas with her husband and son, she thought.

Then she remembered that they were not alone in the cabin. An old Navajo woman and her granddaughter and grandson were with them. How could she face people not part of her? She brought her hand up from the bed and looked at it. How could she look so healthy when she had been living like a wild woman?

The realization hit her hard, as if she'd fallen out of a Douglas fir. Something was about to happen, something unusual, wonderful, scary, more magical than when she flapped arms and flew over lava.

She tried to shake thoughts flooding into her from out of her head. Did she want to change? She was getting older. Her son was a teenager. Even if she wanted to she could not have another baby. She had missed Juniper's baby years.

The humming had a rhythm. It rose and rose above her bed, above the treehouse, into the sky, a great symphony wrung from Gaia, Mother Earth, the great mother, the planet's living being.

Groaning from effort, Sheena got out of bed. It was Christmas morning, she told herself again. She wondered how she even knew it was Christmas morning. Then she remembered the strange, deep, inhuman voice she had heard in her dream. The voice had told her it was Christmas morning. It had urged her to go to Juniper and spend the day with her husband and son.

But the old woman and girl are with them, she thought to herself.

Without thinking she moved to her clothes rack. Rory cleaned her clothes, she thought. When she was inside her dream, living her forgetfulness, he cleaned them. Otherwise they would be caked with filth. Why did he live in the collapse? Juniper could not be happy not living in town. He deserved a life where he could have friends and things to do. She shook her head. She was achieving sanity.

Could she face her husband, son, the old woman, and her granddaughter and grandson? It was Christmas morning. Maybe the humming was the song of angels. Maybe God had decided to work a miracle.

She dressed quickly. Where had the clothes come from? she thought. Long dresses and trousers? Underwear, socks? Shoes and boots? Rory could not be making much money living so far from town. She did not think he had a car. She'd seen him walking with Juniper to catch the bus to town.

She'd have to face the old woman and the girl, she decided. It was Christmas morning, a day for miracles.

They were opening presents when Bill decided. He and Carson would wait until after lunch. Their parents would lay down for a nap. He'd steal his and Carson's guns out of the cabinet their dad kept locked by getting the key his Mom had in her purse. Then they'd head into El Malpais.

Sam, Lily, and Juniper would be at Juniper's cabin. Today was when they were going to see dragons. Bill snorted beneath his breath. Dragons! What a joke! He'd have to watch Carson to make sure his brother did not go crazy. They would scare the three dragoneers, not hurt them, but at least they would have something to do other than sitting around waiting for the axe from court to fall. They had little to lose. Not much to gain either, he told himself.

After unwrapping presents Bill and Carson went outside. Carson said he wanted to see if Sam was still hanging around. They had seen him hide behind trees and watch them all day yesterday. When Bill broached the idea of going to Juniper's, Carson looked him like he was nuts.

"You crazy?" he asked. "No car, and it's a hell of a long walk. Dad's gonna keep the truck keys with him. He knows how easy it is for us to manipulate Mom. He won't be taking chances."

"What do you have better to do?" Bill asked, putting a sarcastic edge in his voice. "Sit around watching Sam watch us?"

Carson was silent as he looked at the hill. Sam was not there. Maybe he was opening presents. Carson knew Sam and his family were different from the Lowders. What was puzzling was why Sam was a sad sack. Sam's Mom and Dad had always been good to all three of them, taking them fishing and trying to interest Carson and Bill in reading. As far as Carson could tell, Sam's parents were much easier going than his parents, especially Dad, who could go off and slap them around any time they irritated him.

"What the hell," Carson muttered. "If Sam can get to where he thinks he's going to see dragons, we can. After lunch," he said. "You're sneakier at getting into Mom's purse. We'll get guns and go, but I'm not settling for a twenty-two. We're not hunting rabbits. I'm taking Dad's thirty-ought-six. If you don't like that, I won't go."

Bill stared at him. Carson stared back, defiant.

"We're only going to scare them," Bill said. "We're in enough trouble. Hurting one of them will make it worse."

"If you don't want me to go, I won't," Carson smiled. "We can sit here all day."

"You got to promise we'll only scare them," Bill said again.

"It's a damned long walk," Carson countered.

Bill shook his head. "I'm not going if you're taking the ought-six," he said.

"Chicken?" Carson laughed.

"Smarter than you are," Bill answered.

Carson sneered and shook his head.

"Twenty-twos," he said at last.

"A deal," Bill said carefully, watching his twin, trying to see what he was thinking.

"Get the key without getting caught, and we'll go," Carson answered.

"No ought-six," Bill said again.

"We'll go; we'll go," Carson said.

"Okay," Bill said.

"Okay," Carson answered, his voice enthusiastic. He hit Bill on the shoulder.

Bill groaned. What had he done to deepen their troubles? He would never learn.

Chapter XXIX

In the dream a coal black dragon hovered above a huge mountain. Strong winds blew a river of flowing snow over a saddle between two peaks. He could tell he was dreaming because he had never seen a mountain. In late evening light it looked unreal as shadows spilled east from every rock and mound in the earth. The dragon glowed in light as it twisted its monster head, hovering, looking for some danger not in sight.

Suddenly, beneath the black dragon, out of a cavern near the summit, an immense, iridescent lavender dragon rose angrily toward the hovering giant. The black dragon straightened its body and snapped toward the rising lavender, nostrils flaring rage.

The lavender breathed a seemingly endless flame, trying to scorch the black's underbelly, but the black twisted and evaded the fire, pointing its head toward the lavender and breathing out its own flame. Claws extended out of four-toed front and hind legs. The lavender slashed at the black, but the black was already out of range, positioning above the lavender, ready to slash downward with all its body's force.

The lavender roared so loud the peak echoed with enraged sound. Air smelled of sulfur even in gale force winds. The black folded wings, hurtling toward the lavender. The lavender twisted, but the black's claws raked its neck. Blood fell toward the snow river in a small, dripping stream. The lavender screamed, flapping upward to position above the black. The black, having failed to land a fatal blow, twisted out of its hurtling fall. The bleeding lavender hurtled, screaming toward the black's right wing. The black roared. Wind howled around the peak's summit.

Simalucroix woke. His hearts were beating so fast they seemed ready to jump out of his chest. He was breathing heavily as he fought off the dream's power. Winnigan, Fruchault, Jennfer,

Straaglon, and the four latest winged dragons, Pruchaldras, Ssinssifra, Willwandria, and Craagladon were surrounding him.

Simalucroix did not recognize where they were in the caverns. He remembered looking for Ssessensin and her followers, calling out to her in endless chambers, enraged she was determined to keep fear of the outside alive for another generation. Once he had sensed her and moved toward her, determined to wake in the elders the fire discovering Juniper in the great cavern had woken in him, but in the end he had stopped, so exhausted he had to end his search.

He had been foolish. He could see that as he stared back at whirling dragon eyes. Dragons had not needed protective circles for many generations. Simalucroix had let emotions rule him when he had told Juniper that he and winged dragons would come from out of the caverns on Christmas.

He had dreamed of lifting wings in silver moonlight and rising in a rush of power and wind above the lava fields he had seen through Juniper's eyes. He had dreamed of using the old dragon ability to heal humans and starting an era when dragons would be free of the deep caverns to fly, achieving a brother and sisterhood of sentient beings based on an understanding of how rare sentience was in a universe of dark matter, black holes, and empty space.

He and the dragons had listened to human news for years and were amazed at what humans had discovered and accomplished. Surely humans, as a society, if not as individuals, had learned to value sentience enough to appreciate dragons. In some societies they had grown enough to accept differences among themselves.

But were his dreams safe? If he and the winged dragons were to climb to the surface, getting past Ssessensin, Syllabrie, and the elders following them, would dragonkind survive the storm of revelation that would follow? Perhaps Juniper, his family, and friends could keep the dragon's secret, but Simalucroix knew that neither he nor anyone else could ensure that. News spread instantly among earth's humans. Even Juniper wanted him and dragonkind to stay hidden, afraid that what the Lowders had done to him was a sign of what could happen to dragons if they revealed themselves.

Simalucroix reached from the dragon circle to Juniper and touched his mind. He was in his cabin with Father, Lily, and Grandmother. Simalucroix started to speak to Juniper, but silenced himself.

"I did not find Ssessensin," he told the dragons surrounding him. "She and the others will try to keep us from the surface."

The winged dragons seemed relieved to hear his voice. Body tension lessened. The circle's tightness loosened as one and then another relaxed vigilance.

"The decision was made when we found our wings," Craagladon, the youngest said, his voice determined.

"There will be more dragons with wings," Winnigan added. "This will not be the end."

The vision of dragons battling in ancient skies flashed through Simalucroix.

"We do not want war," he said.

"The elders do not understand," Craagladon said. "Their traditions are past."

"It is Christmas day above ground," Jennfer said. "Christmas carols are playing on their radios. I have learned to hear them."

"Tonight your dream comes true," Straaglon said to Simalucroix. "We will fly in the moon's light. We will become surface dragons again."

"I was chosen leader by a conclave of elders," Simalucroix said. "I don't want to be the leader that undoes what Grilgax accomplished. I am starting to fear what I started."

"We won't let fear stop us," Winnigan said. "It is no longer your decision, but the decision of all who have used the conclave's power to discover wings."

"For generations we have not known dragons still had wings," Jennfer said. "Now we know we have stagnated underground. We have used tools and thought deep thoughts, but have not grown like humans as they have reached beyond earth to the moon's surface. We need to face our fears and grow into dragons again if we are not to be animals living beneath the earth's surface. We need to face our limitations if we are to grow beyond them."

"But the dangers..." Simalucroix said.

"We will face them," Craagladon answered.

Willwandria turned her head and looked back at the small cavern's entrance.

"Ssessensin and Syllabrie will be at the only place they can stop us," she said. "There are not many of them. We've waited long enough."

The young, sensuous dragon turned from the circle and walked into the lava tube that led to the great cavern. Winnigan, Fruchault, Jennfer, Straaglon, Pruchaldras, Ssinssifra, and Craagladon followed.

Simalucroix, for a moment, held back. He looked into Juniper's mind. Unbelievably, Juniper was looking at his mother, Sheena.

"Simalucroix," Winnigan insisted from the lava tube.

"I'm coming," Simalucroix mumbled.

As he moved toward the lava tube, strange rustlings began all over the caverns. Simalucroix looked around him, but could only see winged dragons walking without hesitation toward the great cavern.

Chapter XXX

By ten o'clock Sammy and Lily's grandfather were at the cave. Lily and Juniper were outside waiting for them when Sammy came up over the collapse's rim. Seeing Grandfather made Juniper queasy, but he told himself that Christmas was for families. Grandfather was part of Lily's family even if he was not to be trusted.

Sammy was carrying a huge backpack of presents. When Juniper realized what they were, his stomach churned. Why had he not thought about making presents? Christmas had come to mean something different than presents to him. It had come to symbolize the risk dragons were taking in a world with Lowder brothers. Watching Sammy cheerily shoulder his load made Juniper feel his failure to think beyond his concerns. Lily, looking at his face as it fell when he figured out why Sammy was carrying the backpack, laughed at him.

"Don't worry," she said. "No one expected you to bring presents. I don't know when you would have shopped or made anything. We've been with you every day for weeks."

"But I didn't get you anything," he confessed, half yelping.

Lily looked at him strangely as Sammy and Grandfather paused halfway down, resting before going down the final flight of stairs.

"Christmas is not about presents," Lily said. "It's about being together. If you bring dragons, you'll have brought a present no one could ever forget."

The mention of dragons caused Juniper to reach out in his mind again. He felt a touch from Simalucroix, but then it was gone. Christmas day had come, but nothing seemed right. A crisis was happening in the caverns, although Juniper could not imagine what it could be.

Would Simalucroix come to the surface? Juniper admonished himself. He would be upset if the dragons did not come. Lily was so determined to see Simalucroix. Then there was Sam... Would Sam come? Why had he not made sure Sam knew he and Lily were at the cabin?

As Sammy reached the collapse's floor, smiling and hugging his little sister, Juniper's thoughts faded. If Sam did not come, he and Lily would go to Sam: Tomorrow morning--if Sammy would see them.

At the cabin Father and Grandmother had finished baking chocolate chip cookies when Juniper and Lily, followed by Sammy and Grandfather, came into the cabin. Grandmother went and put her arm around Grandfather.

"I'm glad you're here," she said. "Merry Christmas."

The old man smiled shyly. He did not say anything, but looked pleased.

Sheena slowly made her way from the treehouse across the lava flats. She stopped at the Douglas fir where she had startled Juniper the night he had walked toward her after she had warned him away. She wondered what had possessed her. Why would either Rory or Juniper welcome her? She sat on the tree's low branches, trying to find courage.

The humming intensified in her head, as if it were forcing her to a decision when what she really wanted was to be alone. Her life had been stranger than a normal person would have believed possible. How could she change and walk a more normal path? What would she do when she encountered the old woman and girl? She had not met anyone strange to her for a long time.

She had once gone to movies and malls where strangers thronged. But that life had died a long time ago. She had no idea about how she could face her son or people closer to her son than she was. Twice she started to walk from the Ponderosa toward the treehouse, but then turned back.

She had often faced down nightmares:

> In the night
> I wrestle
> with the dark ones:
> Huge, man-like shapes
> so great
> my mind cannot
> contain them.
>
> Again and again
> the wrestlers come.
> I try in vain
> to avoid them
>
> until
> the anger in my heart
> wells up inside me.[4]

    She often ran so fast nightmares faltered behind her as she exulted in moonlight, snow, or rain, triumphant in escape, but she could remember no nightmare as frightening as trying to walk to the cabin to greet her husband and son.

    If she took a dozen steps away from the cabin, then stopped, the humming grew so intense her heart thundered with pressures more powerful than fear. She could not face Rory, Juniper, the old woman, or the girl. It was impossible! She was not sane. She was not presentable. Who knew how long it had been since she had had a bath?

    At last she gave up and walked boldly and swiftly toward the cabin. She would not let Rory put his arms around her and then run. She would force herself to stay and see what happened even if she had to go back to the Grants hospital.

---

[4]"Dark Ones," a poem by Ethel Mortenson Davis.

Rory was frying slabs of Christmas ham glazed with wild honey gathered by Lily's Grandfather from hives he kept near fields of sunflowers. He turned toward the door. Sheena, looking as skittish as a new-born colt, was standing, looking into the cabin prepared for Christmas dinner. Without thinking Rory dropped the spatula into the frying pan.

"Shee…Sheena?" he asked.

Juniper's heart pounded. His throat had closed, and he could not breathe. Lily, sitting on the floor close to him, looked from Sheena to Juniper.

Sheena did not bolt from the door to freedom, but held her ground half in and half out of the cabin. She was sweating even though it was cold, a breeze carrying a hint of snow. Grandmother, looking amazed, as if experiencing a miracle, rose from where she was sitting beside Grandfather.

"I am April Smallhand," she said softly. "This is my husband, Jared Smallhand, my grandson Sammy, and my granddaughter Lily. I want to thank you for a Christmas none of us will forget."

Sheena heard the old woman talking, but could not make sense of her words. She looked from Rory to Juniper. They looked as shocked as she felt. The sound and smell of sizzling ham, the breathing of people as they adjusted to her standing in the door letting in cold, the warmth she experienced only when driven to start a fire in the small pot-bellied stove Rory had installed in the treehouse, were so frightening she could barely keep herself in place.

"I want to come home," she said in a clear, firm voice.

She was so beautiful she lit up the cabin. Rory stepped toward her, but stopped.

"You said yesterday you loved me," he said, surprised to hear his voice.

Sheena moved imperceptibly backward, her body moving toward the collapse.

"I want to come home," she said again.

She looked at Juniper. Juniper felt half faint. This was more frightening than when he had been surrounded by dragons. Was he experiencing a miracle? Was his mother healing?

"You are home," Rory said desperately, feeling her starting to run away. "You are home and welcome, loved, cherished, loved…" he said.

"I don't know these people," she said softly. She turned.

"Mother!" Juniper said, startling himself. "You met Lily, on the hill above the treehouse. You talked to her…and me…" His voice trailed off.

Sheena half-turned back toward Juniper and looked at him. She smiled. Her eyes were not wild like they had been every other time she had looked at Juniper—at least every time Juniper knew she had looked at him. They seemed to be pleading for…Acceptance? Understanding?

"I know," she said, then turned to run.

Rory's heart was in his throat. Should he try to stop her?

"Mother!" Juniper said again. He was standing up from his chair.

Sheena stopped and looked at her son again. He was tall, probably taller than she was, young and vibrant, handsome. She could see why the young granddaughter was attracted to him.

"I love you, Juniper," she forced herself to say. "My son…"

Juniper felt desperate. What could he do? He had felt so alone for so long. Now Lily, Father, Grandmother, Sammy, even Grandfather, and Sheena surrounded him, filled him, strangely enough, with a feeling of himself.

"Tonight," he said. "I want you to meet us at the treehouse at moonrise."

A vision of Sheena, face alight with moon shadow, standing in a Douglas fir, eyes fiery with magic, hovered in front of him.

He surprised himself. "Dragons will be there," he said.

Sheena smiled. "I live with dragons," she said enigmatically. She turned again.

"I'm coming with you," Father said. He hesitated. "If you'll let me…"

Sheena stopped again, her hand ready to let go of the door. Father held his breath.

"I'm not ready for company," she said softly. She paused for a moment that seemed as long as eternity. "But I will welcome my husband," she said.

Rory, oblivious of Christmas dinner, face ecstatic with emotions built from years of waiting and hope inside hopelessness, grabbed his Levi jacket and followed Sheena out the door.

"The treehouse! By Four Windows Cave! At first dark!" Juniper said as the door closed behind Father.

When Father and Sheena were gone, Grandmother moved to the stove. No one spoke. Lily, standing, put her hand on Juniper's shoulder. Juniper impulsively hugged her to him. His mind buzzed with thoughts that flitted and danced so quickly he could not capture them. His mother had seemed rationale, sane, afraid, and determined to see them after all the Christmases that had come and gone since she had left. How did he feel? Angry? Frustrated?

"I'm hopeful," he said softly, turning to look at Lily. Lily smiled.

"That was the witch of El Malpais," Grandfather said. Grandmother was putting the finishing touches on the Christmas table. "Why did Rory take off like that?" Grandfather asked.

Grandmother closed her eyes.

"You're experiencing a miracle and don't see it," she told her husband quietly. "And you're sober."

"I don't suppose Rory's eating Christmas dinner with us," Sammy said. He smiled.

"When the spirit's fed the way his spirit is being fed," Grandmother said softly, her voice filled with wonderment. "Food can wait."

"Simalucroix is going to come," Lily said. "We're going to be there, and Father, Sheena, Sam, and maybe Sam's parents. The dragons are healing us, and they aren't above ground yet."

Juniper reached out to Simalucroix again. What was happening in the caverns? He wanted to tell him about Sheena and what had just happened. There was no sign Simalucroix heard him or even realized he was alive.

"Come," Grandmother said. "This is as festive a feast as we'll ever have."

Grandfather looked at his wife as if she was going crazy, started to say something, saw the look in Sammy's eyes, thought better of what he was going to say, got up, and quietly sat at the table.

Juniper held back. "Father," he said.

Lily tugged at his hand. "We'll take food to him and Sheena," she said. She looked worriedly at him. "If you're up to it."

Juniper, hesitantly, smiled and let her lead him to the table. He did not like having Christmas dinner without Father, but he knew that if Father believed he could put his family together again, he would skip meals for a month and never miss them.

Strangely enough, he also felt as strong physically as he had before he had ended up in the hospital. Even if the dragons were in turmoil, he was being healed.

"Merry Christmas," Sammy said as he sat down.

Grandmother sat and bowed her head.

"Thank you for this time of signs and miracles," she said as she began their prayer. "Thank you for blessings spreading from this place into hearts and spirits all over El Malpais and beyond…"

Chapter XXXI

Sam waited until after Christmas lunch to ask his parents. As the opening of presents and meal preparations went forward he grew increasingly nervous as he thought about the importance of what he was going to ask them.

He knew his mother would be upset. She valued Christmas above any other time of the year and tried hard to get everyone into her Christmas spirit. Her idea was that Christmas, Easter, and other holidays were pauses in life when family ties were strengthened, and people remembered who they were as family.

For years Sam had hated holidays. He always tried to keep depression at bay for his Mom's sake, but after an hour or two of trying, the pressure of trying would build, and depression would crash down like a dark wall he could not walk through. The wall was forever.

This year, because of Juniper, Lily, and the dragons, things were different. He knew Juniper and Lily were at Juniper's cabin celebrating Christmas and waiting for evening to come. He was not sure how he could be so certain in his knowing. No one had told him that Juniper had gone home, but he knew anyway. He and his Mom and Dad had to join them if he was to see dragons.

They had gone into the living room so that Mom and Dad could sit by the lighted tree and enjoy hot cinnamon tea and enjoy each other and their Christmas presents. That tradition had started when Sam had been a toddler and still wanted to play with his toys for hours on end. Sam did not try to explore his new I Pad, but sat in front of the tree, looking at his parents. His Mom noticed first. Then Dad noticed and looked at him and then at Mom.

"What?" his Dad asked.

"I want to visit Juniper," Sam said. "I'd like you to come with me."

"On Christmas?" his Mom objected.

"Juniper's my best friend," Sam answered.

Dad smiled and reached over and took Mom's hand.

"Christmas and friends go together just like family," he said.

Mom looked into her husband's eyes and smiled.

"I guess they do," she said. "Friends and family. It's been a good Christmas." She dropped Dad's hand and got up. "If we're visiting, especially down the Cairn Trail, I'd better get ready."

Dad looked at Sam.

"Are Juniper and Rory expecting us?" he asked.

Sam looked inside himself. He could almost hear the right answer, as if someone was coaching him who had access to his innermost self.

"Juniper, Father, Lily, and Lily's Grandmother," he said. "They're waiting for us."

Mr. Maryboy had not smiled so much since Sam's sickness had started. He was always worried, trying to find magic to heal Sam.

"I'm glad you and Juniper have become good friends," he said. "It's a strange family out in the lava fields, but I like Juniper, and Rory has reasons for living where they live." He got up from his chair and stretched. "I'd better put blue jeans on," he said. "Mom's right. The Cairn Trail doesn't lend itself to town shoes, dresses, or slacks."

Sitting by the tree, its lights glowing in afternoon sunlight, Sam felt good. He was going to be there when dragons came out into the world.

Ssissensin and eight followers, all over one hundred years old, gathered at the lava tubes Simalucroix and the winged dragons had to pass through if they were going to reach the earth's surface and moonlight.

"Six of us will position ourselves to breathe fire when they come so no one dares pass without getting scorched to death," Ssissensin said. "We'll take turns. One will breathe fire, then another, then another, each one eating stone before it's their turn again. We should be able to stop them without killing them."

"How long can we keep that up?" Raararriton, a dragon even older than Ssissensin, asked. "Dragons haven't exerted themselves with fire like that since coming to the caverns."

"As long as we need to," Syllabrie answered grimly. "Hopefully not long. Hopefully Simalucroix will show good sense. He was a leader who showed he cared about dragonkind. Hopefully he will come to his senses and protect us again."

"We'll use fire as long as we need to," Ssissensin said, her voice deep. She paused. "Simalucroix's awake. They're moving."

"It's not sunset on the surface yet," Winton, the youngest of them said.

"They know we're here," Raararriton said. "They won't know how long it will take to get past us."

"They won't get past us," Ssissensin promised. "Not now. Not ever." She looked around at the grim faces surrounding her. "We have to prepare," she said.

Syllabrie started humming. One by one the others joined their voices to hers. Dragon song drifted through lava tubes into caverns leading to the great cavern and the dark river. The song grew increasingly powerful even though only nine were singing.

As the sound grew louder and louder, Ssissensin felt herself growing. She had never felt so determined and powerful. A sharp, fierce pain split along both sides of her large back. No, she thought to herself, no!

Pain enflamed her back as the humming grew louder. Ssissensin felt increasingly powerful, more and more like a dragon that had flown skies at night above a moonlit peak rising jagged and dark from valleys. She felt the blood of a thousand, thousand generations of dragons flowing through veins, hearts, and spirit. She felt old wildness, old power, and certainty. She was the most powerful, awe-inspiring creature alive. She rose on hind legs, skin glowing with power, and spread immense wings, roaring above dragon song, sending her voice rumbling toward those who would oppose her.

Syllabrie was the first to see the red wings. They separated from Ssissensin's hide like hidden jewels. As Ssissensin rose up, Syllabrie's singing faltered. The others stopped humming. The dragon song was silent, but Ssissensin was roaring her challenge, mocking those foolish enough to embrace the dragon bold enough to overturn years of caution and plunge dragonkind into an unknown they had fled millennia ago.

Ssissensin stopped roaring and looked around her. The dragons following her were silent and watching with swirling eyes, a hint of fear in the way they had moved away from her when she had risen to her hind legs. Her great dragon head was less than an inch from the small cavern's ceiling. She looked at them with power and contempt.

"No one will pass.," she said. "No dragon will see the surface. No one will pass this place until I am dust on the floor."

Her voice was deeper than before. She dropped to four feet and looked defiantly at her followers. Syllabrie, frightened of her old friend, was the first to recover.

"I'll not let you down," she told Ssissensin. "I won't be as fierce," she said in deference to her old friend. "But we will be every bit as brave."

"There are eight winged dragons on the other side," Felisson, an ancient dragon who had not spoken to that point, said. "Every one of them can be as fierce as Ssissensin. Everyone can breathe fire further than unwinged dragons can."

"A small group can hold narrow passages indefinitely," Syllabrie answered. "All we need is willpower and courage."

Ssissensin looked at Felisson, her friend for a hundred and fifty years, her eyes blazing determination and ferocity.

"What would you have us do, Felisson? Let them pass to the surface and stir up humans who have evolved beyond where they were in the arts of destruction and war when Grilgax led us underground?"

Unperturbed, Felisson looked up at the great dragon and smiled, his face hideous when he showed great rows of teeth.

"Would you like me to join Simalucroix?" he asked. "A leader selected by a conclave? Weren't you there when that happened, Ssissensin?" he asked. "Were you not part of those who selected him?"

"Creleigh should have been here," Raararriton said. "He was driven away by the madness of dragonkind fighting dragonkind. He wanted dialogue, not war."

Ssissensin hissed. "Are you cowards beneath your hides?" she asked. "Afraid of young dragons not old enough to question their elder's wisdom?"

Raararriton and Felisson did not take their eyes off Ssissensin.

"Stop this!" Syllabrie demanded. "We cannot risk our future on emotions. We have to use our minds and understand the risk the young-in-eggs face if this madness of going to the surface does not end!"

Raararriton shook his great head.

"I hope we are not wrong," he said. "I am old and have been wrong before."

"You're staying then?" Felisson asked.

Raararriton did not take his eyes off Ssissensin's glaring, whirling eyes. "I don't believe in our leader's contempt," he said carefully. "But I am not sure I want to face the danger dragonkind will face if Simalucroix follows his passions to the surface."

"You'll join Syllabrie, both of you," Ssissensin said coldly. "I will hold the larger passageway here."

Syllabrie looked and felt relieved. Could they hold the passages? Ssissensin claimed they could, but there were nine winged dragons in their prime strength against nine dragons long past their prime, only one of whom was winged. Simalucroix was no weakling or fool. His determination would be hard to oppose.

Ssissensin's face grew hard as she listened to movements in the great cavern.

"They're coming," she announced.

"Come," Syllabrie said quickly to Raararriton, Felisson, and Winton.

Raararriton and Felisson stared at Ssissensin and did not move. Ssissensin glared at them. Go, she said behind her mind shield. Go. Syllabrie looked at them one last time, then looked at Winton. Winton nodded; they walked to the opening where the cavern's roof sloped downward.

Raararriton took his eyes off Ssissensin. The old female dragon is mad, he thought to himself. We are led by a mad dragon. Feeling ill, he followed Syllabrie. Behind him Felisson grumbled deep in his throat at Ssissensin. Raararriton, who had known Felisson since he had hatched on a day when more dragons had risen out of warm earth in the birthing cavern than had ever been born before, felt his old friend's disquiet. Could their cause be right if their leader did not deserve their trust?

Realization struck him; he stopped. He had seen Ssissensin, Syllabrie, all nine of them, himself. He was seeing the cavern! He had never seen anything in his life. He, like all dragons, was blind. In the earth's darkness they had given up sight. He had seen Sissensin's hide glow as she reared above them, power coursing through as red wings separated from her hide.

Should they be seeing? he asked himself. Were even those holding to ancient traditions becoming more than they were? He wondered if Felisson realized he could see. The cavern dark did not make the ability to see seem obvious. Raararriton looked at the dark cavern. He could hear better than he could see. He wondered what the outside would look like. Then he knew what was driving Simalucroix, the power of the great leader dragon's dream.

Felisson had stopped behind him. Raararriton, feeling his friend's confusion, forced himself to move beside Syllabrie in front of the tube they were to defend.

Grilgax had been wise, Raararriton told himself. Ssissensin was not wise, but the elders still had to protect Grilgax's heritage. Humans had been too powerful during Grilgax's time, but were more powerful now. He sighed as the four of them, Syllabrie, Raararriton, Felisson, and Winton, breathing deeply to stoke fires deep in their guts, sat silently, waiting for Simalucroix to come.

Chapter XXXII

At dinner Juniper could hardly sit still. He fidgeted and tried to participate in Smallhand table talk, but all he could think about was Father and Sheena. Sheena had been wild for so long, chasing Father with an axe, chasing Juniper into a blowhole, haunting lava fields like a beautiful, unearthly spirit, searching for who knew what as she went from Douglas fir to Douglas fir. Now, on the day Simalucroix had promised to come from the caverns, yet another crisis had ensnared his family.

Sheena had acted half normal when she had opened the cabin's door. Father had gone with her, hoping, Juniper knew, that the witch he had helped keep alive for so long could again become his wife and Juniper's mother.

Juniper did not know that people could change. He was not sure changes, other than those dragging people into maelstroms of discontent and pain, could happen. Could dragons come out of the earth and heal humans? Could humans heal humans? Father had gone beyond human effort for Sheena for years, and Juniper had not even known the witch of El Malpais was his mother.

Then there was Lily's grandfather, Juniper thought. He glanced up at the old man who was smiling at Lily. Lily's eyes were bright with anticipation and excitement, although she kept glancing at Juniper, forehead wrinkled with worry. Grandfather looked like a kindly old man wondrous in his spirituality. His round face, haloed with white hair, wrinkles of wisdom surrounding twinkling black eyes, seemed healthy with knowledge of who he was and how he fit into the universe. Still, he lost control of himself regularly, retreating into alcohol, and Grandmother and Lily were left with ugly bruises.

Why? Juniper asked himself silently. Why?

As soon as dinner was completed, food still filling Juniper's plate, Grandmother and Lily cleared the table. Grandmother looked at Juniper.

"We're going to need water for washing dishes," she told him.

Juniper nodded, grabbed the water bucket by the door, and went to the cave's spring. When he came back Grandmother smiled.

"Thanks Juniper," she said, motioning to two tinfoil covered plates. "You and Lily need to find your mother and father if you can," she said. "This is Christmas, and by my lights, not having Christmas dinner comes close to failing to live life."

The relief Juniper felt at being ordered to do what he wanted to do was immense. He poured water into the stoppered sink and took the plates. He looked at Lily, who was already opening the front door, smiled, and the two of them went outside.

"Do you think they'll be at the treehouse?" Lily asked as they climbed the stairs. "Are you going to be okay to walk that far?"

Juniper shrugged. "Who knows?" he said. "Sheena's unpredictable." He was so excited he did not even think about the pain that still made his rib cage ache.

White snow on black lava and wind above the collapse's rim made the earth spotted. Even the sky, pale winter blue, stretched splotches of white, gray rimmed clouds from horizon to horizon. The food would be cold long before they got to the treehouse.

Neither spoke as they walked across the lava's rough surface. Juniper's lungs started hurting before they had gone a quarter mile, but he said nothing to Lily and kept moving.

Juniper stopped before the hill's rim where the pinyon tree stood, a frost of snow on bristling needles. Juniper stared at the cloud mottled sky. Images of Sheena and Father ran through his head.

"You okay?" Lily asked when the lava flats' silence seemed too immense.

Juniper looked at Lily. He thought about when he had first approached her at school, heart in his mouth. She had rejected him, but then had become a true friend and more than a true friend. He squared his shoulders and topped the hill.

The treehouse was empty. Pools of unmarked snow wrapped around the Douglas fir's trunk and front steps.

"What now?" Juniper asked, disappointed, even though he had suspected Sheena and Father would not be there.

Lily did not hesitate.

"We leave the food," she said. "We'll never find them until they want to see us. We'll go back to the cabin and wait." She looked at the sky. "In the end we'll gather where Simalucroix wants us to gather."

Somber, worries flitting through his head, Juniper nodded. "Okay," he said, his voice barely audible. "It doesn't seem right, but okay."

Lily looked at him strangely and put her arm around him. "This is going to be a good day," she said. "A magic day."

"There's trouble in the caverns," Juniper responded. "I feel it. It feels like a terrible battle is about to happen."

Suddenly Simalucroix was in his mind, his emotions powerful and alien. Simalucroix was getting ready, with the other winged dragons, to battle an elder female dragon called Ssissensin. Ssissensin was powerful and might block the winged dragons from getting to the surface, although the winged dragons were determined. They were not coming primarily to help Juniper, his friends and family, but to make a new future for dragonkind, a future Grilgax had left behind when he had led the epic journey into cavern's darkness.

The insight staggered Juniper. He had thought, he suddenly realized, that Simalucroix was coming to the surface for his, Lily's, and Sam's benefit. He had ignored what Grandmother and Simalucroix had told him.

Lily was right, he realized. The lava wilderness was too big. They could look for Sheena and Father for a long time even if he had ideas about where they might be. He sighed. Life was not simple. Inside the happiness Lily had brought was the danger of Lowders, Grandfather's schizophrenic nature, the complexity of dragon motivations, whirlwinds of signs and prophecy, and confusion about Sheena and the fact that she was his mother.

"Let's go," he told Lily.

On the way back to the cabin, not far from the Cairn Trail, Juniper stopped and rested against a rock without snow. Lily came up to him and took his hand. He was hurting badly. Juniper looked into her eyes and wondered if he could love anyone, even Father, more than he loved Lily.

"Simalucroix talked to me back at the treehouse," he said, searching for something, though he did not know what, in Lily's eyes. Lily waited.

"Simalucroix and the others have their own reasons for leaving the caverns. Reasons different from what I told you Simalucroix told me. The caverns are getting crowded. They want to see moonlight the way their distant ancestors did."

Lily smiled. "Makes sense," she said.

Juniper stood up from the rock, and Lily leaned against him, her body warm through their layers of clothes. Juniper shook his head.

"I thought we shouldn't endanger them by needing to be healed."

"Doesn't surprise me," Lily said. "We've seen more signs than anybody else in history. The signs have something to do with the universe's balance. The signs couldn't be about just us, any more than dragons and their affairs could be about just us when they are as intelligent as humans are."

Listening to Lily, Juniper's universe expanded. He saw how one thing linked to another, each link alive in chains that created a beautiful complexity of life and existence that made all life, including his own, possible.

"You're smarter than me," Juniper said. "I've known that since you came to Ramah High School." He paused. "But the truth is, I feel like I've stumbled into a fantasy that refuses to go away. I don't know what to make of dragons and signs and you and your family…" He paused again.

Lily held up her hand and shushed his thoughts. Voices were on the Cairn Trail.

"Who could that be?" Juniper asked irritably. He did not want his and Lily's conversation to be interrupted.

"Sam!" Lily said. "Sam coming to meet Simalucroix on Christmas day!"

Juniper looked toward the Cairn Trail. The voices were closer. He and Lily waited, and then Sam, his mother, and father climbed a small ridge east of them. Sam was in the lead. As he topped the ridge he saw Juniper and Lily and waved, looking excited.

Juniper and Lily started walking toward their friend. Juniper had not thought enough about Sam since leaving the hospital. He had been too busy trying to figure out how to get over his injuries so that he could climb the Cairn Trail to home and the dragons. He felt guilty. He could have gotten Donald or Father to stop at Sam's house on their trips to the lava fields.

"How are you Sam?" Lily asked when they got within talking distance. "All better? I can see it in your eyes."

"It's Christmas day!" Sam exclaimed. "I upset Mom. She wanted to spend Christmas at home, but I talked her and Dad into bringing me. I couldn't miss my chance to see Simalucroix. This is a once in a lifetime deal for sure."

Lily hugged Sam, and Juniper reached out and shook his hand. Lily left Sam and went over to Sam's parents who were struggling over the uneven, sharp ground.

"I'm Lily," she told Sam's Dad.

Sam's Dad and Mom smiled. Sam's Mom walked up to Lily and hugged her.

"I guessed as much," she said. "Sam talks about you and Juniper all the time."

"You're here with Sam to see the dragons?" Lily asked.

Mr. Maryboy looked at Lily, then at Sam, with the disbelief Juniper had seen in Father's eyes when he had first talked about dragons. Sam's Mom turned and warned Mr. Maryboy with her eyes.

"I'm glad you brought Sam," Juniper said. "Christmas wouldn't be complete without all of you."

"Sam kept after us," Sam's Dad said. "We couldn't say no."

"I did too," Sam confirmed. "I told them I had to see you if Christmas was going to be complete. Otherwise I'd think Christmas was worthless. That got to Mom, and so," he said, lifting his arms. "We're here!"

Juniper looked at the sky. They had eaten a late dinner, and winter days were short.

"We'd better get back to Lily's family," he said.

"Don't we need to go to the treehouse?" Sam asked. "Didn't Simalucroix say something about the treehouse?"

Lily laughed. "We've got to get my family first," she said. "Then we'll visit Sheena and Father at the treehouse. We'll have to be careful, though. Sheena, Father, and Juniper can run through lava after dark. The rest of us have to have good flashlights and pick our way carefully." She turned. "Come on," she said enthusiastically. "We're not far from Juniper's."

Sam took Juniper's arm and tugged him after Lily. The Maryboys, looking perplexed, followed. Those supposed to be gathering were gathering, Juniper thought in amazement—in the same way signs had appeared as they had walked to the cabin, one after another.

Out ahead of his parents, Sam bounded forward in excitement. "I can't believe Christmas is finally here," he said. "I'm going to see dragons. Simalucroix! Dragons!"

Chapter XXXIII

Bill and Carson crossed Chain of Craters Road into lava mounds jumbled into an impossible barrier. Carson had got the 30.06 and twenty-two minutes after Mom and Dad had gone into their bedroom for their Christmas nap. Mom had left her purse on the drawer in the house's front foyer, and he had picked up the leather bag and grabbed the cabinet's keys. Five minutes later he had the guns, handing the twenty-two to Bill.

Even though it was cold both Bill and Carson were sweating after following an impossible trail through lava. They had discovered the path when they were kids, delighting in hiding from Mom when their Dad was at work as she desperately tried to find them. She always avoided the lava since that was the last place two boys would dare to hide. But it was only marginally easier to navigate twisted piles frozen into sharp peaks above their heads, rounded swells bunched in fiery waves and cooled into twisted, fantastical shapes a mad artist had gleefully sculpted into curlicues, crevices, dips, lines, and flips, than it was to climb cross-country outside the trail.

For a long time neither spoke. They knew their father, his energy and determination endless, would be looking for them in a rage. Though they would have told anybody who would listen that they were tougher than nails and more incorrigible than Tasmanian devils, neither wanted to face him. In the basement he had a weight room he used when he had a few moments alone. He not only had an explosive temper, but was also the strongest man Bill and Carson knew. If their father guessed they were heading into El Malpais, their adventure would quickly end.

At last Bill stopped and said the obvious.

"This is tough going," he said. He looked at the pale winter sky. "Truth is I don't know where we are either."

Carson sneered. "Your own backyard, and you don't know where we are." He spit on black lava near a small pinyon sprouted in a crevice where soil from rains had accumulated.

Bill snorted. "I suppose you know which direction to go to Juniper's," he said.

Around them the landscape looked the same in every direction. Mounds of lava had made the place where they had entered the lava fields disappear. The sun was falling toward evening, so they could see which way was west, but that was their only clue.

"We go north," Carson said. "Sooner or later we'll find the Cairn Trail. As long as we don't drift west toward Four Windows and Big Skylight caves, we'll be okay. The danger is west of the caves, away from the trails."

"Remember that man and his grown daughter who got lost in here?" Bill asked. "They never found them even though they used dogs and helicopters. They say they were experienced hikers too." Thoughts of death sobered Bill. He looked at his brother. "You're not going to do anything dumb with the ought-six," he said. "Are you?"

Carson looked at Bill and smiled.

"Jealous you only got the twenty-two?" he asked. He pointed the ought-six at the sky and swung around. "I see a dragon!" he exclaimed. "Bang!" he said. "Bang! The dragon's dying!" he laughed. "The great old beast is dead!"

Bill shook his head, smiled, but did not laugh.

"We're not here to hurt Juniper, Lily, or Sam," he said seriously. "I was bored and wanted to get away from the house, not hurt anybody."

Carson looked into his twin's eyes. He was hard, cold, unfeeling.

"They're sending us to jail," he said. "God damned wimps are putting me in jail."

"Hurting them won't do any good," Bill said, heart suddenly in his throat. "It'll make bigger trouble. Sometimes we've got to stop and think."

Carson shook his head.

"You feel good?" he asked. "The way we feel when we're alive?"

Bill did not feel good. He felt half dead even though there was excitement in defying Dad. Usually fear of his father drowned out other emotions. Sometimes he welcomed fear when he was down, even if his father was swinging at him. But since they had bought meth that first time, he knew what Carson was saying. He did not feel alive. He did not give a damned about anything but meth: Not jail. Not his family. Not Christmas. Not Carson. Not even himself.

"I'm not ready to spend the rest of my life in jail," he said.

Carson hummphed. "You can get meth in jail," he said confidently. He saluted the sky with his middle finger and snarled. "You can get any fucking thing you want in jail."

He stalked north, making his way around a jagged peak of lava. Bill stood still. He had started this adventure, but was not sure he wanted any part of it. Maybe he should turn around and face Dad's wrath. Maybe that was easier than dealing with his brother's insanity. Carson topped a small mound and disappeared. Without thinking Bill moved quickly toward where Carson had disappeared.

Inside the caverns Simalucroix, beside the underground river with Winnigan, Fruchault, Jennfer, Straaglon, Pruchaldras, Ssinssifra, and Craagladon, paused when he felt Ssissensin become a great dragon with wings.

"This is a time of legend," Jennfer said.

"I do not want a dragon war," Simalucroix replied. "The caverns are too small. There are too many of us. A war could accomplish what Grilgax avoided, extinction of the dragon race."

"Ssissensin and Syllabrie are determined," Winnigan said. "They believe we're wrong, that the outside brings doom. They are honorable elders even if I do not agree with them."

"We will not avoid fighting and still make it outside," Fruchault said. "Ssissensin is a great dragon, with wings. She sees herself as a leader protecting eggs and the young. She will be hard to get past even if we battle her. She has always been fierce."

"The time has come for dragons to face their outside destiny," Winnigan said quietly. "I would prefer not to battle elders. I would prefer to honor them, but we're too many for the caverns even though we have expanded the underground. The only choice is to destroy eggs before the young are born, or face whatever we find outside. Ssissensin and Syllabrie do not see that. They are still living in their youth. I am not going to see eggs Craagladon and I have made destroyed. I am going to live to see what happens to my daughters."

"But war," Simalucroix said. "Not among dragons! We have lived in peace a long time!"

"You made war when you allowed the young human to see us," Craagladon said. "You awoke knowledge of dragons in humans after we had become legend and superstition."

Anguish rose in Simalucroix. "Was I wrong?" he asked plaintively. "Have I failed?"

Jennfer and Pruchaldas spread their wings, ghostly tips touching the roof of the passage.

"We welcome becoming great dragons," Pruchaldas said loudly, his thought echoing into the minds of dragons all over the underground. "We rejoice in our wings."

"You are a leader out of legend," Jennfer said. "We are following the path you have set no matter where it leads."

Simalucroix, still anguished, looked into seven sets of whirling eyes around him. He was silent, but sighed deeply.

"Way leads on to way," he said. "A human poet said that."[5] He turned. "Ssissensin will be more dangerous with the power we felt after first gaining wings. We might as well face our fates."

He stalked off, the others following him.

Sheena and Rory sat on a large stone above Four Windows Cave. They had hardly spoken since leaving the cabin, but had walked across the lava fields as if they could walk away from their lives' strangeness.

Sheena had stood on the hill above the treehouse. Feeling a sharp pang inside her chest, she glanced quickly at Rory and then stalked through wilderness to the cave with its large, dark mouth. She wondered what Rory was thinking as she led him to and fro without purpose.

At last, for the first time since he had called after her when she had left the cabin, Rory spoke. "We're together," he said.

She looked at him. "I'm not as crazy as I've been," she answered. She looked into her husband's clear eyes. "The question is, what does that mean to you, me, and Juniper?"

Rory thought carefully about his response. He was frightened he would say something wrong.

"I've always loved you," he said at last, not knowing what else to say.

"Angels have been humming to me," Sheena blurted out, her voice stilted. "They won't leave me alone. They've been healing me." She stopped, tears filling her eyes. "You're still here. You and Juniper. I'm frightened of the other people. Juniper's in love with the girl."

"Frightened that Juniper's in love with Lily?" Rory asked.

Sheena looked at him. "I kissed you for the first time in forever," she said. "I didn't mean to, but I did. Didn't I?"

---

[5] Robert Frost, "The Road Not Taken."

Rory nodded. "You did," he said. "I kissed you back. You ran like a beautiful, beautiful wisp of wind."

"We're waiting for something, aren't we? Today. Christmas day," she said. "I've known we were waiting since the angels started humming. I didn't think I'd start thinking and feeling again, but I've known."

Rory looked away, trying to keep his feelings' powerful cross-currents tamped down so they would not add to Sheena's skittishness. He did not really know what he felt as he sat having a conversation with his wife, trying to sort out what was happening. His emotions were a storm that tugged one way, then another even though he could not hold on to any current long enough to comprehend his feelings.

"You're sitting with me, and we're talking," he said at last as she looked at him. "That's something I've wanted for a long time."

"Juniper's coming here," Sheena said, her voice stilted and awkward again. "He and everybody close to him. We've got to stay here."

Rory did not know what to say to Sheena's pronouncement. Juniper might come, he thought to himself. An image of a great white dragon materialized in Four Window's Cave's darkness, dancing into sight, and then disappeared.

"What?" Rory asked, startled. He looked again. The cave's mouth, dark behind green, yellow, and orange lichen and boulders, guarded the cave. He thought about Juniper talking about dragons and wondered if the whole family was infected with hallucinations.

"We'll wait here," Sheena said. "We'll wait for the Christmas angels."

The sun blazed yellow and red on edges of puffy clouds as darkness came. In the east the moon rose, enlarged, over the horizon.

Lily got them moving. The Maryboys and Smallhands had gotten along together, and the cabin was filled with talk and laughter. Grandmother, Grandfather, Sammy, and Mr. Maryboy, with Mrs. Maryboy sitting behind him, had inexplicably started a game of pinochle. Lily, Juniper, and Sam hung around outside talking about school and how the Lowders had messed themselves up by getting involved in drugs. For some reason, after Sam's excited outburst on the trail, they did not talk about Simalucroix or dragons. They even ignored the subject of the Lowders.

Then, as sun touched the horizon and flared red and yellow fire, Lily stood up from the rock where she was sitting.

"It's time," she said. "We've got to get there before dark."

Juniper and Sam stood, faces sober with the moment's significance. Would Simalucroix come? Juniper asked himself. He had not talked with Simalucroix in his head since morning. Had the dragons decided not to confront humans and stay in the caverns? Or would they come and change his, the Smallhand's, and the Maryboy's lives?

He looked for Father and Sheena as Lily went inside and started adults and Sammy moving toward the door. The Maryboys objected until Lily looked outside and motioned to Sam. When Sam came inside and said, "It's time," they put down the cards and followed their son.

"Where to?" Lily asked when everyone was standing on the trail.

Juniper listened and called to Simalucroix, but no dragon voice answered. Would Juniper look like a fool in front of his friends after his big talk? The anxiety did not feel true. He thought he should hope the dragons would not fulfill Simalucroix's promise and would stay in their caverns and let Juniper deal with the fallout the best way he could.

"The treehouse," he said quietly.

"The treehouse," Lily repeated.

She walked down the trail, leading the way to the stairs.

Chapter XXXIV

Creleigh was waiting around a sharp corner in a cavern that led to the narrow passages leading to the surface. His whiteness mottled with patches that looked violet even in the darkness. Simalucroix was leading when the winged dragons turned the corner. He stopped, groaning to himself, when he confronted Creleigh lying calmly in the middle of a small cavern. Creleigh had been a friend of Simalucroix's mother and father and had taught Simalucroix dragon lore when he had been young. Jennfer and Winnigan came to stand beside Simalucroix as he looked sadly at his old mentor.

"I was hoping you would not oppose us," Simalucroix told Creleigh at last.

Creleigh looked up at the dragon he had helped make leader during the conclave that had happened so many years ago. That task had not been easy. Simalucroix's father, Wwhhitrapeau, was already near the day when he would breathe his last, and most of the elders believed Simalucroix was too young and untested to solve the overcrowding and restlessness infecting the caverns. A barely discernable feeling hinted that things were going wrong inside the darkness. No one could quite explain in thoughts or dragonspeech what that wrong was, or even clearly say that it existed, but they had felt it.

Creleigh had believed dragons needed young leadership with the energy to chart a new, more ambitious path. He had believed that only someone with the energy of his old friend's son could expand the caverns and move dragons toward a civilization more sophisticated than the one they had made. For centuries dragons had explored the caverns and lived on creatures bred to the dark river or that had ventured to where dragons lived. They had built a few new caves or structures, but preferred poetry, songs, and dragon lore to progress and making lives better.

Wwhhitrapeau, participating in his last conclave, was not sure his son should rise to leadership. He was proud of the son he had fathered with his mate Windrow, and even believed his son could one day aspire to leadership, but was afraid Simalucroix was too steeped in poetry, song, and lore, too cautious for dreams Creleigh believed him capable of accomplishing.

In the end, during the longest mindspeak conclave ever, Creleigh had prevailed, and the first dragon in generations who had not participated in the choosing conclave was chosen. Simalucroix, stunned, looking even younger than he was, assumed a leadership for which he was unprepared.

His first years had been uninspiring, and Creleigh had privately worried he had made a mistake. He had been surprised at his ability to put Simalucroix's name into consideration, but now the old dragon stood in the powerful young leader's path to the surface, a place Creleigh had never dreamed any leader would dare go—at least during his lifetime, and wondered what he should do.

After staring at his protégé, Creleigh sighed.

"I fear for the destiny of dragons if you continue climbing," he said softly.

"Ssissensin may hold passages leading upward," Simalucroix answered. "I felt her gaining wings. She is powerful." He paused. "You are powerful too. Maybe more powerful than Ssissensin."

The old dragon did not move. Behind him he felt, in caverns branching off the cavern they were in, young dragons gathering from all over the massive underground. He could feel their listening and eagerness to follow their leader.

"Ssissensin has given her followers the ability to breathe fire chains," Creleigh said. "They don't know, but I watched as they searched dragonspeak backward to find ability not present since Grilgax's generation died. She has more power than any dragon for centuries. You and your winged followers may die in your attempt, throwing the caverns into dragon war."

"We are going to the surface, elder," Jennfer said. She spoke out-loud rather than in mindspeak, her voice harsh and echoing in the cavern's small space.

Once, according to lore, dragons had normally spoken out-loud, sang songs, and used powerful voices to express their lives' euphoria, but in caverns echoes and small places made dragon voices disconcerting. They had long mastered the art of mindspeak, separating public from private thoughts with consummate skill.

"What of humans?" Creleigh asked Simalucroix, ignoring Jennfer's challenge. "If they were too powerful during Grilgax's time, they have grown more powerful since. How will we survive their knowledge of our existence? I have looked into Juniper's mind since he was here. News of our existence spreads--more rumor than knowledge yet, but how long can we keep our secret if we spread wings into wind and soar in skies like our ancestors soared?"

"I have obsessed over that question," Simalucroix answered. "I have thought about what we can do as eggs crack open and new life comes out of the shell into darkness. I have thought about emotions that led the conclave to allow eight of us to gain our wings. I do not know what will happen when we spread wings and fly into the light of tonight's moon.

"Can we maintain our secret and keep ourselves alive in these caverns? Once we lift wings can dragonkind stand imprisonment underground any longer? When I sensed Juniper's mind for the first time and felt his fear and knew he was likely to see dragons, I felt a stirring that has led to this moment.

"We are dragons the way ancient dragons were dragons. Dragons were never afraid of dark places, but, as you taught me, Creleigh, when I was just out-of-the-egg, dragons were once free, living lives in skies as well as in underground places. I believe our destiny is made of moonlight, sunlight, and darkness rather than darkness alone. I will face Ssissisen and her chains of fire."

Creleigh looked at his young leader without speaking. The dragons with Simalucroix tensed and prepared for battle. Simalucroix stared at his old mentor, eyes whirling with emotions too complex to understand. At last the old dragon turned away.

"You want to come out?" he asked.

Scores of young dragons poked heads and long white bodies out of the warren of small passages where they had been hiding, listening.

"What's going on?" Winnigan demanded, her out-loud voice angry.

"There will be no war," Creleigh said, his voice sounding old and tremulous.

He walked toward the two passages that led to the surface. Behind him young dragons flowed, a river of white backs, toward where Ssissensin, Syllabrie, and their followers waited.

"Only the winged ones are to face danger!" Simalucroix roared.

Neither Creleigh nor the young dragons paid attention to him. The cavern filled with the smell and sound of dragons. Toward the end of the line, one young female stopped and greeted Simalucroix.

"You are our leader," she said so softly her out-loud voice could barely be heard. "We want sky freedom as well as a cavern home. We are not afraid of humans."

She moved quickly to catch up with those in front of her. Simalucroix did not hesitate, but moved after the river of young dragons. Winnigan, Fruchault, Jennfer, Straaglon, Pruchaldras, Ssinssifra, and Craagladon followed.

Ssissensin was humming tension when suddenly, as if he possessed a dragon magic long forgotten, Creleigh was on the other side of the passage she was guarding. She had been so involved in building up rage and strength she had not felt the hundreds of dragons lined up behind Creleigh. Except for Creleigh, they were all young. The old male stood, eyes swirling, and looked at her curiously.

"Are you joining or opposing us?" Ssissensin demanded. She used her out-loud voice and amplified it with her mindspeak's ferocity.

"The young dragons are coming through," Creleigh said calmly.

"I can't allow that," Ssissensin said, putting all her force behind her words. She cast out her mind and felt winged dragons moving behind the young dragons and Creleigh. "The winged abominations cannot hide behind you."

Creleigh stared intensely at her. She felt his accusation in his whirling eyes. "Are you prepared to kill dragons too young to be guilty of the crime you believe Simalucroix and his followers are guilty of?" he asked. "What of your own wings? Do they make you an abomination?"

"You can't come through!" Syllabrie, from the other passageway, screeched, her voice shrill and insubstantial even though she tried to be loud.

"Who's going to stop us?" Creleigh asked. "Who will spill innocent blood and start a war that will destroy us more surely than being revealed to humans will?"

Ssissensin hesitated. She felt the young dragons' pressure concentrated in a way she had never felt during her long life. Her mind whirled as wildly as her eyes, searching for an answer to the dilemma facing her.

"You forced Simalucroix's leadership on the conclave," she accused. "You warped what the conclave would have decided! He was too young! Too inexperienced! Too full of himself!"

Creleigh sighed. "I don't know where this will end," he said gently. If I could I would stop Simalucroix and the others. I met with you to come up with a plan to bring them to their senses. I am afraid of what they are about to do, but your rage has set a course of doom, and I stand with the young."

"The young are fools!" Syllabrie hissed from the other passage.

"We are willing to chance freedom," a young dragon behind Creleigh said.

"We have courage," another one added.

Simalucroix, standing behind the young dragons, uncertain, torn, thinking he should call the Christmas flight and the meeting with Juniper, his friends and family, off, told himself that if they did not go forward, they would not go forward for generations. Humans would not grow weaker as dragon generations passed. He looked at the winged dragons beside him.

"You are going to have to decide," Creleigh told Ssissensin. "You will spill blood or allow what you consider unthinkable to happen."

"You are twisting events the way you twisted the conclave," Ssissensin warned.

Creleigh stepped into the passageway. Young dragons rushed forward to be beside him, then ahead of him, eyes whirling like his, Ssissensin's, and her followers' eyes. Dragon eyes had not whirled for centuries, but the caverns were alight with dragons' eyes.

Ssissensin breathed a long burn of fire at Creleigh. Flame stopped short of where he was. He closed his eyes, but did not stop. Young dragons surged toward the flame. Ssissensin stopped flaming, choked back anger and rage, and backed away.

"No!" roared Syllabrie. "No!"

Within moments young dragons had surrounded Ssissensin and the dragons with her. Moments later Syllabrie and those with her were backed against cavern walls. Creleigh stood still in the press of dragon bodies flooding into the passageways leading toward the earth's surface. The young dragons, after they had captured Ssissensin's followers, lined cavern walls, but did not go further. They stood as if making a parade line for Simalucroix and the winged dragons.

Simalucroix, stunned that what he had dreaded had not come to pass, led Winnigan, Fruchault, Jennfer, Straaglon, Pruchaldras, Ssinssifra, and Craagladon through the narrow chamber to the larger cavern beyond. He kept turning his head from one side to another. The young dragons' eyes were whirling with joy.

"Thank you," Simalucroix said over and over again. "Thank you."

"We'll wait here to find out what the outside is like," one voice said.

"We did this for ourselves," another said.

"Dragons have a heritage of freedom," yet another said. "We are going to live the way dragon lore says we should live."

Simalucroix reached out his mind that had been so intent on events and felt Juniper walking away from the treehouse.

"We're coming," he said to his young human friend. "We're through!"

The excitement in Winnigan, Fruchault, Jennfer, Straaglon, Pruchaldras, Ssinssifra, and Craagladon was so wild it almost burned the air around Simalucroix.

They were going to fly above caverns, above earth, in the moon's light! They were going to experience what dragons had not experienced for centuries. Instead of sulfur air and the deep earth's endless cold, they were going to feel surface air and wind on Christmas day.

Chapter XXXV

"We're through! We're coming!"

Simalucroix's voice thundered triumphantly in Juniper's head. The sound was so strong and unexpected Juniper stumbled, causing Lily to grab his arm. She looked at him, alarmed.

"Simalucroix," he explained.

The hill above the treehouse was less than a hundred yards away. Juniper listened. "Not the treehouse. Four Windows Cave," he said suddenly. Lily stopped, putting her hand up in the air. Sam stopped too. Juniper veered off the treehouse path and walked toward Four Windows Cave. His excitement dulled the increasing pain in his ribs and legs. Sam's parents, Grandmother, Grandfather, and Sammy stared at him, confused.

"Follow Juniper," Sam said quickly.

Sam and Lily moved off the trail into lava fields, making sure they kept Juniper in sight as he climbed a small hill and descended into a gully.

"They're coming," Grandmother said softly, joyously.

"Who's coming?" Grandfather asked, irritated to not know what was happening.

"Dragons," Sammy answered as he took his grandfather's arm.

The Maryboys hesitated, wondering why the young people had changed direction. They looked at each other, concerned that Sam had gotten them into something they would rather have avoided.

"We're getting too old for this," Mr. Maryboy grumbled.

Mrs. Maryboy did not say anything, but kept her eyes on the rough ground.

Juniper could hardly breathe from excitement. He had prayed this day would never come, but now that it had the world seemed brighter and more hopeful than ever. He felt as if he had misused his body in ways that would never heal, but his exhilaration, responding to Simalucroix's exhilaration, was so powerful he felt as if all his emotional burdens had disappeared. When he looked back and saw that even Lily and Sam were having trouble keeping up with him and that Grandmother, Grandfather, and the others were even further back, he stopped and caught his breath.

The earth was darkening. The sky was Prussian blue. The moon was bright, but in its first quarter, a dark crescent hollowed out in a field shining with stars. We're not going to see them come out of the cave, he thought. It's too far.

Sheena vibrated from the humming more powerfully than ever before. She felt like a crystal whose skin was so translucent Rory could look into her and see her heart, liver, and kidneys.

"Angels are coming," she said softly. "Oh, they have white wings!"

Rory, sitting beside her, felt strange. He had followed her to the treehouse and then Four Windows Cave, hoping to start a conversation. He had an instinctive feeling that if they could talk the years of their madness could end. They could begin a new life together. At one point Sheena had stopped not far from the treehouse and looked at him with normal eyes.

"I'm becoming sane," she told him. "I don't know why, but I don't feel like a beautifully plumaged bird flying among the stars."

She had turned and finished walking to the treehouse, ignoring Rory. As soon as they had reached the treehouse, her normalcy had faded. She touched the stairway banner Rory had spent hours sanding and polishing and said, "You made this." She looked at him, frightened, grabbed his hand, and ran toward Four Windows Cave. "They're coming," she said.

"Who's coming?" Rory had asked.

But Sheena had not answered, tugging at him until they were running side by side over the lava fields.

During the run Rory felt optimistic, then afraid, that this interlude with Sheena meant nothing. When they passed where they would have to turn to reach Big Skylight Cave, he started hearing the humming Sheena was hearing.

At Four Windows Cave Sheena climbed up on a huge, smooth boulder above tumbled stones where a climber could climb into the collapse. She sat, took Rory's hand, and said, "Hush." He sat, silent, trying to deal with humming vibrating in his bones as Sheena stared at the cave's opening.

"There's a battle, but the angels will win," she said.

She put her finger on Rory's lips when he tried to ask her to explain. He could feel her vibrating beside him as she pressed hips and sides against his warmth.

"Juniper's coming," she said softly. "The angels told him to come."

Rory did not speak. He was afraid to speak. Sheena did not look normal, but luminous, shining with light streaming from cold lava, making her burn as brightly as the descending sun.

"What's happening?" Rory asked at last. "Are you okay?"

Sheena turned to him and smiled so radiantly his heart expanded. He could almost hear the music Sheena was hearing, but it danced just beyond his hearing, tantalizing, beautiful, and powerful. He was no longer afraid, but as excited as Sheena. But what was he excited about?

Sam was the first to spot Bill and Carson. They were too far away to be seen clearly, but they were climbing one of the higher hills to see where they were. Carson was outlined against the sky. Sam could not make out who the two figures were, but the second he saw them he flinched. He and Lily had been moving swiftly, trying to keep up with Juniper while looking behind them to keep his parents and Lily's grandparents in sight.

When he slowed, Lily, beside him, moved ahead. He looked back toward his parents and saw Mom touch his Dad on his shoulder, then gesture at Sam. His Dad swiftly moved ahead of Mom, catching up with Grandfather. The sight of Carson sent a surge of anger through Sam. He caught his breath and cursed when Carson pointed toward them. He had a rifle in his right hand.

Lily had slowed too.

"What's wrong?" she asked Sam over her shoulder.

Sam pointed, although he kept moving to make sure they did not lose sight of Juniper.

"The Lowders?" Lily asked.

Sam nodded. "They have guns," he said.

Carson and Bill climbed off the hilltop. They were invisible against black lava in the growing darkness.

"There's not much moon," Lily said, still moving, but looking around. "I've never been out here after dark."

Sam looked at Juniper who had stopped, waiting on the crest of a rise.

"We're almost to the cave," Sam said. "I was out here with Juniper when we were younger."

The miracle was that seeing the Lowders was not depressing him. He had not forgotten about the dragons, but he was angry. He was often angry at himself and sometimes at his family, blaming them for the sad state of his life. Why couldn't they pay more attention to him? Why did they have to live so far out in the boondocks?

But this anger was different. It was not aimed at him, his life, or his emotions, but at the Lowders, their guns, and the teasing and bullying that had marked him from the time the three of them were old enough to establish who was strongest. They would not hurt Juniper again, he vowed, nor him, nor dragons.

He surged past Lily. She looked strangely at him. Behind them the Smallhands and Maryboys kept struggling over the rough landscape.

"Hurry! It's getting dark!" Lily called.

Her voice was tiny inside the landscape's hugeness.

Juniper was waiting, his slender body outlined against lingering evening light. Sam's mother was the furthest behind. His father had moved in front of Grandmother who was not even breathing hard as she moved across dips, plunges, and rises. Grandfather was slightly behind her, but seemed to be as strong as his wife was. Sam was half running toward Juniper, waving his arm south toward where Carson and Bill were. Juniper looked at Sam, but kept turning and looking west—as if he could see Four Windows Cave from where he stood.

Lily breathed deeply and forced herself forward. She felt as if she had taken a physical beating. She wondered how the Maryboys were taking the punishment. Grandmother and Grandfather were always strengthening themselves as they went about daily tasks in the canyon. They walked everywhere. The Maryboys lived no such life. They prized the comforts they had earned.

The fact the Lowders were in the wilderness was troubling, but this was not the school cafeteria. Out here Juniper, his father and mother, had the advantage. What was amazing, Lily thought, was how Juniper moved over the lava. He had bruises all over his body. He had to be hurting. He was only days out of the hospital. Still, he had to wait for them. That he would wait said good things about him, she thought. He would not abandon them regardless of circumstances. He's somebody worthy of love, she told herself.

Sam's father was just behind her now, breathing hard. They were all getting closer to where Juniper waited.

Juniper could not see Four Windows Cave from where he was standing. He knew he was too late to see the dragons come out of the cave. He was responsible for those following him.

"I'm not going to make it to the cave in time to see you emerge," he told Simalucroix in his thought.

"Father and Sheena are there," Simalucroix answered.

"Mother and Father," Juniper whispered out-loud. Thinking about the two of them waiting beside the cave made him smile. Father had waited to be at Sheena's side for fourteen years.

Sam was within shouting distance. He was waving south.

"The Lowders!" he shouted.

Juniper looked toward where Sam was pointing, but could see nothing. He felt the Lowders, though, and saw them through Simalucroix's eyes as they struggled with growing darkness. Fear shivered up and down his back. He could see Lily's backpack filled with books coming at his head as Carson grinned.

"Light," Simalucroix said, wonder in his voice. "The surface dark is lighter."

Juniper glanced at the moon's horn.

"The moon is small tonight," he told Simalucroix.

"We're coming!" Simalucroix exhalted. "The eight of us are coming! The young ones are looking at light through our eyes!"

This is Simalucroix's night, Juniper thought. The night of the dragons.

He could hear Sam's hard breathing as he crossed the rock bridge between two collapses yawing darker than the evening's darkness. Lily was just behind him. Mr. Maryboy was just behind her. Within moments Grandmother, Grandfather, and Mrs. Maryboy were in sight.

As Sam came up to him, shouting that the Lowders had guns, Juniper, forcing the Lowders and everything else from his mind, turned toward Four Windows Cave. He could hear Simalucroix's and the dragon humming song vibrating through the lava around him.

Why did the Lowders have to show up? he asked himself.

Sam, then Lily, came to where he was standing. Sam bent over, breathing hard. Lily smiled at Juniper so brightly his heart jumped.

"They're almost to the surface," Lily said. "I see it in your face."

Sam, startled, straightened and looked at Juniper, then at the sky.

Mr. Maryboy came running up the rise, his face ashen.

"Sam," he gasped. "Sam."

Sam turned toward his father and smiled.

"The dragons are almost here," he said.

His father, in spite of the lava's sharpness, knelt painfully on the ground as Grandmother, Grandfather, and then Mrs. Maryboy, looking stronger than Mr. Maryboy, came to the crest of the rise. Grandmother looked shrewdly at Juniper, then at the skies. The humming had become so powerful even Mr. Maryboy's face wrinkled in puzzlement.

"Sam?" Mrs. Maryboy asked, looking toward the cave with Sam, Lily, and Grandmother.

"Toward sunset," Grandfather said out-loud, his voice deep and powerful.

Juniper could feel the push of Simalucroix's wings.

Chapter XXXVI

As the cavern widened, Simalucroix spread wings and almost flew over the rising floor, folding, spreading, pushing down, moving powerful legs, singing the dragon song along with Winnigan, Fruchault, Jennfer, Straaglon, Pruchaldras, Ssinssifra, and Craagladon, climbing, climbing, and climbing, telling Juniper about his powerful joy, sending vibrations into Sheena as she healed, moving as swiftly as wind, creating a wind behind him, singing, singing, and singing…

Surface light shined from the moon and stars. He could see moonlight out of Four Window Cave's oblong opening into the forbidden place, the place dragons had fled generations ago. He pushed as hard as he could, wondering if he could fly, wondering if never-used wings would know how to lift him out of the cave.

The jumbled smells of living plants, animals, and sky assailed him. He moved faster and faster, straining toward the cave opening. Suddenly he was there, into light, into the movement of air as it sang across black lava fields into a world unlike the world of caverns and small passages. His two hearts thundered; his singing roared into flame as he rose out of the collapse, wings laboring up and down, flying becoming song, flying becoming Winnigan, Fruchault, Jennfer, Straaglon, Pruchaldras, Ssinssifra, and Craagladon as they too pushed until they moved like wind. Wings strained into wind, rising into moonlight, starlight, faint hint of earth light, soaring past Father and Sheena, going over the heads of Juniper, Lily, Sam, Grandmother, Grandfather, Hilda and Lester Maryboy.

They were flying! Flying like dragons of Grilgax's time, like Simalucroix's great great great grandparents, ancestors dating back to the time when dragons lived in swamps and caves, battling strange. two legged humans that dared come to their lairs. Dragons that became sentient in order to combat humans, living, loving, dying, and growing toward days when they would soar above forests and plains into high mountain caves and freezing snow fields.

Eight dragons soared above Ssissensin and Syllabrie, above conclaves, dragon singing, talking, hunting, eating, digging, scratching life from caverns and dark earth. They soared into skies so bright eyes whirled faster and faster, singing dragon eye songs, the song of dragon hearts alive in a way only told about in stories, in fear of humans, in fear of dragon nature that demanded flight and the beat of double hearts singing in concert with the beat of dragon wings.

They were flying! Flying! Flying!

As the moon's tipped horn poured silver light
Onto the backs of dragons' ghostly hides,
Eight dragons shined in silver, soaring flight
As wings and double hearts at Christmastide
Sang freedom into lives too long confined
By cavern dark and fears of humankind.

The dragons flew! The dragons flew!
Wind sang its breath beneath stretched wings.
They felt and smelled the earth and wind and knew
How dragons once had lived like sentient kings.
The dragons flew! The dragons flew!
Their double hearts beat true! Their hearts beat true!

Life bloomed above a troubled, tortured earth.
Ecstatic, dragons sang of dragonkind's rebirth.

When Simalucroix and seven dragons erupted from Four Windows Cave's mouth, Sheena, whose heart had been beating faster and faster, stood on the rock she was sitting on with Rory. Her excitement reached an unbearable crescendo.

The shining creatures rising into the sky were not angels. Her mind groped for an explanation. Then it came to her. She was looking at dragons! She had been hearing dragonsong, not angelsong. It was Christmas night, but dragons, not angels, were flying above the earth.

Beside her Rory was standing with his mouth open. Dragons? Juniper's dream of dragons conjured in deep caverns alive? For years he had longed, with a longing burning his insides, for a chance to sit with Sheena and start weaving a life lost together again. Sheena had not shied from him or threatened or screeched at him all day. They had tried to talk to each other. His impossible dream had started to haltingly, awkwardly, come true, but now another dream was intruding, his son's dream of dragons.

What was the name Juniper had used? Simalucroix? Were he and Sheena talking because he too had gone insane? He stood beside his wife and drew her close to him. Dragons were in the skies above El Malpais! Was this a Christmas of miracles? Or madness? He squeezed Sheena's shoulders so hard he was hurting her.

He forced himself to loosen his hug when she flinched and looked toward the east. Juniper was coming down the slope dropped into the depression where Four Windows Cave's collapse was. He was looking at the sky, stopping, jumping, shouting.

"Dragons!" he was shouting. "Dragons in moonlight!"

Lily, the elderly Smallhands, and Sammy were with him along with Mr. and Mrs. Maryboy. Father looked from his son to the dragons flying in a confused mêlée over the lava fields. They bobbed up and down as they beat wings and swooped toward the ground, one dragon flying below, then above another in humming exhilaration.

Dragons, Rory thought to himself. Dragons!

Sheena looked up into her husband's face and wondered why she had not realized how much he loved her. Dragons were in the sky, and instead of moving away from her and jumping up and down and shouting the way her son and his friends were, he was holding onto her as if he would never let go.

How could the heavenly humming that had disturbed her nights for so long come from dragons rather than angels? Dragons could not heal human beings the way angels could. The flying dragons were not anything like angels even though white hides gleamed like angels' wings.

Without thinking she put her head on Rory's shoulder and tried to melt into him while staring, stunned, at the skies.

"We're flying! We're flying!" Simalucroix exulted to Juniper as he came out of the cave.

"Lily! Sam!" Juniper cried as Simalucroix soared above them into the faint moonlight. "Simalucroix!"

Lily saw the dragons as Juniper yelled. They're real, she thought to herself. She started shouting. Sam, beside Juniper and Lily, stared as eight dragons rose higher and higher into the sky. His mother and father were sitting on a fallen tree trunk, their mouths open. Lily's Grandmother was smiling and crooning to herself. Grandfather was looking at his wife, a little frightened, amazed, filled with a deep spirituality that allowed him to feel every animal, plant, and stone near him, all of them singing earth's song, the song dragons were singing as they cavorted like children in the sky.

But no dragons are near the Navajo, he told himself. The white man has brought something new, again. He did not know whether to celebrate or mourn surprises coming out of the earth.

Grandmother looked from the dragons to Juniper and her granddaughter. She felt the power of the signs they had experienced. She did not believe the signs' meanings were clear yet. No human had been meant to see a dragon in the lifetimes of their children's children's children, but now dragons were present. Her perceptions of Mother Earth, Father Sky, and the beings of earth and sky had changed.

"Welcome sky children, earth children," she said. "May your paths be strewn with beauty. May your hearts beat true inside the glory of earth and sky."

She looked at her foolish husband and smiled. He was stunned. Dragons had taken him out of his life, and he was constructing new understanding. He's not going to drink anymore, she thought. He is a thinker. This is not understandable without prayer, contemplation, and deep thought. Lily's, Sammy's, and my life will be better.

She looked at the sky and smiled more brightly than before.

"Thank you," she called to the dragons. "Thank you!"

Sammy's, Mr. Maryboy's, and Mrs. Maryboy's heads swirled like dragons' eyes. Sammy kept shouting nonsense at the sky. He could feel the great beasts' song and feel their intelligence. He felt their celebration entering him, causing him to celebrate.

Mrs. Maryboy kept looking from the dragons to Sam. Sam was excited, alive in a way she had never seen him before. It was like he had shed old skin the way a bull elk shed antlers in the spring. She put her hand on Lester's arm and squeezed.

"Is Sam going to be all right?" she asked.

Lester looked into her eyes. He had always loved Hilda—from the moment when they were kids, and he had seen her on the dance floor at Pine Hill High School's gym at prom. Sam's depression had been hard on their marriage. They each blamed themselves, and they moved through days as if they could hardly stand to touch themselves, nonetheless each other. Was that time ending?

Sam tugged at Juniper's shirtsleeve. "Are they going to land?" he asked. "Am I going to meet a dragon?"

Juniper's parents walked slowly around the rim of Four Windows Cave's collapse. Juniper looked into the sky and tried to pick out Simalucroix. He thought he could make him out, even as high in the air as the clutch was. Simalucroix seemed more powerful, his wings lifting him higher than the others.

"Are you going to land, Simalucroix?" Juniper asked in his head.

Simalucroix's deep, thundering laughter rumbled.

"There is healing to do for this gift," he said. "The young are amazed. They are looking through our eyes at the outside world. Ssissensin and her followers are afraid and upset, but the young are forcing them back into caverns. They want wings so they can fly. We'll land," he said. "You have promised Sam he will meet a dragon.

Chapter XXXVII

When Carson came out of a depression and walked around a small mound and saw eight white dragons rising into the sky, he almost dropped the ought-six.

"God damned," he said quietly.

His heart hammered in his chest. He felt excited. He had not felt excited except when using meth for months, ever since the day he and Bill had run into Snuffy Christian sitting below the rock cliff above Inscription Rock Trading and Coffee Company and Ancient Way Café and got their first dose of heaven. He could hardly believe he was beyond the mind numbing, vague dullness of everyday life. He felt alive even though he had not had a hit since he and Bill had beat the hell out of Juniper in the school cafeteria.

Bill walked around the mound and stopped. He looked toward where Carson was looking and dropped the twenty-two.

"Holy shit," he said. "Sam was telling the truth. Those are dragons."

"No fucking dragon can possibly exist," Carson said. "We're hallucinating. Sam couldn't know what he was talking about."

Both stared as dragons flew over, under, and around each other, then stilled into long glides ended by more wing aerobatics. Bill had never seen anything so beautiful in his life: The slender quarter moon, the Milky Way smearing sky with stars, the coldness of Christmas night in El Malpais wilderness. For the first time in he did not know how long Bill felt good. His body did not seem so hungry with the restlessness that made him want to freeze into rock while moving aimlessly around.

Carson looked speculatively at the cavorting dragons.

"Those animals are pretty far away, aren't they?" he said.

Bill looked intently at his twin. Carson's eyes were feral.

"You're not going to kill a dragon," Bill said, voice intense. "No human has ever seen a dragon. They probably only exist in this wilderness. They're beyond endangered, and you're not going to kill one."

Bill turned his eyes from the dragons and looked at Bill. Bill, for the first time in his life, saw Carson's craziness clearly.

"Killing a dragon is a sportsman's dream," Carson said, keeping his voice casual. "Why shouldn't I be the great white hunter? Maybe it'll make me famous. Hell, the world doesn't know dragons exist. When we kill one, they'll forget about throwing us in jail."

Bill looked at the dragons again. They're beautiful, he thought. Wild. "Nothing's going to keep us from jail," he said bleakly. "Killing an endangered species will make it worse."

"They know we're here," Carson said. "They see Juniper and his friends and family and us. Just think, they're smart, and an animal. I can be the first man to kill one outside of storybooks. Doesn't that heat your dick?"

"Carson," Bill warned.

"They're gonna go to Juniper," Carson said softly. "We have to get closer. They're too damned far away." He turned and grinned at Bill. "Come on," he said, expecting Bill to follow.

Carson moved quickly toward where Juniper, the Maryboys, and Smallhands were standing. Carson's crazy, Bill thought to himself. He's always been crazy, and what have I done every time? He expects me to be inside his craziness. Thinking about Carson, he sighed. He was going to jail. He did not feel good about himself or what he'd done or was doing. He'd led the way plenty of times, but Carson always outdid him. He shook his head and followed Carson.

Sam's face, alight with joy, changed. He looked puzzled, then frightened. He held up his left hand toward Juniper.

"No, no," he said. "You have to tell Simalucroix not to come. Not now."

Juniper looked at his best friend, confused.

Lily was looking at Sam too, but her face was as filled with foreboding as Sam's.

"Sam's right," she said. "Carson and Bill."

Father and Sheena, looking happy, had traversed the collapse's rim and were climbing to where the rest of them were.

"Dragons, Juniper!" Father called out. "You really found dragons!"

"Not angels, Dragons!" Sheena called out on the heel of Father's voice.

"Courage," Grilgax had said, the strength of his words echoing through them. "We must have the courage of life until either humankind murders themselves on fields of glory and gore or they evolve into beings intelligent enough to accept our intelligence. We can clutch our eggs and cherish our young even in this darkness, and we can explore what being a dragon means."

The force of his hospital vision hit Juniper so hard he sat on the ground, looking up at Grandmother.

"You have to stop them from coming to this spot," Grandmother said, kneeling down beside Juniper, looking worried. "Sam and Lily saw the Lowders. They have guns."

"But where will the dragons go?" Juniper asked. "This is the only passage to where they live."

Panic was rising into pain. Father and Sheena were suddenly kneeling beside him with Grandmother.

"What's wrong?" Father asked.

Sheena was looking at him with concern, love, and sanity in her eyes.

"He has to tell the dragons to stay away. They can't die!" Sam wailed.

"They won't die," Sheena said. "They are too intelligent to die."

"Juniper?" Father asked, trying to get Juniper to talk.

Juniper was searching in his mind for Simalucroix. For a moment he could not find the dragon, but then Simalucroix soared higher than he had up to that point, pivoted from the moon toward Juniper, and glided toward the humans on the rise. One dragon after another followed their leader, each one so graceful they looked like they had spent lifetimes flying.

"Don't worry, little one," Simalucroix told Juniper. "I believe it will be all right."

"Humans with guns are trying to kill you," Juniper said, feeling breathless even though he was speaking in his mind, not outloud.

"I see them," Simalucroix answered, coming closer and closer.

"They're crazy enough to kill you," Juniper said, trying to get Simalucroix to take off into the sky again.

"Perhaps," Simalucroix agreed.

He suddenly realized he was coming in to his landing area too fast; he flared wings outward, slowing his descent.

Carson was breathing hard as he ran over the rough ground. He stumbled twice, but caught himself and kept going. He felt powerful with the 30.06 in his hands. Bill had hesitated when Carson had taken off and was fifty yards behind him. Carson smiled, covering as much ground as fast as he could. He was close enough to see the euphoria on the rise. He glanced at the sky and saw the dragons wheeling in a group and gliding toward Juniper.

Now or never, he thought to himself. Was he close enough for a good shot? He could make out white dragon hides in the darkness, but he had no idea how close they would fly to him. He would have to shoot at moving targets. The hill's rise would block his line of sight when they landed beside Juniper.

A small blowhole was to the right of him. He needed to be higher to get a better shot. The dragons glided in fast. He jumped to the top of the hole and put his belly over the small opening. It felt uncomfortable, but he put the ought-six against his shoulder. He tried to calm his heart. He would miss if he did not calm down. He'd killed too many elk, deer, and even a bear to not know that lesson. He put his cheek against the rifle's stock and aimed at the dragon in front. It would be a long shot, but he could be deadly. He was a great hunter.

Behind Carson Bill was running for all he was worth. He had lost ground to Carson, but not that much. He had thrown his twenty-two down in an effort to run faster. When Carson jumped up the blowhole, Bill's heart leapt into his throat. Carson was going to kill a dragon.

Bill felt stranger than he had ever felt in his life. The largest dragon, ahead of the others, was looking at him. He had no idea how he knew the dragon was looking at him, but he felt whirling eyes drilling into the spirit of who he was. He gasped. Carson tracked the dragon with the ought-six. He was ready to pull the trigger. Bill shouted as loud as he could and jumped. The ought-six roared, shattering silence.

"Fuck! Fuck!" Carson raged. He was sitting on the blowhole, glaring at Bill who had grabbed Carson's feet. "You made me miss, you asshole," Carson snarled.

"I kept you from messing up," Bill replied. "Again."

Carson's face was a storm of hatred and rage. He pointed the ought-six at Bill's head and put his finger on the trigger. Bill let go of his brother's feet and cringed, waiting for the explosion that would end his life.

Carson sighed. "You're a fucking wiener," he said. He sounded as tired as a human being could sound. His shot at the dragon had drained him. "You know that?"

He looked toward where the dragons had gathered on the rise. In spite of the darkness they could still be seen. Carson had been wrong when he had thought he would not be able to see them after they had landed. They looked as if their hides absorbed moonlight and starlight and reflected it back at the sky, giving them a faint glow. He shook his head violently and looked speculatively at his rifle, then pointed it away from Bill's head.

Bill was his brother, after all.

"Fuck it," he said again. He got up, looked disgustedly at Bill, and spat, sliming his brother's head. "Loser," he said. "Fucking loser." He looked at the dragons, looked back at Bill, and sneered. "I don't need you," he said. "All you'll ever do is hold me back."

He jumped off the small blowhole and, without looking at Bill again, stalked angrily into the darkness. Bill, shaking, feeling himself cringe while he waited to hear the ought-six's report, watched Carson walk away from him.

He'd have to wait for daylight to go home, he thought. It was cold. Let him go, he thought. He'd be better off without Carson finding trouble that inevitably sunk them both. He put his head in his hands, feeling Carson's spit in his hair. He sighed and started to sob, no longer able to control himself.

Between his sobs he could almost hear his Dad telling him to be a man and grow up so they wouldn't be ashamed of him.

Chapter XXXVIII

The Maryboys were frightened. As one monstrous shape after another found a place near Juniper and flared huge white wings and extended thick legs to land, both Maryboys glanced nervously at the sky and then at Sam, too frightened for speech. Dragon smell drifted through the air, sulfuric, with a hint of exotic lizard, neither pleasant nor unpleasant, but unmistakably different.

Sam was gleaming from excitement. He was going to meet Simalucroix at last! Lily, standing beside him and Juniper, eyes shining, was as calm and accepting of the impossible moment as if it was part of who she was. She was excited, but had stillness as placid as Ramah Lake's surface when there was no wind. Her grandparents were holding each other as Simalucroix flared his wings and whooshed toward them, his landing clamoring as he extended claws toward earth.

Sheena took Rory's hand when they were halfway up to the clearing where Juniper was. Father could not close his eyes because of the ground's roughness, but felt like he could sink into a bliss he could not remember experiencing. As one dragon after another landed, followed by Simalucroix's hugeness swooping toward Juniper standing calm before the fierce-looking beast with whirling eyes, Sheena moved even faster. The two of them reached Juniper, Lily, Sam, Lily's grandparents, and Sam's parents as Simalucroix's feet touched lava.

Inside Juniper's head Simalucroix said, "Your mother first."

"What?" Juniper asked.

"Watch," Simalucroix answered, twisting his neck so that he was looking at Sheena.

A rifle's report echoed through the wilderness. The Lowders had fired a gun, but Simalucroix seemed amused by the sound.

"That's done," he told Juniper. "Carson has failed. He won't try again."

The others, under the spell of seeing dragons, heard the shot, but did not register what it was. Father felt protective of both Sheena and Juniper. He pulled Sheena to a stop when she moved toward the huge beast in front of them. He was unsure what to do. Juniper was not afraid of the dragon, but Rory wanted to run for cover, preferably with his rifle in his hands.

The humming in Sheena was so powerful she felt as if every pore in her skin was alive to powerful forces beyond her control.

"Come," the great dragon said in her mind. "You're not a Christmas angel," she said, half accusing.

Great eyes whirled dark colors into her spirit. The dragon laughed. Its laugher was deep and beautiful. She tried to let go of Rory's hand. She had been gripping it so hard her hand was sore, but as she relaxed her grip, Rory's grip held on to her. She could almost feel him pleading with her to not take the chance of getting closer to the dragon.

"I am Simalucroix," the dragon said. "Your son's friend. Come, touch me."

The command was so compelling she tugged strongly at Rory. He held her back. He did not say anything, but tried to pull her away from the white monster in front of them. Juniper and Lily saw what was happening and moved to Father.

"It's okay, Father," Lily said. "It's Simalucroix. He's here to heal Sheena."

Juniper touched his father's shoulder, and Father, not knowing why, let go of Sheena's hand. She did not move, but turned to look at Rory, Juniper, and Lily. They're family, she thought to herself. She looked toward where Grandmother and Grandmother held each other as calmly as if they expected what was happening to happen. They're going to be family, she thought.

She moved away from Rory, Juniper, and Lily toward Simalucroix, reaching out her hand, feeling heat emanating from the dragon. When she touched Simalucroix the humming vibrating through her stopped. She gasped, its absence a void inside who she was becoming. For a moment she stood touching the great dragon, trying to find something inside she had lost a long time ago.

There are no miracles, she thought to herself. Not even at Christmas. The disappointment she felt was as sharp as a honed knife's edge. We have to keep ourselves—or what counts in life, those who love us, disappear.

She pulled her hand away from Simalucroix's warm hide.

"I cannot help you," the dragon said calmly. "You can help yourself."

"The humming," Sheena answered, talking out-loud. "Where has it gone?"

"We are still singing," another dragon voice answered. "But you are stronger than the singing now."

Jennfer, on the rise's crest above the humans and Simalucroix, walked toward them. Sam was staring at Sheena and Simalucroix, then at the other dragons. He was smiling as if he had found nirvana.

"Sam," Jennfer said, grabbing Sam's attention, talking in his head. "I am Jennfer."

Sam laughed, startling his parents who had unconsciously backed up the rise. Unthinkingly they were moving toward a dragon moving toward them. When Sam spoke they stopped. Their eyes widened even further than when they had first seen dragons rise into night skies.

"Rory? Juniper?" Sheena said. "Can I come home?"

Father, whose heart had pounded uncontrollably as Sheena touched Simalucroix, was so startled his heartbeat slowed down. He looked at his wife with a look containing years of waiting, pain, and hope, dreams deferred and then deferred again.

"I don't need the treehouse anymore," Sheena said.

"Hello Jennfer," Sam said in his head, communicating the way Juniper did with Simalucroix. "I'm pleased to meet you."

I've met a dragon, Sam thought to himself. Just like Juniper, I've met a dragon.

Lily smiled so brightly, as Sheena touched Simalucroix, she shined like the dragons were shining in moonlight and starlight. She could feel dragons spirits around her, the storm of emotions roiling through her grandparents, the Maryboy's fear and amazement, Sam's absolute delight, and Juniper's curiosity as he watched his mother and father and what was happening to them.

She could feel the profound change in her grandfather, as if, suddenly, he had jumped out of himself and now looked at the universe in a different way. The dragons' earth magic was strong. It pulsed in a stream that made people alive and more related to the earth than before they had confronted dragons.

Sheena stepped from Simalucroix and reached out to Rory and Juniper. Juniper reached out his hand. Rory, unsure, stunned that Sheena had touched Simalucroix and then turned toward him, feeling his world changing in ways he had dreamed about for so many years, was slower than his son. Seeing Juniper reach out, he put his hand out too. My God, he told himself. There are miracles.

He looked at Simalucroix. The dragon's great eyes whirled at him. Stars, galaxies, and volcanic fires spewed ash and smoke in great, ferocious bellows into the sky, the eruption's heat so great trees spontaneously burst into flames.

Thank you, he told Simalucroix. Simalucroix, exultant from aboveground freedom, spoke into Father's mind.

"You're welcome," he said, then let rumbling laughter and joy reach out with a force that nearly knocked Rory off his feet. Juniper, hugging his mother, the witch who had haunted his childhood from the branches of El Malpais' Douglas firs, laughed to hear Simalucroix's laughter and see the joy on his mother's and father's faces.

How had it all happened? he asked himself. How had he gone from feeling lonely, lost, and angry in a hostile world of school hallways and people who did not like him to this moment of triumph when the universe was filled with love?

Suddenly Lily, hypersensitive to what was happening inside the dragons and everyone around her, hugged Juniper, pouring her love into him. Sheena and Father reached over to touch her, accepting her, and images of her parents, black hair and black eyes, faces filled with their lives, materialized. They were smiling in a way they had seldom smiled, proud of her and Sammy.

Sammy, not long after the dragons had landed, had sat on the rises' sharp lava. He watched his grandparents, feeling love's intensity beneath their everyday surfaces. His Grandfather had been so wrong so often, only sometimes pushing back disappointments and acting wise beneath his surfaces, Sammy had grown alienated from the only significant man left in his life. Living inside alienation had been the only way he could live a life where he could protect Grandmother and sister and try to be the man he wanted to be.

He did not want to drink like his grandfather or father and beat those who loved him and die in a whiskey bottle or a fiery car accident that left children lost and bereft of life. He wanted to be steady, someone there the way men should be there, a strength women and children could come to when bad things happened. Watching his grandparents, glancing at Lily embraced by Juniper and Juniper's parents, feeling dragon song alive around him, feeling Sam walking toward a dragon coming down the hill, he smiled. The world is going to be different, he thought. Better.

As Sam reached Jennfer and touched her warm hide, the other dragons walked toward the two of them. In less than fifteen minutes Sam was surrounded by dragons. His mother, getting used to the impossible, looking at her son's ecstatic face, feeling beneath ecstasy calmness and strength Sam had never had before, relaxed. The Christmas miracle swept over her. She had always believed in miracles.

"What's it like being a dragon?" Sam asked Jennfer.

"What's it like being human?" Jennfer asked.

The sound of dragon laughter was so loud it rang into the wilderness. Sam laughed too. He had friends who were dragons, he thought to himself. Friends he could laugh with, who enchanted him. For a second, worry about depression flitted through him, a dark shadow, but he did not feel his old obsession with his failures. He did not feel the anger accompanying his feelings of failure.

Inside the dragon circle, great eyes whirled at him, dragon smell powerful in his nostrils. He felt different, stronger, and more alive than he had ever felt. What Bill or Carson said no longer meant anything.

"Being human's a difficult thing," he told Jennfer. "You never know who you are, or at least I don't, and you're always trying to find some way to be well."

"We came from the caverns," Jennfer said.

"Our ancestors saved our kind," Winnigan said.

"You like dragons, don't you?" Fruchault asked.

"It's good to be in starlight, moonlight, with wind beneath your wings," Jennfer said. "It makes you feel more alive."

Mrs. Maryboy walked toward the dragon circle around Sam. Mr. Maryboy pulled back, reluctant to approach the huge beasts. He had gotten control over his fear, and he was adjusting to the shock of seeing mythical beasts surrounding his son, but he had no desire to follow his wife.

"Are we going to be friends?" Sam asked inside the circle.

"Sam is going to be better," Mrs. Maryboy whispered fiercely. "We need to be beside him."

"We are already friends," Straaglon said. "We are outside friends."

The dragons' deep joy swept over Sam and everyone on the rise again.

Mr. Maryboy, feeling joy rather than fear, for the first time since seeing the dragons, walked into the circle.

Lily, still hugging Juniper, fulfilled in a way that seemed like it could stretch over a lifetime, looked at Simalucroix looking toward Sam and his parents.

"Thank you," she said.

Simalucroix's great head turned solemnly toward Lily. Grandmother and Grandfather, hand in hand, had walked over to their granddaughter. They could not take their eyes off Simalucroix as he bent his head close.

"The world has changed. The signs were true," Grandmother said quietly.

"But where is this moment going to lead?" Simalucroix asked out-loud.

Juniper reached up and impulsively touched his friend's nose, taking his arm away from Sheena and Father.

"Toward the future," he said. "Out of caverns and into light."

"We're not strong enough for sunlight," Simalucroix answered.

Juniper smiled. "You will be," he predicted, "and humans will get used to dragons."

On the hill Sam's laughter rang out as his father and mother tentatively walked into the center of the circle where seven dragons stood.

Chapter XXXIX

When Bill stopped sobbing he got up from the cold, wet ground. It was Christmas, he thought, and he felt awful. He could not remember feeling anything but a boy's excitement about Christmas before. He looked at the rise, now invisible in the dark, where dragons, Juniper, Lily, Sam, and their parents, including the witch of El Malpais, were. All except one dragon clustered in one spot. They looked like they were floating, illuminated, in sky above the earth.

Bill felt a strange humming in his head. He could not get rid of it even though he shook his head vigorously. He was lost in El Malpais, he thought to himself.

He wondered about Carson. He could see the coldness in Carson's eyes when he had pointed the ought-six at his head. He had seen that look just before Carson had started kicking Juniper when Juniper had collapsed unconscious to the cafeteria floor.

Bill had been scared, he realized. Scared of his twin brother. He wondered why Carson had taken his eyes away from him, cussed, and walked away, not paying attention to him, the dragons, or Juniper and his crowd. He wondered if Carson could find his way out of El Malpais. A lot of people had died in lava country. Some of those people had lived near the wilderness all their lives just like Carson and Bill had.

After a while Bill started wondering what he was going to do. Carson was gone and would be avoiding him. How they had gotten to where he was physically at was a mystery to him. He had struggled to follow Carson who had seemed to have a compass in his head.

The thought of dragons befuddled him. The humming in his head, he thought, wasn't real. He couldn't think. What were dragons doing alive in the twenty-first century on Christmas night? He shook his head, trying to get rid of the humming.

What was he going to do? The question made him sick to his stomach. He had no idea what the answer was. Juniper, his family, the dragons, and the others would not welcome him if he could get through the lava between him and them, he thought. But what else could he do if he wanted to survive? The lava flats were deadly. He did not want to die. He wanted to see his parents again.

He got to his feet. He had no choice, a strange voice said inside his head.

He walked toward Juniper, Lily, and Sam. Maybe they would treat him better than he and Carson had treated them. He wondered if the humming in his head had anything to do with the dragons.

In the wilderness, already a half mile away from Bill, Carson was half blind. The slim moon did not give enough light to keep him from stumbling over tangled lava. The weariness that had swept over him when he had pointed the ought-six at Bill's head, considering whether to kill the brother who had been the closest person to him in his life, or not, was being replaced by a fiery rage.

Dragons, he thought contemptuously. Sam had been telling the truth about dragons. He should have beaten the hell out of Sam rather than Juniper. He would have never heard of dragons that were actually alive. He should have beaten Sam and Juniper and then jumped Lily. It would have served that smart bitch right.

He had left Bill and his family behind. The realization made him stop and look around. Bill had been a pretty good brother, he thought, but tossed the thought away.

Dragons should not be alive in the world, he thought. Dragons had never existed. They were a myth. They should not exist now, especially when Carson knew about them. He could see eyes whirling with evil that swirled around and around in his head.

No one would believe him if he told them dragons existed, he thought. He had to keep them secret. He was not going to jail. He knew Bill was. Bill was afraid of Carson now. Carson saw Bill's blank fear looking up into his eyes after knocking his shot at the dragon astray. Bill would not slow Carson down by following him. I didn't kill him, Carson thought. He's still my brother, alive.

He knew where he was going, as if there was a line between him and the Ancient Way Café. He would get to the highway, catch a ride, and take off toward Mexico. Mexico was not so far away, and nobody would bother with him there. His father had taken him and Bill to Ciudad Juarez once. Mostly it was gangsters, drug heads, and drunks. He'd fit in there. The only question was which kind of bad he was going to be.

Dragons should not exist, he thought. They were myths, not real, abominations. They are an affront to me as a real human being.

He thought about Bill on the ground, looking up at him in terror. He knew Bill had no idea about how to get back to the house. Bill had barely been able to keep up with Carson as he followed feelings through the wilderness to where the dragons would be. Poor sucker, Carson thought.

"The god damned dragons shouldn't exist," he said out-loud, startling himself.

He raged through the night toward where he would hitch his ride and start his journey toward Mexico and freedom.

THE END

Thomas Davis is Provost at Navajo Technical College, a tribally controlled college on the Navajo Nation. He has served as the President or Acting President of three tribal colleges.

He is a poet, scholar, and playwright known for his work for tribal colleges, sustainable development, and high performance computing. He lives with his wife, poet and artist Ethel Mortenson Davis, and two dogs, Pax and Juneau, in the mountain community of Continental Divide, New Mexico.

His last books were *Sustaining the Forest, the People, and the Forest* published by State University of New York (SUNY) Press (2000), a non-fiction case study of how the Menominee Indian Tribe of Northern Wisconsin have practiced sustainable forestry and sustainable development; *Salt Bear*, published by Four Windows Press in January 2011, a novel for young people about mythological creatures of the American West, including salt bears, jackalopes, and a cactus buck; and *The Alkali Cliffs*, published by Four Windows Press in January 2013, an environmental novel placed in the 1950s that tells the story of the Smith families' struggle against the building of a rendering plant next to their small farm in North Delta, Colorado.

He has given poetry and dramatic readings at schools and universities throughout the United States as well as in Canada, Australia, and New Zealand.